LIGHT AS A FEATHER

LIGHT AS A FEATHER

HELEN DUNNE

ORION

First published in Great Britain in 2002 by Orion,
an imprint of the Orion Publishing Group Ltd.

Copyright © 2002 Helen Dunne

The moral right of Helen Dunne to be identified as the
author of this work has been asserted in accordance
with the Copyright, Designs and Patents Act of 1988.

A CIP catalogue record for this book
is available from the British Library.

ISBN 0 75283 809 1

Typeset at The Spartan Press Ltd,
Lymington, Hants

Printed in Great Britain by
Clays Ltd, St Ives plc

The Orion Publishing Group Ltd
Orion House
5 Upper St Martin's Lane
London, WC2H 9EA

To Gordon and Patricia
– with love and gratitude

ACKNOWLEDGEMENTS

Once again I'd like to thank my patient editor Jane Wood, her assistant Sophie Wills and my ever-enthusiastic agent Ali Gunn. They may have had some concerns along the way with *Light As A Feather*, particularly when I kept missing deadlines, but their guidance and support proved invaluable. Thanks also to Carol Jackson and Philip Patterson, and all the team at Curtis Brown.

Apologies to those friends that I neglected in order to finish another chapter. Trish and Paul, Stephanie, Jackie, Bernadette, Wendy, Rachel, Sheila and Yasmin – you've all been stars. Thanks to Marcella and Garrett for permission to borrow their names, and for their blatant promotion of me to all their friends. A big drink to Emma and Liz for their help – I know you both won't say no.

And finally, I owe so much to my mother Lily. She has helped out in so many ways, and I truly appreciate it. To John, Anna, and Liz – I sense another dinner!

SLIMMING TIP ONE

Imagine yourself in a bridesmaid's dress

My best friend Liz is glowing. Her jet black hair shines like an advert for dandruff shampoo and her blue eyes sparkle as she lifts her wine glass to mine and clinks. In the twelve years that I've known her she has never looked quite so excited, although that day we spotted Brad Pitt walking around Soho *without* Jennifer comes pretty close.

Last night, Jason, her boyfriend of three years, popped the question. In twelve months Liz Jackson will achieve her dream – to be married by thirty. On Saturday the happy couple are to meet the priest to discuss the arrangements. Isn't it thrilling? she gushes. Aren't you just so excited?

Yes. Yes. It really is. And I really am. Truly. I'm positively *thrilled*. It's just that right now, at this very moment, I'm finding it *rather* difficult to concentrate. Could we just rewind? Go back to that moment when my heart stopped. You want me to be your bridesmaid? Me? In a satin dress? Let's not think meringue. Let's think *blancmange*.

I keep a smile locked on my face as I hail the waiter. On autopilot, I act as best friends should and order a bottle of house champagne. Liz protests at the extravagance – she's now saving for a wedding – but I stress this one's my treat. After all, I need something to deaden the images of me, Orla Kennedy, thirty and spinster of this parish, shoe-horned into a brides-maid's dress. I hesitate for a moment. Perhaps two bottles would be better.

'Could you put another one on ice?' I ask the waiter, as he

re-emerges with a bottle of Dom Pérignon (since when was that house champagne?) and two chilled flutes. 'To you and Jason,' I say chirpily, lifting my glass in the air, as I try to blank out the vision of me standing in the receiving line at the wedding, welcoming guests. The struggle to keep the bouquet balanced in front of my stomach with one hand as I shake with the other. The guests searching for something complimentary to say and avoiding the *big* issue. Me smiling pleasantly as one guest congratulates me on my bouquet. Grinning while another mentions my elaborate hairstyle, shoes, and jewellery . . . anything but the dress that bulges where it shouldn't. And then finally, the ultimate faux pas. The guest who asks when the baby is due. I quickly fill the glass again. 'Destined for each other,' I fawn.

OK, so I'm not huge. When I check in for flights, they don't actually remove a few pieces of luggage to ensure that the plane gets airborne. Just medium fat. The sort of fat where the buttons on blouses need to be sewn on really tight and you then can't make any sudden movements. Where designer labels are left in jackets, but the telltale tag with a figure on it is removed. Where you never discuss your vital statistics with anybody, just in case some mathematician gets hold of them and works out that your body surface could cover eight squash courts. It's hardly surprising that I'm not exactly jumping for joy at Liz's news.

'That's so sweet, Orla,' replies Liz. 'And you're not upset that I didn't ring you first thing this morning?' I shake my head. If I'd had any more warning, I'd now be flat on my back after my fourth bottle. 'I just wanted to tell you face to face. To see your reaction.' Paint on a smile, Orla. Quick. 'Can you imagine? I just didn't guess. I was tucking into my popcorn at the cinema and bit on something really hard – a ring! Isn't that romantic?'

'Just as well it's never happened to me. I'd probably swallow it.'

'Ah, don't be silly, Orla. Stop putting yourself down.' Liz glances down at the solitaire rock sparkling on the third finger of her left hand, stroking it gently with her thumb as if she still can't believe it's there. 'Jason did try to get down on one knee, but the people behind complained so we had to wait till the film was over.'

'Which film was it?'

'*Gladiator*. A special showing at the Screen on the Green in Islington. I found the ring during the Battle of Carthage, just when the woman's body is sliced in two.'

And who says romance is dead?

'So, come on. What were his exact words?' I shrug off my own fears and gear myself up to hear about the moment my best friend said 'yes'.

'Oh, it's a bit silly really.' Liz waves her hand dismissively. 'Just a joke we have between us. You'll think we're ridiculous.'

'I won't. Come on, my best friend getting married, leaving me on the shelf. The least she can do is to give me some of the juicy bits.'

'He said that he chose the ring because it sparkled like my smile.'

'That's lovely.' I glance at the diamond, watching the light reflect on its surface. 'And he's right, but is that all?'

'No,' she admits, hesitantly. 'He asked if I wanted to change my domain name.'

'Eh?'

'Well, he is a website designer,' she says defensively. 'Personally I thought it was really sweet, and that it showed a lot of imagination and thought. It was so appropriate for him.' Exactly. 'Anyway, we rang our parents the moment we got back to our flat. They're thrilled – already talking about what colours they're going to wear. My mother wants oatmeal; Jason's mother figures butterscotch.' God, even the outfits make me feel hungry. 'And for the bridesmaids I thought green. What do you think?'

I think Incredible Hulk. 'I don't know, Liz,' I say tactfully. 'Isn't green meant to be unlucky?'

'God, you're right.' Liz tops up our champagne glasses. 'What about red?' I shake my head vigorously. Revenge of the killer tomatoes. 'Purple?' Like an overfed Pope. 'Yellow?' A walking melon.

'What about black?' I suggest hopefully, gulping down another glass. Black is slimming. 'Or something with a nice vertical stripe?' Liz looks at me in horror. 'I don't mean like a deckchair,' I add hastily. 'I was thinking something more subtle.'

Liz puts her half-empty glass onto the table and looks carefully at me. 'Are you not happy about this?' she asks finally. 'Don't you like Jason?'

'Yes, of course I do. He's lovely. You make a great couple. Seriously. It's just that . . .'

'I knew it. You think he's a nerd because he's into computers.' She slumps back in her chair in dismay.

'No!' I protest, attracting the attention of an elderly couple on the next table, who tut pointedly and shake their heads. The ostrich feather brooch on the woman's lapel quivers with disgust. 'Don't be so silly. Why on earth would you think that? Honest. It's just . . .' I pause, but Liz leaps in, feet first, mouth wide open.

'Oh my God, I'm being so tactless.' She grabs my hands, almost knocking over my champagne flute in the process. 'Orla darling, some day these roles will be reversed. You'll meet somebody just like Jason' – I shudder at the thought – 'and we'll be discussing your wedding plans. It will happen to you. I just know it.' She gives my fingers an extra squeeze. When do words of wisdom from your best friend sound like patronizing guff? Oh yes, I've just realized. When she sees two point four children and a company car on the horizon and you still haven't left the harbour.

'Liz, thanks for the words of hope,' I reply, 'but you've got hold of the wrong end of the stick. I'm quite happy with my life as it is.' What's a little white lie between friends? 'Anyway, you forget. I've been seeing Sebastian.'

'Oh God, yes. How long is that now? How's it going? I'm being so selfish hogging the conversation.' Liz settles back into her chair, desperate for the gory details. Well, she's virtually a married woman now. They probably don't have sex any more. So we do have something in common.

I met Sebastian three weeks ago in the Bishop of Norwich, a spit and sawdust basement bar on Moorgate, just five minutes' walk from Browns Black, the investment bank where I work as a press officer. I was out with Patti de Jager, the department's graduate trainee, and we were moaning about our boss, Tabitha. The witch. I know it's a harsh epitaph and not one I'd normally use . . . but, hell, she's even named after one. As a child, in fact, my favourite programme was *Bewitched*. I used to sit there in front of the television and imagine wrinkling my nose to make a kitten appear. As for Tabitha, her head is so far up her own arse that if she ever were to wrinkle her nose . . . it just doesn't bear thinking about.

Patti and I were discussing strategies on how to deal with Tabitha, ranging from decapitation, wrapping her in a hessian sack and throwing her down Niagara Falls, to exiling her to a world in which she could only wear high street fashion. Well, we were on our second bottle. And, besides, when you read what they did to witches in medieval times, I think we were positively Samaritan-like. It was only when Patti knocked her third wine glass onto the floor that I noticed we had an audience. Three City boys, propping up the bar. One plucked a glass from a wire rack above the bar, grabbed a new bottle and came over. It was Sebastian – and he was gorgeous. And psychic. Patti's glass-breaking antics had completely depleted our second bottle. Obviously we hadn't drunk it all. Had we? Patti and I were immediately smitten, particularly when he went back to the bar and returned with two packets of crisps. I hardly noticed that my scarf had moved from its strategic position hiding my cleavage, and that a baby's bottom was now revealed to the world, but he certainly did. And, wonder of wonders, he asked for my number.

'It's going really well,' I tell Liz. 'We've been seeing each other for just over three weeks – I'm not quite at the stage where I feel I can ring him up unprompted – but it's good.'

'And?'

'And what?'

'Is he, you know?' Liz winks at me. 'Is he good?'

'Good?' I play dumb, stalling for time because I know how Liz is going to respond to the truth. Sebastian Egan, gorgeous blond Adonis, has yet to make a move on me. Obviously we've kissed, but he hasn't tried it on once. Not even a roaming hand. I must admit it's a mystery, but I'm sure there's a simple explanation. Sebastian's the only guy I've been out with since school who hasn't tried to get me into bed the first night he pays for dinner. Even at school there was Paul O'Fagan – and he'd only paid for a Wimpy. 'Oh, that? Well, we haven't yet. It's early days,' I add indignantly, in a what-sort-of-a-girl-do-you-think-I-am voice.

'Since when did men worry about social niceties? So, you're playing hard to get?'

'He respects me,' I say defiantly. 'He wants us to get to know each other before we go any further. I think it's rather sweet.' Grab the dessert menu before she realizes I'm lying.

'Really? He hasn't tried to adjust your horizontal hold?' I shake my head. 'Well, I think that's weird. Are you sure he's not gay?'

'*No*. Of course, he's not gay,' I shriek. The couple on the table beside us are busy listening in. I glare at them until they turn away red-faced. Still listening, though. 'Anyway, Liz, we're not here to discuss Sebastian.'

'Perhaps he's married,' she interrupts, her face horrified at the thought of a man betraying the precious vows she's about to take.

'Listen to me. He's not married.' I say the words slowly. 'I've seen his flat. There are no wives in it.'

'But you've not stayed there.'

She's like a dog with a bone. Gnawing away. OK. It's time to get mean.

'I don't want to be your bridesmaid.' There. Said it. Don hard hats. Wait for sky to fall in.

'Sorry?' Liz looks dazed at my announcement. 'You don't want to be . . . but we promised. At university. I was going to be yours and you were going to be mine. Is that it? You don't want me to be yours?' She clasps her hand over her mouth in horror.

'No, don't be silly. It's just . . .' Time for second bottle. I gesture to the waiter. 'Come on now, Liz, can you imagine me in a bridesmaid's dress? Be honest.'

Liz looks at me and for one fleeting moment I can see that she's considered it. Probably even conjured up the same images that I have, although I suppose only my fertile imagination has come up with the one where my ample bosom casts shadows in the wedding photographs. But then it's gone. And now when she looks at me, I can tell that she's being genuine. Our friendship is deeper than weight issues. She really doesn't give a fig about my size.

'Orla, I am asking you to be my bridesmaid because you're my closest friend. You could be twenty-seven stone and stark naked so long as you follow me up the aisle and grab my flowers when required.'

'I'm not that heavy,' I say indignantly.

'I know that, for God's sake. I was just making a point.' Liz is irritated. She expected a bit more of a rapturous response from her best friend, who, she seems to forget, is paying for two bottles of Dom Pérignon. How much more rapturous can a friend be? 'But what size are you? Eigh—'

'Don't even go there!' I hold up my hand in protest. 'And you're wrong. Try one down from that.'

'Sixteen.'

'Shh,' I glance around quickly to check that nobody's listening.

'What's wrong with that? Didn't I read somewhere that sixty per cent of British women are over a size fourteen? Besides, if you lived in America you'd be a twelve. Look, we can try on every dress out there until we find something flattering that you feel comfortable in.'

'But . . .' I search for another excuse.

'But nothing. I wish you realized, Orla, that when people meet you they don't see your weight. Have you looked in the mirror recently? I'd die for a complexion like yours. Look, we made a pact at university and I am not letting you get out of it. Can't you see what having you by my side will mean to me?' She continues on the guilt trip. One-way ticket. No turning back. 'If you're that bothered, you could try to lose some weight before the wedding. You have twelve months.'

Twelve months? She might as well say twelve years. I've had so many twelve months since my sixteenth birthday and I never managed to lose weight in any of them. But I realize how determined Liz is that I will be her bridesmaid. Because she has never, *never*, mentioned my size before. Liz is a true friend, who gives the correct answers to all the standard questions. For example, does my bum look big in this? No, of course not. Is this jacket too tight across the back? Of *course* not. Do I look like a beached whale in this swimsuit? The correct reply, in *emphatic* tone, is most definitely not.

This last response demonstrates the depth of a friendship. Any hesitancy before response indicates that a friend is actually considering the question, which implies an element of doubt in their mind. A rushed 'Don't be silly' indicates a friend who has actually spotted beached whale similarity, but is trying to cover up. But an emphatic answer, which dispels all doubt, indicates that the friend is a true one who never sees the weight on your frame. A bit like those husbands interviewed in slimming magazines who express complete surprise that their wives have shed half their body weight and are now ten stone, insisting all along that they never noticed her size. Even when they had to buy two airline tickets because she didn't fit into one seat.

'I suppose I could try to lose weight,' I say hesitantly. 'I mean, I know all about dieting. I read all the books and magazines. I know the diets for blood types, sad types, and not my types. Ask me the calorie content of anything.'

'What about the F Plan? One of the secretaries at work went on it and lost loads of weight.' Liz is beaming. She can see I'm relenting.

'Hmm, you obviously never went into a lift with her,' I reply. 'Or stood down wind. The F doesn't only stand for fibre, you know.'

'Protein only? Isn't that the latest Hollywood fad? Jennifer Aniston went on that.'

'Gives you bad breath.'

'And Brad Pitt married her.' Liz shakes her head in wonder. 'I know, what was that diet Minnie Driver used to slim down? After that film when she had to put on loads of weight? I seem to remember it proved very successful. She went on all the chat shows to disclose her secret.'

'Yeah. She said she ate less and moved around more.'

'Why don't you try that?' asks Liz. 'Doesn't sound hard.'

'She was being ironic. All diet books say that to lose weight you should basically eat less and take up regular exercise. Minnie Driver didn't invent the Holy Grail. It sounds easy, but it isn't. Dieting is very lonely.' I stop to ponder the dessert menu. 'I really need somebody to diet with.'

'Well, I could do with losing a few pounds . . .'

'Liz, that's not what I meant. Think how I'd feel when you shed your two pounds, knowing that I've got four more stone to go. No. I need a sort of support group. You know, people in the same boat as me. Like Alcoholics Anonymous,' I say, mouthing at the hovering waiter, '*Crème brûlée*. Anyway, let's change the subject. Dieting is just *so* boring to talk about. And *I* have some news. My mother rang today.'

'Your mother rings every day,' interrupts Liz, as she hands back the dessert menu to the waiter, saying. 'Just coffee.' Traitor. 'Black. No sugar.' Turncoat.

'And a large cappuccino for me,' I add boldly. 'What?' I catch

Liz's eye. 'I'm only talking about dieting. I couldn't start today; it's a Wednesday. Diets have to start on a Monday. Everybody knows that.' She nods patiently. 'Well, Mum rang and had the usual five-minute rant about how she would never be a grandmother. She's obsessed with my biological clock.'

'Which hasn't been wound up for a while.' I glare at her. 'Sorry. Which of your old schoolfriends has just given birth?'

Liz knows my mother only too well. My mother Mary lives in Clontarf, a seaside town on the north side of Dublin, in the redbrick house that I grew up in. She rings every day to keep me in touch with the local gossip, and to check I'm not doing anything I shouldn't be.

'Deirdre O'Grady. We were in junior class together when I was five,' I explain, shifting back in my chair to allow the waiter to place the dessert cutlery and my *crème brûlée* in front of me. 'Apparently Mrs O'Grady now has six grandchildren, which my mother thinks is an ideal number of offspring from two children. She says Mrs O'Grady is blessed. Anyway, Mum was ringing about Finn.'

'Don't tell me. Your brother's got his girlfriend pregnant. Well, at least that takes the pressure off you.'

'What girlfriend? Sure, do you know any women willing to put up with a barely house-trained twenty-eight-year-old, who thinks antibacterial cream is a relative from Cork?' I tap my teaspoon firmly on the caramelised top of my *crème brûlée* and wait for a fissure to develop, allowing entry into the luscious dessert. 'No. I'll give you a clue. My mum's said eight rosaries over the past two days and even went to confession with Father Andrew. She blames herself.'

'Don't tell me. Finn's gay?'

'Worse than that. You're obsessed with men being gay.'

'He's impotent?'

'And he'd tell my mother? Anyway, why would she blame herself for that?'

'I don't know. Maybe she's praying that you'll both save yourselves for your wedding night. It seems to be working with

11

you and Sebastian. I give up.' Liz lifts her coffee cup to her lips. 'He got a parking ticket? Bought a Britney Spears album?'

'He's become a Buddhist. Finn Kennedy, former head altar boy of the parish of St Ignatius in Clontarf, has become a Buddhist. Imagine.'

'No! How has your mother taken it?'

'How do you think? She feels that she's failed in her role as a Catholic mother. She's tendered her resignation from the church cleaning team and her position on the St Vincent de Paul fundraising committee is under review.'

'And your dad?'

'I think he's used it as an excuse for an extended stay in the pub.' As a child, I thought my father, Dermot, was a sailor, as every night he would announce he was off to the yacht. In fact, The Yacht was the pub at the end of the road. It was only when I was an adult that I wished he had sailed away.

'But it's not your mother's fault,' protests Liz. 'He's a grown man, responsible for his own actions.'

I snort at the idea of my brother being responsible for anything. 'Get this: He learned about Buddhism through a chat room – and my mother bought him the computer. Apparently he's been on-line for months learning about enlightenment. She's only just got the phone bill.'

'That's it,' Liz exclaims, leaning over to dig her teaspoon into my *crème brûlée*. My very last mouthful. Has she no respect for our friendship? 'Have you ever thought of a dieting chat room? Where you could chat to other people trying to lose weight.'

'Do they exist?' I ask doubtfully.

'I don't know, but they should. If people chat on-line about Buddhism, I'm sure they must chat about calories.' Liz puts her thinking cap back on. 'And if they don't, why don't you start one?'

I almost spray my coffee all over the linen tablecloth. 'Sorry? I thought you just said I should start a chat room.'

'I did. Admit it, you know what to do – all the tricks and tips, the calories, which diets work, which ones don't. And,' – she pauses for effect – 'my boy . . . fiancé,' – a quick smile at the unfamiliar word – 'knows how to set up websites and chat rooms. I can publicize it through my magazine . . .'

'You write about finance,' I interrupt.

'I'll think of an angle,' Liz adds dismissively, 'and you work in a press office, you know all about publicity and advertising and everything.'

'For Browns Black. An investment bank.' I enunciate the words. Liz doesn't seem to be taking anything in. Must be the lack of sugar in her meal. 'Not for dieting websites or chat rooms or whatever.'

'Oh, come on.' She throws back her hands in exasperation. 'Live a little. You could become the world's first ever dieting chat room millionaire.'

'Or the world's first ever dieting chat room loser.'

'I don't know, Orla. One minute you're talking about losing weight and needing a support group, and when I come up with something that might help you achieve that, you put up all the barriers,' snaps Liz.

'I don't.'

'You do. It's like when you ring me on a Monday to say you've started a diet, then ring back on a Friday to say you've stopped one. Because you had to go to some journalist lunch and found yourself inextricably pulled towards the most calorific main course. What do you call it? The Fat Force.'

'It's a real phenomenon,' I say defiantly. 'My eyes glaze over at the words "grilled" and "poached". I've told my optician about it.'

'And what did he say?'

'Order salad.' I pause. 'When am I actually meant to run this chat room?'

'What's to run? You're always complaining that Tabitha leaves you in charge of the phones during the lunch breaks when hardly anyone rings anyway. Why not operate a chat room then? Tell clients it's only open between noon and two. If anybody walks past your desk, it'll look as if you're working on the computer producing press releases or whatever it is you do.'

13

'What about Patti?'

'She's your ally. She's hardly going to snitch on you. Besides, from what you've said in the past, I don't think she actually notices what's going on after lunch. *And* I've just thought of the perfect name,' she adds, glancing at the brooch on our neighbour's lapel. 'Light as a feather.'

It seems as if I've only just fallen asleep when the phone on my bedside cabinet starts to ring. I look at the illuminated dial of my alarm clock. Who on earth calls at three in the morning? My mother, that's who. The only woman who thinks there's a time difference between London and Dublin. I curse the day that I loaded my correct numbers (work, home, mobile, pager) into her phone's memory.

'Hello,' I croak into the handset.

'Orla? Is that you?' My mother's voice echoes in my ear.

'Who else would it be at this time?' I sigh and pull myself up into a sitting position, fluffing up the pillows under my head. This could be a long call.

'Well, I don't know. You hear such strange stories about what happens in London. People living in squats and all that. Are you alone?'

'Of course I'm alone. It's three in the morning. Even the milkman doesn't pop round at this time.'

'Are you awake then?' If she were sitting beside me, I would thump her. 'Did you not get my messages? Sure I've rung five times tonight already. I even said it was an emergency. Why didn't you call me?' Because I just fell into my bed after my night out with Liz and didn't once look at my answer machine or check my mobile phone. And God only knows on which bus I left my pager all those weeks ago. 'It's Finn.'

'What's happened?' My heart thumps fiercely in my chest

15

cage as the protective elder sister genes spring into action. 'Has there been an accident? Is he all right?'

'He . . .' My mother pauses. I can feel panicky little tears welling in my eyes. 'He's . . .'

'Mum. Tell me. Don't hold back. I can take it.'

'He's . . . he's run away.'

My tears evaporate. 'He's twenty-eight,' I finally say, frustrated. 'Twenty-eight-year-old men don't run away. They move.'

'You sound just like the Garda, who incidentally won't do anything for twenty-four hours. Why do they call themselves an emergency service? I don't care what you all say. My Finn ran away. Earlier tonight.'

'Why would he run away?' Best to use her terminology.

'We'd been talking about his Buddhism thing.' My mother pronounces Buddhism 'Booedhissem'. 'Marcella told me yesterday that Buddhists shave their heads, wear orange dresses, and walk up and down streets banging cymbals together. I just couldn't bear it if Finn shaved his head, he has such lovely curls, and I was worried about the cymbals. Your brother hasn't a musical note in his body. Even St Ignatius's choir rejected him, and they took that Grimes boy who was mute. How's he going to cope with this silly nonsense? I only asked him,' she adds defiantly.

'I think Marcella has got her wires slightly crossed. She's mistaken Buddhists for Hari Krishna followers,' I say patiently. 'Finn can wear whatever he wants as a Buddhist and he doesn't have to play cymbals.'

'Now he's run off, probably to have one of those mass market weddings,' my mother continues. Ignoring me. 'I couldn't bear to see him married in a church with fifteen thousand other couples. I mean, where would your Aunty May sit? She's so small. Wouldn't be able to see a thing over all the heads.'

'Mum, those are Moonies. I can't see why he would run off if you only asked him about cymbals and shaving his head,' I admit. I can think of lots of other reasons though.

'We also had a small argument about this little statue thing he had. Short fellow with a bald head and huge belly. At first, I thought he'd bought it because it looked like your daddy. But then he put it on the mantelpiece in the front room, under the picture of Pope John Paul II, lit a few candles, and started chanting at it. Well, you wouldn't chant at your father, would you?' Not unless it was last orders. 'And then Finn said it was a Buddha. I mean, being so close to the Pope and everything, I didn't know if it would bring bad luck on the family or what. And Marcella said I should have the priest over to bless the house. Exorcize it.'

'And that's why Finn left?' Why does my head ache so much? It can't just be the alcohol, can it?

'He got very upset when Father Andrew arrived. Said that I didn't understand him, or his need to express himself. He said that he couldn't experience true enlightenment in this house.' My mother tuts at the memory. 'Sure how does he think two children were conceived?' Whoa, Mum. Have you been at the Amaretto?

'That's all Finn said?' I interrupt quickly.

'Pretty much. Then he went upstairs, packed a bag, told me that he'd be in touch and that I should cancel his subscription to *GQ*. I'm glad actually. Some of the outfits those girls wore.'

'Did he say where he was going?' Deep breath, Orla. Remember she's old. It's her hormones.

'Not exactly, but about two hours after he left, he rang and asked for your address. And where you worked. I don't know who he was with, but they were very rude. Kept interrupting while he was making his call.'

'Like an announcer, perhaps?'

'I don't know. But now you mention it, could be.'

'Could he have been at the airport? Or a station?'

'Aye, might have been.' My mother sounds surprised. 'Oh Orla, what should I do? It's times like this when one really needs the comfort of grandchildren. Did I tell you that Mrs O'Grady now has six?'

'Yes.'

'Mrs O'Grady asked about you when I saw her. But I told her

that you weren't interested in men, or settling down. That you were a career girl in London. In public services.' Great. Now the neighbours aren't sure if I'm a lesbian or a prostitute.

'Public relations, Mum, I've told you before. Look, there's nothing we can do at the moment. I'll call you if Finn gets in touch, but right now it's' – I glance at the clock – 'almost three thirty and I really must get back to sleep. I've got work in a couple of hours.'

'How can I sleep knowing that my only son is lying in a ditch somewhere?'

'If I know Finn, he'll probably have booked into a hotel room while he sorts himself out,' I reply patiently. 'Worrying about him isn't going to change anything. He's a grown man. He'll cope.'

'Thank goodness I let him join the scouts when he was ten. He might just remember some of his old survival techniques. Did he ever get his badge for lighting a fire with two sticks? Can you remember, Orla?'

'Mum,' I say, trying to keep my voice calm, 'Why don't you make yourself a mug of hot milk and go to bed. Is anybody else there?'

'Your father. He's in the kitchen having a nightcap to calm his nerves.' There's a surprise. 'It was a complete shock to him. He thought Finn had been gargling to get rid of a sore throat. Never realized he'd gone' – she spits the word – 'Booedhissed.'

'Mum, I'll talk to you tomorrow. I'm sure that Finn's fine. He's just making a point. Anyway, you get to bed now. OK?' I put the phone down as my mother starts to cry. I am wide awake now. Finn's probably sleeping on one of his friends' floors tonight and will return later when he thinks he's made his point. Hoping that Mum will welcome him and his statue back into the family home. It doesn't surprise me that he's turned to Buddhism. Finn is one of those people that never seem happy. Always searching for something else. He's just drifted since graduating from university, one employer to the next. He's between jobs at the moment. Maybe Buddhism is

18

what's been missing from his life. Maybe it'll give him a purpose.

If only I'd been going out with Sebastian for a few weeks more. I'd feel that I could call him tonight with this family crisis. Ask him to come right over and allow me to cry on his shoulder. I pause for a moment. Perhaps this is just the thing for Sebastian and me. Perhaps I haven't shown how much I need him. Perhaps he really does want to sleep with me, but doesn't think I'm ready. Should I call? My finger suddenly takes on a mind of its own and presses his number in my phone memory. One. It rings. Once. Twice. Three times. Ah, perhaps he's not in. Four times. Five times. Answer phone. No. Definitely not in. I hang up without leaving a message.

I don't remember him mentioning plans. It's probably one of those 'quick drinks' with colleagues that suddenly turn into a mammoth session. Like the night he met me. We all ended up in Soho, at Dick's in the Atlantic Bar until three. Me and Patti, Sebastian and his two colleagues, Darren and Nigel. The three men took bets on everything. The colour tie of the next person entering the room. What would be the first word the waitress said. The easiest one hundred pounds I ever won. Sebastian said he spends the day betting with colleagues and clients. On our first date he'd won so much that he splashed out on vintage champagne and oysters, and confided that he was in line to win a five thousand pound bet with his boss. 'Stick with me, girl,' he'd winked. I sure planned to.

It's definitely too late to ring Liz – she's probably comatose by now. We left the restaurant in a giggly state and hailed a black cab to take Liz to the 'man I love'. I took a little while to explain to her that, while drivers of black cabs may pride themselves on finding anywhere in London, they are not actually psychic. In the end, the driver insisted that I accompany her, while she held her head out of the window sucking in the fresh night air, vainly struggling not to throw up. That's the problem with people who are too slim; they haven't enough fat to absorb excessive amounts of alcohol.

Jason answered the door to their flat in Islington in his Bart

Simpson pyjamas. And Liz wonders why I sometimes think he's a nerd. He simply swept her into his arms, took the plastic carrier bag filled with vomit, and thanked me for looking after her, before carrying her through to their bedroom. The nasty-deep-down-buried-so-far part of me guiltily imagined him throwing her onto the bed, with a sharp comment about women drinking. But the jealous-this-probably-happened-instead part imagined him carefully undressing Liz, slipping the covers gently over her, before fetching a pint glass of water and a bucket to place by her side of the bed.

I've tried to diet, but all it does is make me bigger. They always have to start on a Monday, and so each Sunday I would empty my fridge of any fat-laden goodies that might tempt me over the coming months. Well, you can't throw them out. Not with all the starving children in Africa that my mother used to talk about. And then I would fret that it was quite impossible to begin a diet without one last binge, otherwise I'd get withdrawal symptoms and end up ruining the process. So I'd pop down to the local curry house, the Bengal Tandoori, or Binge All Tandoori as I preferred to call it, and order a takeaway onion bhaji, chicken tikka masala, pilau rice, keema nan, a few poppadoms with mango chutney, and a portion of sag aloo. The last item only because I know that it is important to get greens into a healthy diet. Unfortunately, I popped down so often that it has now become a standing order. Delivered every Sunday evening at seven thirty. Just in time for Coronation Street.

The bank I work for negotiated a very cheap corporate rate with a local gym, so I joined. It's lovely. Wonderful pool, couple of studios, four squash courts . . . at least, as far as I can remember. It's been a long time since I visited. I went for the induction session and met a very gorgeous young man, dressed in a polo shirt that revealed his taut muscles and six pack stomach – he looked like a walking Action Man – who advised a programme that involved running three times a week for twenty minutes or so, a spot of stepping and a spin class or two plus a couple of leisurely swims. He told me that I would eventually look like Kate Moss. I started on the rigorous programme, until one day while surfing at work I discovered a website that revealed the calories burned off by each exercise. Indeed, he was right. I could eventually look like a supermodel. It would just take eight years, four months and three days – give or take a few hours. Well, it's hard to find motivation after statistics like that so I settled back into my old ways. And added another stone.

I can't believe that Liz and I wasted so much time tonight discussing setting up a dieting chat room. How absurd. Why didn't we just consider liposuction? When Liz wakes up, the two of us will just have a good old laugh about our drunken conversation. I mean, me setting up a chat room? It's a ridiculous idea.

Slimming tip four

Ask yourself what you're going back to

The phone rings on my cluttered desk. It's a welcome relief. I'm drafting a press release on a ten million dollar property deal that the bank is doing in some obscure part of Slovakia. I rub my temples. My head is throbbing, spinning with the heady mixture of tiredness, concern about my brother, and a complete lack of interest in what I'm doing. I spent an hour this morning trying to understand this deal, then another hour trying to explain to Sven, the investment banker in charge, why it will not be necessary for him to get a haircut today. *Newsnight* would not be calling.

Investment bankers. They seem to think that just because they earn a lot of money and are fêted within Browns Black, they are actually important people in the outside world. I spend a lot of time massaging their egos and managing their expectations. Explaining why if it's a choice between them, Tom Cruise, Prince William or Charlie Dimmock on the front page of a newspaper then their chances aren't great.

Sven seems to have the most difficulty grasping this principle. He can't understand why a woman who is known for her water features and an inability to put a bra on can achieve so much notoriety. He's Eastern European though, so I think the whole concept of page three has passed him by. He arrived last year from some obscure bank that I'd never heard of, but smiled and nodded politely when he named it, and has been one of the most regular visitors to the press department. If I get his name into a newspaper he is the happiest man in the world.

And if it happens to quote one of his pearls of wisdom his ecstasy knows no bounds.

Unfortunately, I've managed both achievements only twice. One was a mention in the *Financial Times* that Sven had joined the bank and the second was in a feature piece on what it was like to change jobs when they quoted his views on how traumatic it was. Like moving schools when you're thirty-five. Since then the newspapers have been a Sven-free zone and, judging from today's deal, I can see why. It's very dull.

I glance at my watch – noon – and answer the phone. 'Orla Kennedy speaking.'

'It's ground floor reception here. East entrance. We have a man waiting to see you. A Mr Finn Kennedy. Shall I send him up?' No, he does that well enough himself.

'I'll come down,' I sigh. 'Could do with a short break. Tell him I'll be there in a few minutes.' The return of the prodigal brother. I stretch my arms out in front of me, locking my hands together until the fingers click. A passing secretary looks over in disgust.

Finn is studying one of the huge paintings that adorn the marble and glass reception area of Browns Black, a stuffed rucksack by his feet. The massive canvas is covered haphazardly with yellow and red splodges, and a squiggly lime green line shoots from the bottom left-hand corner to the top right-hand one. I glance at it in despair. Modern art is the passion of the bank's chairman, and the reception area is littered with paintings and sculptures. Only last week I stopped a journalist stubbing out his cigarette in one of the latest acquisitions, and last month there was almost a diplomatic incident in the bank when the chairman returned from a three-week trip to the Far East to discover that his pride and joy, a twenty-foot painting that had just won a major prize, had been hung upside down. Personally I thought it looked better, but then I think Tracey Emin's unmade bed looks exactly like mine.

I tap Finn's shoulder. He turns, smiles wanly, then returns to stare at the canvas. 'What does this picture say to you?' he asks.

'That some artist is having a laugh,' I reply, without properly looking, 'at Browns Black's expense.'

'You can't mean that,' he shrieks, stabbing his finger at the centre of the painting. 'Can't you see your inner self in it?'

'Nope,' I say finally, staring once again at the painting, 'but if that really is my inner self, then I might just book a colonic irrigation.'

Finn turns back to me. 'I suppose this is a by-product of discovering Buddha. I can now see deep into myself, in a way that wasn't possible before.'

'Yes, I've heard about your self-discovery,' I reply, carefully examining him to see if I can spot any differences. But he looks the same as ever. Not particularly bad-looking, but not particularly good-looking. Finn's tall, with the well-built physique of a rugby player, and a cropped hairstyle to downplay his receding hairline. He's the sort of person that you would notice in a bar, think 'he's nice', then two minutes later have forgotten all about. Today he's wearing jeans, a crew neck sweater, with a denim jacket tied around his waist.

'So Mum has rung?' He shrugs, a little awkwardly.

'About eight times.'

'Did she say anything?'

'No, kept putting the phone down without a word.'

'Really?' To think we're related.

'No, not really. She's worried about you. Finn, you could at least have told her where you were going. She won't have slept a wink last night. I mean, this is the woman who rings me every day in October to check that I've started taking Vitamin C to fend off cold germs. Have you any idea what she's going through since you walked out? I had her on the phone at three this morning fretting about you. She thinks you're going through a midlife crisis at twenty-eight.'

'I'm sorry.' He has the grace to look embarrassed.

'Where did you sleep last night?'

'I went to the airport, booked the flight, then checked into a bed and breakfast nearby. I suppose I should have rung to say that I was safe, but, Orla, she doesn't appreciate what I've discovered. I just couldn't stay there. You do see what I mean, don't you?' I nod in a trying-to-be-Cosmopolitan-sister sort of way. 'Dublin is just *so* claustrophobic. I mean, the neighbours were blessing themselves when I walked past them in the street. Nobody understands me there.' Or here. 'All this Celtic leopard stuff. Irish people are now so obsessed with material wealth, they don't understand about the Eightfold Path that we should follow.' I nod again. 'I mean, one should work to affirm values and moral behaviour, to enhance our environment. You do understand, don't you?' Another right-on-let's-eat-hummus nod. 'I just had to come to London. I can be myself here. Find like-minded people, who care about ethics and the right way. So it's all right if I stay with you?'

I must truly be enlightened because I saw that one coming a mile off. Still, no point in giving in easily. Aren't people meant to suffer for their beliefs?

'Finn, I have a one-bedroom apartment. I haven't got the room.'

'I just need to further discover my inner self, Orla. I thought of everybody you'd understand.' Ooh, sneaky move. Pull on my sophisticated heartstrings.

'I haven't even got a sofa . . .'

'The floor will be fine. More than fine. Buddha teaches us that we learn through suffering. Actually he also says that we should refrain from using comfortable beds.' He smiles. 'And I won't be any trouble. Honest. You'll hardly know I'm there. I know how to wash up now and Mum has shown me how to turn the vacuum cleaner on.'

'Well . . .'

'OK, so I don't know what else to do with it. I can learn. I'll even cook dinner tonight.' Ah, the fatted calf. Now here's a man after my own heart, even if he is only thirteen stone. I pass my brother my keys, and scribble down my address on Goswell Road.

It's a street filled with a mismatch of architecture that stretches almost from London Wall in the City – where the remains of a Roman wall guarding the entrance to the area still survive – to the Angel in Islington. A location I hated in my childhood when I landed on it playing Monopoly because it was *so* cheap. How things change. Today Islington is filled with trendy wine bars, restaurants, antique shops and expensive boutiques.

Finn takes in all the information, nods, then asks, 'And do you have any spare cash? The flight and the bed and breakfast cost more than I thought. Capitalism, the scourge of our modern society.' He shakes his head ruefully, extending his hand. 'Thanks, Orla,' he said, as I take five ten-pound notes out of the wallet that I brought down just in case. 'I promise you won't regret this. I'll make myself useful. I just need time to find myself. To establish my focus of appearance and being, to find the appropriate concentration . . .'

'OK, Finn, I get the message.' I put my hand up to stop him bleating and push him towards the exit in the appropriate direction of Goswell Road. 'I won't be late. Oh, and a word of warning, tuna and green peppers don't agree with me. Just like Mum.'

I ring my mother the moment I return to my desk. She isn't happy. She'd just finished sorting out his bedroom and discovered he'd left behind all his thermal vests.

'Will you keep an eye on him? You know he's got a weak heart.' The one he invented to get out of cross-country running. 'And he can't eat muesli. Or marrowfat peas. Or—'

'Mum, I've got all that. I have to go,' I interrupt. Sven is hovering by my desk, a trio of ties in his hand. 'He just needs some time to sort himself out. You know Finn. He'll be home next week when he discovers Hinduism.'

'No. Isn't that where they wear turbans?'

'It was a joke, Mum. Look, I'll call you,' I promise, replacing the receiver.

Sven holds up the ties. There's a navy one, a green one with anchors, and a really disgusting multi-coloured one that looks like something Liz threw up on last night.

'Which one?' he asks.

'For what?' I look at him blankly.

26

'The photograph.'

'Photograph?' Even blanker.

'Patti said that you'd managed to get my deal on the front page of the *Financial Times* tomorrow.' Is that above or below the collapse of that major industrial company? 'And they'd like a photograph.' How about one of Patti's autopsy since I'm going to murder her. I glance over to her desk. What a surprise. She's out to lunch.

'I think she got confused with another story we're working on,' I explain diplomatically. He looks crestfallen. 'But the green tie is very nice. Looks like you've won a Blue Peter badge.' It's his turn to look blank. 'That's a good thing, honest.' Patti's phone starts to ring. 'I've got to answer that. Sorry. Everybody else from the department is at lunch.'

It's not strictly true. Tabitha has been in a strategy meeting all day with Giles Heppelthwaite-Jones. He's the kingpin of Smiths, a City-based public relations firm, who comes in to see Tabitha once a week and tell her – for the bargain price of three hundred pounds per hour plus VAT – how Browns Black can improve its press coverage. His advice this morning (which Tabitha made him repeat to me) was to get more mentions in the press. Increase column inches, as he put it. I don't know how we'd manage without him.

Giles is the only man I know who can make a walrus seem blessed with good looks. He's rotund, with an enormous red nose that encroaches deep into his cheeks, thread-veined from years of excess. He keeps his greying hair permanently slicked back with Brylcreem and just oozes grease. I've met him many times over the past three years – fetching him coffee, taking his coat, listening to his pearls of wisdom – but if he was asked to name me, he'd have to phone a friend.

I grab Patti's receiver, half-knowing what is coming.

'Orla, is that you?'

'Yes, Patti. Where are you? And what have you said to Sven? The poor man is distraught.'

'Who? Oh he wassh annoying me. Kept ashking about photographs.'

'Are you drunk?'

'Don't be shilly. I jusht don't think the fisch agreed with me. The journalist I'm with feelsh exchactly the same. We feel a bit shick. Gonna go home. Can you tell Tabitha?'

'All right, but Patti, listen, you've got to be in tomorrow. Tabitha and Giles are off to Royal Ascot. I'll be by myself otherwise.'

'Yeah. Oh, almosht forgot. Sebastian rang.'

'When?'

'Thish morning. He's at an off-shite meeting. Will call tomorrow. Keep Friday night free. Said something about anniversh, anneever, oh hell. Shelebration.' Bless her. I just hope Patti's fish was ice cold and arrived with a plump cork in its mouth.

SLIMMING TIP FIVE

Take it upstairs now

I have just grabbed a bacon and egg roll from the nine o'clock breakfast trolley when Tabitha calls me into her office. Damn. It'll be cold by the time I get around to eating it. Just like the much-heralded meal that Finn prepared for me last night. A ham sandwich. Apparently my microwave is so completely different from the one my mother owns that he was unable even to put a ready-made meal into it. He blamed it on London Electricity. Said their wattages were imperial and he was only used to dealing in decimal. And, by the way, did I have any more cash for him? He was really surprised at the price of a sliced loaf. And Parma ham. Whoever heard of such prices? Where did the local delicatessen get it? Italy?

Giles is already sitting on one of the four reproduction Chippendale chairs that surround a long mahogany table at the side of Tabitha's massive office. The table is strewn with screwed-up pieces of paper. A thesaurus lies open at one end. Giles is wearing a morning suit, all ready for a day at Royal Ascot, and an oval pink card swings on a silken thread from his lapel – an invitation to the Royal Enclosure. He glances at me without a flicker of recognition.

'Orla Kennedy,' I prompt. 'Junior press officer.'

He smiles vaguely.

'Orla, could you sit down?' Tabitha is sitting behind her big desk reading a sheet of paper, pencil in hand. She is wearing a jade green, silk shift dress embroidered with little cherries, and her hair is swept up into an elegant chignon. A matching hat with a huge brim, filled with bright red, artificial cherries, lies on the desk. 'Giles and I were in extremely early this morning. There's been something of a crisis.' Don't tell me, Tabitha, you broke a fingernail? Or perhaps Giles was unable to break wind with his customary regularity? 'I was called late last night by a reporter. Apparently there are rumours out there that this bank has suffered trading losses.'

I look at her in shock. 'Has it?' I've worked in the City long enough to know that trading losses can cause banks to collapse. A trader, too embarrassed to admit a small loss, can find the temptation to hide his error irresistible, and then that small hole develops into a massive pit. Big enough to swallow the bank up. Everybody remembers Nick Leeson and Barings.

'Of course not,' she snaps. 'We employ some of the best traders in the City. They don't make mistakes. But rumours like this need to be stopped immediately. Giles and I have been in since six this morning working on an appropriate statement.' She turns to him and smiles. 'I don't know what I'd do without the benefit of his experience and expertise.' He smiles graciously, waving off her compliments with a soothing 'Nonsense, darling.'

Tabitha hands me the piece of paper she's been studying. 'This is the bank's response.' I read it. 'Browns Black denies it has suffered trading losses.' However could we have produced such an opus without Giles? 'Now, Orla, whenever any journalist rings about trading losses, you must read that out. Can you do that?' Is this the moment to ask for help with the big words? Probably not. I nod. 'And tell Patti too. Now' – she checks her Palm Pilot – 'you'll have to take a meeting for me later this morning. With' – she glances down again – 'some new analyst who's joining next week. Tony Younger. Completely forgot about him.'

'OK,' I nod.

'You'll need to write a press release about his appointment. Get some articles in the newspapers about him this weekend. Remember Giles's advice; we need to improve our coverage.

I'm depending on you. Get Patti involved.' She stands up, grabs her hat, moves over to the mirror at the corner of her office, and settles it on her head. 'He's been doing voluntary work in one of those Third World places. Oh, what's it called? Name one,' she orders as she reapplies her lipstick.

'Africa?'

'That's the place.' She closes the lipstick and drops it into her beaded clutch bag. 'Imagine. He had three months between jobs and chose to spend it putting in drainage in some miserable country. I mean the man was even given a huge cheque as a thank you just for joining Browns Black, so God alone knows why he didn't just book into a five star spa and relax. Accounts even told me last week that he's set up some sort of charitable save-as-you-earn scheme. What on earth is the City coming to?' She gives herself a final check in the mirror, grabs a matching coat from the stand, and adds, 'Don't worry about pictures, he's bringing some in. And try not to disturb me. It makes you look so amateurish when you ring up on the mobile. What must Giles think?' I glance across at him. He smiles in a can't-get-the-staff way, but says nothing. 'Right. 'Bye.'

I return to my desk just as Patti arrives – a big bottle of Lucozade under her arm. I brief her on the statement we must repeat if asked about trading losses. She takes a little while to memorize it, but, like me, thinks she can cope. I also brief her on the meeting with Tony Younger.

'Orla, I know this is presumptuous . . .'

'That's a long word with a hangover.'

'It was the fish,' she reiterates.

'And the bloodshot eyes?'

'A new fashion,' she replies as she tries to hide the Lucozade bottle in her drawers. 'Look, I'm sorry about yesterday, but I wonder if I could do the press release for this one. I need to learn the ropes. I mean, what on earth can I do wrong? I've seen you draft hundreds of these things.'

'Well . . .' Tabitha did say I was to get Patti involved but . . .

'Please,' she begs, hands clasped to her chest. 'I'll never learn if I don't sometimes get thrown in at the deep end, will I?'

'All right then,' I finally say as my phone starts to ring. 'You have sole responsibility for getting press coverage on this appointment, but we'll do the meeting together. Agreed? And I want to see the press release before it goes out to the journalists.'

She nods as I answer my phone. It's Liz.

'Tabitha has gone to Ascot with Smiths, so I'm minding the shop,' I tell her. 'I'm meeting our new recruit.' I check the name that I jotted down onto my notebook. 'Tony Younger.'

'Tony Younger,' she shrieks. 'Do you know who he is?'

I check my notes. 'A new economy analyst. Highly-rated. Why?'

'Just that he's hot. With a capital H, O and T. Wow. You sure you don't need any journalists to come in and meet him? I can be ready in, er, let me think, hair, bikini wax, defuzzing legs and armpits, make-up—' She pauses. 'In four hours?'

'Too late. He's coming this morning. Anyway you're an almost married woman. But thanks for the offer.'

'Spoilsport. Anyway I was talking to Jason again this morning about our idea for Light As A Feather.'

'Oh that.' Just when I was beginning to think this morning wouldn't be all bad. 'I thought we'd established yesterday it was just all a drunken chat. You know like when we vow to run the London Marathon and do nothing about it.'

'No, that was your interpretation. I'm still deadly serious and Jason thinks we're onto a winner. We spent last night surfing the web checking out the competition.' See, it is all downhill once he puts the engagement ring on the finger. 'Honestly, there's not much out there. I think you could do really well, particularly if you just concentrate on clients in the London area at first.'

'Did you start drinking early this morning?'

'Orla, we're doing this for you.'

'I'd rather a lifetime supply of Twix bars.'

'I thought you said you wanted to lose weight.'

'I did.'

'And you wanted a support group to help you.'

'I did.'

'Well, we're helping you to form one. Honestly, Orla, you could be onto something here. Jason suggests we come round to yours on Saturday morning, after we've seen the priest, to talk it over.'

'But what about Finn?' Ah, the only time in my life that my brother proves useful.

'He can make the coffee.'

'Well . . .'

'We'll be there about eleven thirty. Maybe noon. No later, we're off to see possible reception venues in the afternoon.'

'And if I still think it's a silly idea after seeing you both, we'll drop it?'

'Settled. Now . . . still no chance of a quick meeting with Tony Younger?'

'And you just newly engaged,' I admonish.

'Well, you need somebody to take care of you.'

'I've got Sebastian, remember. Thank you, but I can cope. Speak later.'

I have barely put the phone down when it rings again. My second call in two days from ground floor reception. East entrance. This time it's Tony Younger. Patti volunteers to collect him. 'And remember,' she says as she grabs the security tag that allows her to regain entrance onto the floor, 'you did promise that I could do the press release. No interference.' I nod. 'Great, see you in five.'

Five minutes, my arse. After twenty minutes I begin to worry and make my way to the bank of lifts to check where Patti and Tony have got to. As I pull open the security door, I can hear her.

'And on the left, the door with the sign that has a little man with his legs wide open is the men's loos. As you enter the security door – personnel will get you a special pass – you'll find the drink making facilities on the right. Obviously alcohol is not allowed on the floor during working hours.'

'Patti. What are you doing?'

'Orla.' Patti starts. 'I was just showing Tony where everything is.' She gestures to . . . oh my God. Come to mamma. Tony

Younger is not hot. He's positively boiling. Dressed casually in chinos and open necked white cotton shirt that highlights his tanned skin, he turns to me and extends his hand, piercing blue eyes staring straight into mine. Please God, don't let me have globs of mascara on my lashes. I know I have a Buddhist staying in my apartment, but I'll evict him immediately if you just do this one small thing.

'Tony Younger,' he says. 'Patti here says that you and she will be looking after me today.'

'That's right,' I say, trying to hide my bitten nails. His hands feel calloused in mine. 'Would you like to come through? I'm Tabitha's deputy,' I explain en route to Tabitha's office, 'but it's only a small team. Just us three.' Swallow me up, floor. I'm about as interesting as an empty Rolo packet.

'Tabitha said you'd just done some voluntary work,' I add, as we settle ourselves around the witch's mahogany table. Patti gathers up the scattered waste paper, and throws it into a bin before sitting down. Right next to Tony.

'Yep, that's right. I enrolled with one of the voluntary agencies and offered my services. I'm a fully qualified engineer,' he smiles.

'OK.' I push a notebook towards Patti, who starts taking down salient facts for the press release. 'Engineering,' I repeat as she jots it down. 'What university?'

'Em, Cambridge.' He blushes. 'Do you know, I haven't been asked which university I attended since my first job? Is it relevant?' Shit. I'm looking like an amateur.

'You can never tell what some journalists will ask and we always like to have all the possible answers,' replies Patti. Good save. I look at her in surprise. Then remember it is still before lunch.

'I took a first.' Hmm. No problems offering that bit of information unprompted. I start to re-evaluate my opinion.

'You graduated in?'

'1987. I then joined McKinsey, the management consultants, as a graduate trainee, and became an analyst in the City about five years ago, just when the internet was starting up.'

'You specialize in new economy stocks?'

'That's right.'

'And you're rated . . . ?'

'Em, second in the Boxtel survey and' – he blushes again – 'first in the newswire surveys.' No wonder he's on a multi-million package. Just getting one of those top ratings guarantees a flood of job offers, each one higher than the last. I can imagine the head guys upstairs preening that they've recruited him, despite the cost.

'What about some personal details,' interrupts Patti. 'Age?'

'Thirty-five.'

'Marital status?' She stares straight into his eyes.

'Single.'

'Hobbies?' I cut in, ignoring Patti's daggers glance.

'Jogging.' Not so good. 'Rugby.' Getting better. 'Fine wines.' My kind of man. 'And karaoke.' Retreat position. Back off. I repeat. Back off.

'Er, karaoke? Do you really want me to put that on the press release?'

'Well, it's only a bit of a laugh. I do a mean Tom Jones "Sex Bomb".' I bet you do. 'My friends and I do it after rugby training. To unwind.' He smiles. A little crooked smile, rather endearing. 'Maybe it will appeal to some warped journalists out there.' Patti purrs like a smitten kitten.

'So what can we say about your voluntary work in Africa?' I continue. Patti sighs.

'I was working with an agency that's installing drainage and sanitary facilities in some of the villages in Africa. As a trained civil engineer, I was able to devise plans for the installation of the pipes.'

'Whereabouts in Africa?'

'Somalia.'

'Wasn't that dangerous?' I ask in a wow-I'm-impressed voice.

'I suppose,' he answers in an I'm-a-reluctant-hero voice. 'I'd rather not give any specifics in the press release, if that's all right? It's not like I was the only one out there. There are guys who have been working there for years; I was only a small contributor. They are the ones who should be getting publicity.'

Goodness, an investment banker who doesn't try to claim credit for everyone else's work. He is unique. I remember my manners. 'Would you like a cup of coffee?'

'Well, I know where the drink making facilities are.' He smiles at Patti. 'Shall we wander over?' The three of us stroll across to the coffee machine, where little flashing red lights inform us that the black filter, white filter with one sugar and hot chocolate facilities have run out. Strange how there always seems to be a limitless supply of coffee with powdered milk. 'Hmm. Classy place I'm joining,' jokes the beautiful one. 'What about a proper drink, instead?' I can see his standing going up even higher in Patti's estimation, like mercury rising in a thermometer. 'Is Corney & Barrow where it was three months ago?'

'It was there last night,' replies Patti. 'Ah,' she adds quickly, catching me glaring at her, 'I started to feel a little better after we'd spoken yesterday. Thought a drink might help. Purely for medicinal purposes.'

'Well,' Tony checks his watch. 'It's nearly noon. I know you two ladies are extremely busy, but this is almost my last day of freedom before rejoining the rat race and, while I loved my time in Africa, I did yearn for good old British luxuries. Like a gin and tonic with a slice. Surely you won't deprive me?'

Over our drinks, Tony tells us about his work in Somalia. Occasionally he looks rather distant, as if remembering some traumatic event. He describes the excitement of installing a tap in the centre of the village, miles from the nearest river. The look of joy on people's faces when the tap turned and fresh water spewed out. The elderly women's fear that an evil god was playing tricks. The mothers, used to walking in the searing heat to collect the daily rations of water, dropping to their knees to mop up the puddles under the tap. I glare at Patti, willing her not to make some glib comment.

Tony is remarkably easy to chat to. He has to be aware that he's good-looking, but he doesn't have that conceited attitude that attractive men often have. He genuinely se̶̶̶̶ enjoying our company. And Patti is definitely enjoyin̶̶̶ She's hanging on every word. If she wasn't so conscious of th̶̶ gap between her two front teeth, I swear she would have her mouth open. Dribbling.

He describes how he got into the City and his interest in the internet. His enthusiasm is palpable and yet he doesn't sound nerdish like Jason sometimes can.

'I have a *friend* interested in starting an internet site,' I throw in casually, sipping slowly on my gin and tonic. 'Well, actually it's more a chat room.'

'Really? What does he or she plan to chat about?'

'Em, dieting.'

'Really?' interrupts Patti, hailing a waitress to bring another round of drinks. 'Who's that?'

'Er, Liz.'

'But she doesn't need to lose weight . . .' She stops as she catches sight of my face.

'Well, if you look at how books on diets sell,' says Tony, oblivious to the evil looks that I'm throwing Patti, 'I'd say there's a real market for that sort of stuff.'

'Is a chat room easy to set up?' I ask.

'Well, your friend could buy a software package. It seems relatively easy, but she'd need to get the publicity right and to make sure that there are lots of links with other sites, like health information, to get people to move from one to the other. Kind of like a chain letter. But it's really important to get the site advertised. I mean, there are thousands of other sites out there, so why would anybody choose your friend's? If she needs any help, get her to give me a call.'

'Thanks.' I munch on an egg and cress sandwich.

'But,' continues Patti, 'why would Liz want to set up a dieting chat room?' And why would I want to put a fist in your face? Is this girl a direct descendant of Einstein, or what?

'It could be a sound business proposition,' explains Tony. 'You don't have to sing to set up a music site.' I smile at him. He knows. I'm sure of it. But his face remains impassive.

Suddenly Tony's mobile phone rings, startling me. 'Hi, yeah. Where are you?' he shouts into it. 'OK. Face the counter, round to the right.' He stands up and waves his hand in the air. I turn around, just as the most stunning woman I have ever seen approaches our table. Patti blanches. 'Emmie,' grins Tony. 'Great to see you.' And with that he gives her an enormous hug and a big kiss.

Slimming tip six

Never mention calories in the presence of beauty

I'm meeting Sebastian in Neat, a restaurant on the second floor of the Oxo Tower, on the south bank of the river Thames. The Oxo Tower; the ultimate two fingers to bureaucracy. Banned from erecting advertisement hoardings on the waterfront, the gravy cube makers merely built a tower, and inserted three large windows. One on top of the other. Shaped O, X, O.

Sebastian is sitting on a lilac leather chair when I arrive. Our table is near the open window, looking down onto the calm waters of the Thames. It's just seven and still bright, but within hours London will light up, and from this table we can watch its reflection twinkle across the river.

I had to rush to get here on time. Patti was taking longer than I expected on the press release for Tony Younger's appointment. It took a while for her to calm down when we returned to the office. Tony left with Emmie to go shopping for new work clothes. He had, she told us, lost quite a bit of weight during his voluntary stint. We both smiled politely as she patted his flat stomach and teased about how he needed somebody to help him choose his clothes, or he would end up with the most dreadful outfits. Brains and good taste, she teased, don't always go together. Patti and I laughed appreciatively, my chuckles masking the irrational pangs of disappointment that I felt at Emmie's arrival.

I had to leave without seeing Patti's final press release, although she promised that she'd ring on my mobile if there were any problems. She assured me, as she pushed me into a lift, that she would get the most press coverage ever for an analyst's appointment. Giles Heppelthwaite-Jones and Tabitha would be proud of her, she predicted. I felt awkward leaving her, but I didn't want to cancel tonight. Not our anniversary dinner. Anyway, I tell myself as the maître d' leads me to Sebastian's table, what on earth can Patti do wrong? I've got to trust her.

Sebastian is sitting by an open window, a slight breeze is catching at his hair. He turns and spots me, and any lingering doubts about his inability to be romantic are dispelled at the moment. A smile breaks out across his gorgeous face. Twinkling blue eyes that produce butterflies in my stomach each time they focus on me. Patti can cope, I console myself.

He stands to greet me. A quick peck on the cheek, but I'm sure the maître d' can spot the electricity fizzing between us. His hand on my arm is practically burning through the silk sleeve of my blouse. I'm wearing a new two-piece outfit that looks like a dress, but gets around the embarrassing problem that I have a top and bottom that are completely different sizes. My body always reminds me of that game we played as children, the one with cards of different heads, torsos and undercarriages. You had to swap the cards around until you got the perfect match, but in the process got a buck-toothed vicar, with a bust that Jordan would die for, and legs that wouldn't look out of place on a Chippendale chair.

I think of the game whenever I go clothes shopping. I look in the mirror and see Orla Kennedy from North Dublin. With her Irish colouring, freckles and auburn hair that hangs like a curtain around her face. She's not bad-looking. Like her brother, she's the sort of person that never stands out in a crowd. It's funny how Catholic parents pride themselves on their children's honesty, yet drum it into them that they shouldn't be immodest. It sort of screws you up. So if someone were to ask me what my best feature was I couldn't answer, even though, if I'm honest, I'm rather proud of my nose, which is finely cut and doesn't dominate my face. I would probably have to say something flip, like 'they're all as bad as each other'. It drives Liz mad.

When I look at Sebastian, I can't believe he has any insecurities about himself, even though Liz assures me that everybody does. She frets about her eyebrows, which, if left unpruned for a week, spread across her forehead like a hardy perennial. If pushed, I might admit that I privately believe Sebastian is insecure about relationships. Sometimes he acts so gauche when we're together. So ungallant. He seems nervous about intimacy. I mean, we've kissed. With tongues, as the boys at school might say. We've even held hands in public, although that was an accident. I tripped on an uneven paving stone and Sebastian put his hand out to save me. But he didn't let go. Not for ages.

'Babe, you look nice,' he smiles. Nice. Hasn't he noticed my scarlet lipstick? My perfectly applied eye make-up? Or these killer strappy sandals that even Tabitha would find it hard to walk in? See what I mean? Gauche. But then he looks me up and down again, slowly, causing a shiver to surge through my body in anticipation. Sebastian smiles again, attracts the attention of a passing waiter and orders a bottle of Chablis. 'Very nice indeed,' he repeats, settling back into his chair.

'This is so pretty,' I say, looking out of the window at the dome of St Paul's.

'I did try to get a table in the centre of the restaurant, but they put us here. It's a bit quiet. Sorry,' says Sebastian, as the waitress pours the dry white wine into our glasses. 'Have you got a jacket or anything? It might get a bit cold.'

'I'm fine,' I reply, casually placing my hand over his. 'Don't worry. It's perfect. Besides, I'm sure you'd lend me your jacket if I were chilly.'

'Er, yeah. Obviously,' says Sebastian, reaching for his glass and accidentally knocking my hand off. 'Cheers.'

We clink glasses.

'To a memorable evening,' I say, meaningfully. I've vowed not to bring up the anniversary word unless he does. Play the relaxed game.

'So, how's your week been?' asks Sebastian. We've barely talked this week, apart from a brief conversation this morning to fix up details for tonight.

'A bit unusual,' I reply. 'My brother Finn has turned up to stay and my mother's having kittens back in Dublin.' I explain about my brother's conversion to Buddhism. 'Honestly, there was a spider in the bathroom yesterday morning and he wouldn't let me wash it away. He mounted a rescue attempt. Apparently I don't think enough about the consequences of my actions. As Finn told me, if I plant a mustard seed, then a tomato plant will not grow.'

'Bright cookie your brother,' says Sebastian, obviously confused. 'Is he a gardener in Dublin?'

'It's the Law of Karma,' I explain, sipping on my wine. 'You get what you plant. If you sow kindness through hard work etcetera then you get kindness back.'

'Or a family of spiders come to stay?'

'Don't say that.' I shudder at the thought. 'Finn has completely taken over my flat and he's only meant to be staying there temporarily. He's put his stuff everywhere. Even in my bedroom. I wake up to see a bald-headed fat man looking down at me.'

'What's his name?' Sebastian replies, pretending to be indignant, but the waiter comes to take our order and I can't flirt back.

I check the menu, go through my standard practice of picking out all the healthy, low fat options and then rejecting them, and suddenly stop. I feel a twinge of guilt when I remember that Liz and Jason are coming around tomorrow to help me set up Lightasafeather.co.uk. If I'm going to do it – and I'm quite coming around to the idea – then I have got to be serious about it. I reselect and give my order to the waiter.

'Are you not feeling hungry?' Sebastian asks once the waiter leaves.

'Big lunch,' I lie. 'I had to meet some guy who's starting on Monday and prepare a press release.'

'That explains it,' he smiles. 'I had a bet with myself that you'd go for the "pan-fried veal escalope in a rich creamy sauce with Dauphinoise potatoes".'

'In normal circumstances you'd have won,' I smile, feeling slightly ill at ease at his comments. 'How much did you lose? Perhaps I can make it up to you,' I say daringly, 'later.'

'No sweat.' Sebastian grabs his wine glass and tells me about his week. He's spent the past three days entertaining clients on a golf course. Obviously the clients were delighted. They don't seem to realize that the commissions they've paid Sebastian's company over the past year could have paid for three golf courses. Instead they viewed it as a freebie and everybody loves freebies. Even clients of money brokers. I did try to find out what money brokers actually do, so I could sound knowledge-able to Sebastian, but I couldn't find anybody who could describe their job in one syllable or less.

'Actually it's good that our team got out of the office. It was getting mad, babe,' he continues, reading the wine menu. 'A couple of the young guys did their first trades earlier in the week, and we had to go through the old initiation rites.'

'Eh?' I look at him confused.

'They had to run around the trading floor naked, while everybody slapped them with rulers.' He grins at the memory. The sommelier, who's just arrived to take the wine order, is confused as to what he's just walked in to.

'Did you have to do that? When you did your first trade?'

'Everybody has to do that.' He sounds surprised at the question, but, hey, I thought he was a money broker not a new boy at Eton.

'Even the women?'

'Babe, it's a predominantly male environment. But the women who join know what they're getting in to. We have a different sort of initiation ceremony for them.' He winks. 'And we don't give them nicknames.'

'You didn't tell me you had a nickname,' I exclaim. The sommelier is pretending not to listen, rubbing his cloth over the little grapevine badge that he wears.

'Babe, we all have them.'

'So, what's your nickname?' I ask coyly.

'Donkey.'

Thank you God. 'Er, why?'

'It's a bit embarrassing.' The sommelier stops rubbing.

'Oh, don't be silly. How embarrassing can it be?' I ask. Praying.

'Well, it's not the obvious reason. Beaujolais for the main?' I nod in agreement and he points at the bottle on the list. The sommelier leaves, disappointed that he didn't hear the answer. 'So what about you? Any nicknames?'

'Don't change the subject. Why are you known as Donkey?'

'It's because occasionally, and I stress occasionally' – he looks slightly embarrassed – 'when I get really excited I sort of bray like one.'

'Excited?' I ask. Rewind. This does not sound good.

'Yeah, like when England score a hat trick.' Oh. 'Or when I do a good trade.' Oh indeed. 'Or when' – he pauses, lifts his glass to mine and stares into my eyes – 'I'm enjoying a night of wild, unbridled passion.' Oh my God. How embarrassing. The walls in my flat are paper-thin. And my brother's sleeping in the living room.

'I can imagine,' I stammer, 'that all of those events could prove embarrassing. Some more than others.'

'Oh, I don't know. I think it can add to an atmosphere,' he says, raising an eyebrow. I concentrate on the waiter placing our starters down as a deep blush gradually covers my face. 'So, how's Patti?' Sebastian continues. 'She sounded in good spirits when I called.' He spreads a liberal amount of goose liver pâté onto a thin, crisp melba toast. My taste buds salivate at the sight, and I practically choke on my almost-calorie-free consommé.

'Probably literally,' I reply. 'A fortnight ago she arrived back in the office so drunk she could hardly turn on her computer.'

'I can see that could be a problem.'

'And instead of sitting in her chair, drinking lots of coffee and sobering up, Patti took it upon herself to be useful, and phone lots of journalists just to say hi. The only trouble was they couldn't understand a word she said.'

'Oh.'

'I spent the next day fending off calls from journalists convinced that a deep throat had been trying to get a message through to them about the bank. I'm not sure if that's where the rumours about trading losses came from.'

'I've heard those.' He looks up, interested. 'Any truth in them?'

'Don't know. Tabitha says not, so I have to believe what she says.' Sebastian seems mildly uncomfortable. 'Sorry. Going on too much about work. Let's talk about something else.'

So we do. A couple of hours later I glance out of the window and see London's lights sparkling back at me. It's Friday night. I'm sitting in London, one of the coolest cities in the world, with Sebastian, one of the coolest guys on earth. Could life be any better?

Well, maybe.

Sebastian signals to the waitress. The bill. This is it. I disappear to the bathroom, brush my teeth, check my make-up and freshen up while he settles the account. And then we walk in silence to the lifts. His hand resting protectively in the small of my back. An elderly couple enter before us and the man takes control of the buttons.

'Going down?'

I do hope so.

Sebastian nods. We reach our destination and walk quietly across the cobbled courtyard, through the gates and onto the main road. I don't say anything. We stop and face each other.

'Thank you, babe,' Sebastian finally says, taking my hands in his. He slowly kisses me. Soft. Gentle. No awkward lunging. 'For a wonderful evening,' he continues. An anniversary evening, I want to say. But don't. I just stand there smiling. 'And so educational.' He winks. 'I know more about Buddhism than I ever thought possible.' He kisses me again. 'Shall we talk tomorrow?'

Eh?

He's stepping back from me and lifting his hand. There's a

black cab in the distance, its yellow light signalling its avail-
ability. The driver flicks the headlights. He's seen us.

'I'll call. Promise.'

Call? I look at him, confused.

The cab pulls up. Sebastian opens the door, says something
to the driver, and motions for me to get in. I sit down.

'It's been brilliant. Sorry to be a party pooper, but I've got an
early start tomorrow. I'm driving to my parents in Chester for
their golden anniversary celebrations. Remember? I did tell
Patti.'

'Of course,' I lie.

'You're incredible, you know. Absolutely incredible. It's been
brilliant. Look after yourself. Goodbye.'

He leans into the cab, kisses me one more time, then slams
the door shut, patting the roof as the cab accelerates away,
back to North London. The incredible Orla Kennedy is going
home. Alone. Again. Tears start to slide gently down my
cheeks. I don't turn back to wave.

SLIMMING TIP SEVEN

*Start planning something new
and exciting in your life*

'Orla, you wouldn't guess. We're going to have a choir. It only costs five hundred pounds.' Liz bursts into the flat, all red with excitement in her new Karen Millen suit after her meeting with the priest. 'And a soloist to sing Ave Maria when we sign the register.' She beams at me. 'This is going to be *some* wedding.' I glance across at Jason, settled in my brown leather armchair, and watch the colour drain from his cheeks as he mentally tots up the cost of the wedding that he and Liz have just agreed. 'And the priest agreed with me when I said that the flower arrangements on the altar should be really big,' Liz continues. 'I mean, you wouldn't be able to see them from the back of the church if they were too small. And he was thrilled with my idea to buy a new piece of red carpet to lay in the aisle. The one down there now looks really manky, doesn't it, Jason?'

'Er, yeah.' Jason stirs from his reverie. 'Have you got any coffee, Orla? Preferably strong.' I nod and move into the kitchen to put the kettle on. I feel slow, lethargic. I have barely slept since I returned home last night. 'I've been looking at some slimming websites,' he shouts after me. 'I think this is a really good idea.'

'Oh Jason,' interrupts Liz, seating herself in a wicker chair. 'Can't you hold on for a while? I haven't finished telling Orla about the wedding plans. I was thinking gerberas for the altar. What do you think?'

'Yes, very nice,' I shout back, trying to sound enthusiastic as I gather three mugs onto a tray. 'Milk and sugar, Jason?'

'Yep, two spoons,' he yells. The sound of the toilet flushing echoes around my small flat.

'Oh my God. Is he still here?' Liz screeches before turning to Jason. 'I told you that we should have rung first, but, oh no, you wouldn't listen. Do you want us to go, Orla?'

'That's Finn,' I say simply, placing a tray with coffee things and a plate of biscuits down on the table in front of them. 'Not Sebastian.'

'Did he leave earlier?' Liz continues, ignorant of the knife that stabs my heart with each word she utters.

'No. He didn't come back here.' Silence. Liz and Jason are looking at me, sympathy in their eyes. 'And he's gone away for the weekend. His parents' golden wedding anniversary.'

'Oh,' exclaims Liz, the full implication of what I have just said hitting her. 'But you told me you were going to celebrate *your*—'

'Yes,' I interrupt, 'but I was wrong. Anyway' – I take a deep breath – 'why am I so worried and upset? I have a boyfriend who obviously respects me and is not just using me for my body. It's no big deal that we haven't slept together yet.'

'What's that, sis?' Finn walks into the room, bare-chested with a towel around his neck. 'Your boyfriend doesn't want to sleep with you? Is he gay?' He kneels down on the floor by the coffee table and starts pouring himself a mug.

'I do not have a gay boyfriend,' I repeat indignantly as I walk out to the kitchen to fetch another mug.

'Let's talk about the reason we're here – Light As A Feather,' says Jason quickly. He can sense an embarrassing situation at three paces. 'Come on, Liz, we haven't got much time. Don't forget we're off to see some reception venues later.' Good man. Never thought I would be so glad to see plans for a chat room. He takes out a sheaf of papers from his briefcase and lays them on my coffee table. 'These are a few designs I've drawn up for the site,' he explains. 'I think the key is that, along with the chat room, it should contain vital information on dieting. Like how many calories are in an apple.'

'About sixty,' I reply, nibbling on a chocolate Hob Nob. Sod dieting for men.

'Pint of milk?' continues Jason.

'Three hundred and seventy in full fat, two hundred and fifty-five in semi-skimmed and about one hundred and ninety-five in a pint of skimmed,' I say without thinking. Three people stare at me. 'What. What have I done?'

'Wow, sis,' exclaims Finn. 'Are you one of those people? A whatdoyoucallit? Like the guy Dustin Hoffman played in *Rainman*?' He hides his biscuit beneath his hand. 'What's under my hand?'

Are we really from the same gene pool? I ignore him.

'See, Jason, I told you. Orla knows the calories of everything. What about an ounce of spinach?' Liz looks at me.

'Ah, you should always boil it,' I reply. 'Seven calories for a raw ounce and five for a boiled ounce.'

'That's so freaky, sis.' Finn looks around the flat. 'How many books on that shelf?' Even Jason and Liz are now looking at him strangely. 'You have a real gift from Buddha.'

'I can't see the shelf properly, but I can definitely tell how many brain cells you have.'

'Sure there's no cause to be like that. Just because I was impressed by all those numbers you came up with. What did you call them?'

'Your sister is a walking calorie counter,' explains Jason.

'Really, then how come she's—'

'Very kindly allowed you to stay,' interrupts Jason firmly. He really is Mr Assertive today. Liz must have allowed him a third Shredded Wheat for breakfast.

'Exactly what I was going to say.' Finn realizes when he's beaten. And hasn't got any rent. 'But why are you guys sitting here discussing calories on a Saturday morning? There's cartoons on the telly.'

'Your sister is going to set up a dieting chat room,' explains Liz.

'I haven't agreed yet,' I sulk.

'Wow. That's so cool. Will it be like the chat room where I

found salvation? Buddhistsrus.com?' He rubs the little jade Buddha that hangs around his neck on a leather thong. 'Honest, Liz, it has changed my whole outlook. It could help you to forget how mundane life can be.'

'I prefer alcohol,' she replies.

'And don't forget I can give you a real chat room user's opinion of the site,' adds Finn. 'Looks are so important. I mean, there were some Buddhist sites that set my teeth on edge.' Only some? 'I just couldn't enter them, I was so worried that there would be all these religious fanatics. You know the sort. Always trying to force their religion down your throat. I hate them.'

'Finn's got a point, Orla.' Really? Well, let's hope he sits on it.

'You don't want people to feel too intimidated using the site,' continues Finn. 'To feel embarrassed that they're fat.'

'Who's embarrassed?' I shove my third chocolate Hob Nob in my mouth.

'You need to be sympathetic. Offer considered advice.'

'Orla can do that,' interrupts Liz. 'Remember when you wrote out a diet sheet for me? When I wanted to lose a few pounds before going on a beach. You wouldn't even let me contemplate using the Cabbage Soup Diet as a quick fix.'

'We were sharing a flat at the time,' I point out. 'I was doing it for me.'

'I've done a little research,' says Jason with an amused look at his blushing fiancée. 'Checked out the competition. I think your site needs to include a calorie counter, and perhaps another counter to show how much different exercises burn off.'

'You mean like if I jogged for twenty minutes, it would mean that I could scoff my fourth Hob Nob with impunity?'

'What does an hour of meditation burn up?'

'Your remaining brain cell,' I smile. Finn dives for the last Hob Nob. Retribution. 'What else would it need, Jason?'

'I don't know. Some calorie counted recipes – people seem to need everything spelled out for them – and a couple of quick fix diets.'

'They aren't the answer,' I reply. 'People should aim to lose between one and two pounds a week. Anything else just isn't healthy. It's only water.' Wow. Hark at me. The Doctor Spock of the dieting world.

'That's exactly what you need to say,' smiles Jason. 'Now look at some of these designs. Tell me what you think.'

I lift the top drawing from the small pile. It's a huge feather with little weights hanging from it. The kind that always falls on cartoon characters' heads, concertinaing them into the ground. The feather looks like a fluffy Christmas tree and each weight signifies a different element of the site. At the top of the home page runs a welcome banner, naming the client, and in the bottom left hand corner is their personalized weight resting on a feather.

'That signifies their excess weight,' explains Jason, pointing at it. 'As they shed pounds the weight starts to rise, releasing the feather in stages. When they achieve their goal the feather floats away. I kind of envisaged a moment when they hit their target weight where feathers fall down from the top of the screen for a few moments, you know like when you win at solitaire on the computer and the cards all bounce around.'

Er, never got that far. Aren't newly engaged people meant to have so much more on their mind than designing websites for friends? Jason has put in so much time already that I feel trapped. I can't back out. Can I?

'This is far out, sis,' interjects Finn, looking at the designs. 'Much better than buddhistsrus.com, although the Buddha's eyes did light up when I registered. So, when's it launching?

'I've thought about that,' says Jason. I glance at Liz. Either she's deadly determined that I act as her bridesmaid, or they've run out of things to talk about already. She looks calm, smiling fondly at her fiancé. 'I reckon we can be up and running within two weeks. Once we've inputted all the data.'

'And I'm going to run a piece about people in the City

wanting to lose weight and give the site a plug,' adds Liz. 'Next week. And I'm sure you can pull a few strings in the advertising department and get a few posters and flyers printed. We can distribute them outside some of the City's slimming clubs.'

'How much will it cost?' There. Caught you both out.

'We'd have to register a site, then there'd be some other charges, but I don't think it will break the bank,' replies Jason, before muttering, 'Not like my bloody wedding.'

'I heard that,' shrieks Liz. 'Now come on, Orla. Can you see any flaws?'

'When do I run it? I already have a full-time job.'

'I thought we'd already sorted that one out. In your lunchtime,' says Liz. 'And I can help out on those days you're busy.'

'Hey, I can help too,' interrupts Finn. 'Don't forget I'm an *aficionado* of chat rooms. I could keep an eye on it when you can't. Check for lewd content. Besides I need a job.'

'And I need rent,' I hiss.

'Er, I mean, I need something to do before I find a proper job. Sis, this sounds so cool. You could be one of those dotcom millionaires. We could buy a castle on the west of Ireland. Mix with celebrities.'

'I thought you were beyond worldly goods now, Finn,' says Liz as she gets to her feet. 'Come on, Jason. We've got to get to The Four Seasons by two.' I walk the two of them to the door. 'By the way, Orla, what a great idea to capitalize on Tony Younger's appointment,' she suddenly says. 'Totally inspired. We're devoting nearly a full page to it and we've never done that before. I mean, when John Major took that job at what's-the-place, we only gave it a paragraph. If that.'

'Really?' Goodness. Patti must really have risen to the occasion. I was wrong to doubt her. 'Well, I'm glad that you liked it.'

'Like it! We're thinking of running it as a regular slot. And there's talk that I'll be in charge of it.'

'We just tried to emphasize his good points,' I bluff.

'You certainly did that,' laughs Liz. She hugs me and shouts in at Finn, ' 'Bye there, carry on chanting.'

I close the door feeling more than a little uncomfortable. What on earth did Patti come up with?

Slimming tip eight

The buck stops with you

On Monday morning I realized just how determined God is to punish me for having a Buddhist halfwit as a brother. It started to dawn at seven when the postman knocked with a special delivery from my mother. Two hot water bottles and Finn's bronchial balsam for when he gets wheezy. With special instructions to shake it vigorously before use as it had been in her medicine cupboard for a while. Put it away in a cool place, her note said. Hmm, I could think of another, less cool, place.

Still I never quite appreciated just how vengeful God could be until two hours later when I arrive for work. A massive yellow Post-it note is stuck to my computer screen. It is from Patti. It says just one word. SORRY. In great, big, red letters. With a little kiss in the bottom left-hand corner.

Sorry? What for? I look around for Patti. Her jacket is slung over her chair back and a pile of newspaper cuttings are scattered over her desk. The weekend's press on Browns Black. It should have been photocopied and distributed to all the bank's senior management by now. Is this what the message means? Is Patti trying the old coat-on-the-back-of-the-chair routine? Has she gone home? Did the porridge 'disagree' with her?

I take a step towards her desk, hands outstretched to scoop up the cuttings, when I hear a shriek.

'Orla. In here. *Now.*'

It's Tabitha. She's standing in her office doorway. I look at her for a moment, uncertain. What *is* going on? She sounds angry. There are three people in the office with her. Patti. What's *she* in there for? Giles Heppelthwaite-Jones . . . it really is too early to see him. My breakfast hasn't fully digested. I can see the back of another man, who's gesticulating like a Telly-tubby on speed.

'Did you hear me?' Tabitha screeches.

'Sorry,' I reply. 'Just coming.'

I start towards the office and then my stomach drops. The other person is Tony Younger. And from this distance I can see that he's angry. Very angry. Oh shit, Patti. What did your press release say? What have you done? As I reach the doorway, I know only one thing. Whoever said it was better to con-front one's demons was talking bollocks. Great, big, huge bollocks.

I take a deep breath and enter. Brazen it out, Orla. Smile. Bluff. Lie.

'Tabitha,' I nod at my boss. 'Patti. Giles.' The walrus looks confused. He's sure that he knows me from somewhere, but for the life of him . . . 'Tony.' I walk over and extend my hand. 'Welcome to Browns Black.' Patti buries her face in her hands.

Tony looks at me, but doesn't move to accept my greeting. His face is full of contempt. 'Are you trying to be funny?' he snarls. 'Because I'm having a huge sense of humour failure here.' He turns to Tabitha's desk, and lifts up a copy of Liz's magazine. 'Have you see this?' He waves it in my face.

'Not this week's copy. No,' I say truthfully. 'I've only just arrived.'

'But you know what it says?' snaps Tabitha.

'Of course she knows what it says,' replies Tony. 'She wrote the bloody press release.' I glance at Patti, who stands there looking awkward. Willing her to admit her role. To come to my rescue in whatever disaster this is. 'I mean, you were in charge of it, weren't you?'

'Yes.'

'So, you're responsible for what went into this magazine?' I look at Patti once again. She is mouthing something at me. It looks like 'Please, please.'

'I am.' It's true. Whatever has been published is my fault. I should have supervised Patti. It's my job. I have to check anything she sends out with the bank's name on it. I can't drop her in it, like some playground telltale tit. Patti closes her eyes in relief. I know this job means so much to her. A girl from Streatham who once thought flamenco dancing was the mating ritual of those funny birds that stand on one leg. 'But I haven't read what the journalist finally wrote.'

'Well, I suggest you read it now.' Tabitha thrusts the glossy publication into my hands, and gestures to a small stool at the side of her office. The one she normally stands on to get something off the top bookshelf.

It's bad. Correction. Worse than bad. The new series that Liz talked about so excitedly is entitled 'City Hunk of the Week', and it kicks off with Tony Younger, or, as the article prefers to call him, A BEAUTY. WITH A SENSE OF DUTY. And, just to make matters even worse, the magazine has superimposed Tony's head onto a muscle bound body and you would need an exceptionally strong magnifying glass to read the disclaimer underneath.

'Look.' Tony's angry voice cuts across me. 'I can take a joke like the next man, but that article makes me look like a bloody arsehole. How am I meant to be taken seriously with City institutions when articles like this are being written about me?' He grabs the magazine from my hands and reads from it. ' "Tony's rippling muscles were finely honed in Africa, in a village in Somalia where he single-handedly installed the drainage system." It's not even true,' he adds. 'There were twenty of us.'

'I think we should all sit back and reflect on this experience,' Giles interrupts. 'Learn from it and . . .'

'Learn from it?' explodes Tony. 'I tell you what I've bloody learned, along with thousands of other City workers. I've learned' – he lifts the magazine again – 'that my "rippling muscles set female hearts alight" and that I'm likely to "serenade a woman with a unique karaoke style version of Tom Jones's 'Sex Bomb' ". Give me strength.' And me an escape route. 'But what really gets me is the picture. It looks like I've posed for it and given the whole sodding article my blessing.'

'Isn't it your body?' Tabitha sounds somewhat disappointed.

'Oh, for God's sake. No. Those are not my "rippling muscles".'

'Let's injunct,' Patti suddenly pipes up. 'You know, stop publication.'

'But it *is* published.' Tony gives Patti such a contemptuous look that tears spring to her eyes. 'And I've already had fifty e-mails and phone calls in' – he checks his watch – 'less than two hours.' He turns to me. 'Why did you do this? Why did you make me look like a prat? Did I upset you?'

'No,' I start, but then I can't find any more words. I have no excuse for this. I left early for what I expected to be a weekend of climactic pleasure, which turned into an anti-climax, and this man standing in front of me is paying the price. A man I really liked and admired when we met. I glance at Patti, willing her to come clean. But she keeps quiet, apart from little shaky gulps as she tries to catch her breath through her sobbing. Two round, red patches glow on her cheeks – a telltale sign that she is upset. 'I thought it would attract attention to your appointment.'

'Oh, it did that,' snaps Tony. 'I've already had one of the tabloids ringing me up. Wanting me to be one of its page nine pin-ups. They even offered me the chance to pose with Belinda Bosoms.'

'Really?' pipes up Giles. 'Now that could be a good way to defuse the situation. And I could come along to oversee the photo shoot. Make sure it was all tastefully done.'

'How kind,' replies Tony in a sarcastic tone. 'But how exactly would that defuse the situation? Wouldn't it just *attract* the attention of over three million new people who otherwise didn't even know I existed? Tell me, do you get paid for your advice?' Colour spreads from Giles's nose to the rest of his face. 'There is nothing that *you*' – he stabs his finger accusingly at Giles – 'can do to deflect attention from this. I'm the one who'll now have weeks of ribbing, and every so often, just when I think everybody's forgotten, it'll be brought up. This article will haunt my career.'

'Oh, I don't think so,' says Tabitha. 'It could enhance it.' Go on, Tabitha. Save me. Earn your six-figure salary. For once. 'I mean, women clients will definitely want to do business with you.' I suppose it was too much to hope for.

'I would,' pipes up Giles. 'If I was a woman, that is.' His voice tails off.

'Do you know what the problem is?' asks Tony.

'Is the picture not accurate enough?' asks Patti. Oh God. Why don't you just finish me off now? I thought I was your friend. You wouldn't let a dog suffer like this.

'No,' snaps Tony. 'The picture isn't accurate enough. Because it's not me.' He says the words slowly. 'The big problem is the fact that none of you seem suitably penitent.' He looks at me. '*You* haven't even said sorry. My first day and I'm a laughing stock. I want an apology from all concerned on this travesty. Today.' He spins around and leaves the office.

Within minutes the witch explodes at me.

'What the *hell* did you think you were doing? I leave you to do something so simple that even Patti couldn't mess up and you do this. It's a disaster. That man is one of the City's top-rate analysts. Every bank was trying to hire him and he chose Browns Black. And this is the thanks we give him. If he quits over this, I won't be responsible for what might happen.' Tears are dripping through Patti's hands, which are clasped over her face.

'Now, Tabitha darling, calm down,' Giles interrupts as he swings his legs onto her desk and leans back in his chair. 'I think we should all sit back and analyse the situation. Perhaps some more coffee?' He looks expectantly through the glass wall towards my desk. 'Where's that nice young girl who usually takes my coat and fetches my espresso?'

'I'm here,' I reply.

'Oh, right. Have you changed your hair?'

'No.'

'Oh, OK. Anyway if you wouldn't mind running along and

getting some coffees. Double espresso for me, and if you can find a blueberry muffin . . .'

'Giles.' Tabitha's voice cuts through. 'Orla, fetch us coffees and then go back to your desk while Giles and I discuss what this bank can do to sort out your sorry mess. Really, as if I haven't enough to do. I'm constantly being called about these spurious rumours that Browns Black has lost money trading government bonds.'

'I've had a couple of those,' Patti mumbles. She wipes her eyes with a tissue.

'Really? And what have you said?'

'I just read out the statement you and Giles wrote.'

'See, Orla? It's simple if you follow instructions.' Gee. Thanks, Patti. You're a real buddy. 'Now fetch the coffee. Patti, you go back to your desk and answer the phones.'

We leave together. Patti keeps dabbing her eyes as she constantly mutters, 'I'm sorry. I'm so sorry' while we walk to our desks. 'I couldn't admit it was me,' she finally says. 'I tried, but the words just wouldn't come.' She stops and looks at me. 'I knew that I'd be fired if I admitted it and I really *really* love this job. Please, Orla. Don't hate me.'

'Just don't talk to me right now,' I hiss. 'I might not be responsible for my actions.'

'Honestly, I just thought . . .'

'Thought what?' I spit back at her. 'Just what the hell were you thinking? That Tony Younger would like to be a laughing stock?'

'No, of course not, Orla. Please.'

'Patti, I am really, really angry. I have enough problems in my life without this. Why?' I turn to her. 'Did you want me to get fired? Do you want my job? Is that it?'

'No. No.' She tugs on my sleeve as I start to march off. 'You said that the bank needed coverage. That it wasn't getting enough column inches.'

'And?'

'I just worried that nobody would write about Tony's appointment . . .'

'He's a bloody top-rated analyst. Every bank fought to get him. Of course we'd get bloody coverage. All you had to do was send out a well-worded press release. Do the journalists' jobs for them.'

'I didn't realize.' Patti tries to grab my hand. 'I just thought if I was creative then it would attract more attention.'

'Be creative in your own bloody time.' I snatch my hand back. 'Take up pottery.'

'Orla, please. Don't be nasty.'

'Not another word, Patti. Not another word.' I start to walk away. 'Now, if you don't mind, I've got some coffees to get. Remember?'

'You must think I'm such a bitch.' Patti bites her lip to prevent the tears reappearing.

'No, Patti.' I shake my head. 'I think you're young and naïve, and I was wrong to trust you. But don't worry, it won't happen again.'

As I pass my desk en route to the coffee shop in the Broadgate Circle, I spot two yellow Post-its stuck to my computer screen asking me to call Liz. She probably wants my feedback. Thinks I'm delighted with the coverage. How wrong can she be?

The queue in the coffee shop snakes around the small aluminium tables, which are filled with City bankers getting a quick fix of caffeine to wake them up. Most of these guys will have been at their desks since before seven and are psyching themselves up for the long haul until midday and lunch.

I am just two away from the counter when I hear a yelp and watch one of the bankers at a table hold up the dreaded article and shout to his colleague in the queue, 'Have you seen this? We should put forward Snoopy for next week. I mean, he's just stupid enough to go in for something like this.' My heart sinks. I can only imagine the stick that Tony must be getting.

I have just ordered the coffees, including Tabitha's large latte with soya milk, and picked out the muffin that looks like it has fallen on the floor at some point in its short life, when somebody tugs my sleeve. I turn around praying it's not Tony

Younger. I just can't face another confrontation. It's Sven. He's holding a folder in his hand.

'Not now, Sven,' I say testily. 'I've got enough on my plate today without having to get one of your obscure deals in the newspapers. Can't it wait till tomorrow?'

'It's not one of my deals,' replies Sven. 'It's my personal details. And a photograph. I want to be a City Hunk of the Week. Can you arrange it?'

SLIMMING TIP NINE

Enlist some friends to help you

I'm sitting in Starbucks on Moorgate waiting for Liz to arrive. On one of those brown velour armchairs that look like they're rejects from Vera and Jack Duckworth's living room. A black coffee is on the table in front of me. I'm having trouble finishing it. It's not my drink of choice. Well, it's hardly a drink – it's more like something that people use to protect their garden fence from the elements. But it's got one thing going for it and it's a big plus in my books. No calories.

I'm planning to start my diet proper with the launch of Light As A Feather, but I'm getting a little worried about the initial weigh-in. I just want to shed a few pounds beforehand. Besides, Patti has spent the past three days trying to make amends . . . with Danish pastries, chocolate chip cookies, cafe lattes, and extra creamy cappuccinos.

Tony Younger, on the other hand, has spent the past three days ignoring me. I've spotted him in the bank foyer twice and each time he blanked me. I can't say I blame him. He must feel so embarrassed. The press department has had four requests from local television stations for interviews and a top-shelf women's magazine rang too. They wanted him to feature in the 'Oh my God. Where on earth do you expect to fit that?' monthly slot.

I also heard that all the analysts he works with have changed their screen savers. The torso that wasn't even his in the first place now pulsates on forty-four separate computers. And there's even a rumour that one of them was forced to bribe a security guard after he was caught on camera late at night doing a little pulsating of his own in front of the screen.

In my bag is a pile of flyers that the advertising department ran up for me yesterday. The first bit of publicity for Light As A Feather, although Liz has promised a magazine article this Monday. I'm not going to be mentioned as Tabitha would welcome any sort of excuse to sack me at this moment. If she thought I was distracted with another project, and wasn't around to do her work, there would be hell to pay.

Liz and I are going to distribute the flyers to people as they leave a slimming club down the road. The site is really coming on. I've spent the last few nights inputting the calories of every basic food item I can think of. I've copied them out of a book, so I suppose there's some copyright law out there that I've breached, but how else could I do it? Anyway, somebody somewhere once calculated the calories of each basic food and everybody since has just pinched their work. Well, that's my defence anyway – just in case someone challenges me.

I check my watch. It's six. Liz is a quarter of an hour late. I'm just about to ring to tell her to get a move on when the mobile rings.

'Liz?'

'Er no, dear. Mary.'

'Mum.'

'That's right. Is that you, Orla?'

'How many other women with this mobile number call you Mum?' I answer in an exasperated tone.

'Well, there's no need to be like that. I was only ringing to see how you are.'

'I'm OK.'

'And Finn?' Ah, the true purpose of the call.

'Well, he's a bit chesty. He keeps forgetting to take his cough mixture and he will insist on going out with his hair wet.'

'No. Orla, you must stop him. Don't—'

'Mum,' I interrupt. 'It's all right. He's not really chesty, but he is a grown man and I can't stop him doing anything. Just like you can't stop him being a Buddhist.'

'Don't throw that back in my face. I've been praying to St Christopher, hoping that Finn will find his faith again. Hours, I've spent. Aidan down the road says he's never known a woman more at home on her knees. Says his wife just doesn't have the patience.'

'Mum,' I interrupt. 'I'm in a bit of a hurry. I'm meeting Liz in a moment.'

'How is she? Is her mother delighted that she's engaged? Praying for the grandchildren already? 'Tis every mother's dream you know. Are you off out anywhere nice?'

'We're going to distribute some leaflets to advertise this chat room I'm going to start. The one I told you about. To lose weight.'

'Oh yes, I was going to ask you about that. I know that Finn discovered Booedhiseem by chatting, but how do you lose weight doing that? I mean, if that were the case, your Aunty Molly would be a stick by now. I can barely get a word in edgeways when she's on the phone.' Must run in the family.

'It's sort of more like a support group. Everyone is trying to lose weight, and they chat about the issues and any ups or downs that they're having with people who are suffering the same anxieties.'

'And can you see them?'

'No, Mum, all I can see is the messages they type up.'

'So how do you know if they've lost weight?'

'I don't. I have to assume they'll be honest. Look, Mum, I've really got to go. I can see Liz now. I'll call you later. 'Bye.'

Liz is breathless when she reaches me. 'Sorry, got caught in the office,' she gasps. 'Ran all the way here from Bank. God, I'm out of condition.' She tries to catch her breath. 'It's been so hectic these past few days. I must have had thirty guys ring and send details to get into the City Hunk of the Week slot. I've got to arrange some interviews to whittle them down. Sorry.' Liz catches sight of my face. 'But people really love it and, let's face it, everybody knows who Tony Younger is now. It was an inspired idea.'

'That's not how Tabitha described it.'

'In a few weeks she'll be begging to get your chairman in there.'

'He's eighty years old with a patch over his left eye. He's got more chance of starring in a boy band.'

'I know, but think how much Tabitha would be in my debt. She might even give me some juicy gossip.'

'Tabitha doesn't know any juicy gossip,' I say indignantly. 'She's spent the past few days at Wimbledon entertaining journalists. I've already written one speech for the chief executive that she was meant to do and four press releases. But she picks up the quarter of a million each year. She only popped in for ten minutes yesterday and that was to drop off her Alfa Romeo Spider so I can deliver it to the garage for its annual service.'

'Sounds like *she* needs her annual service.'

'Please, I'm drinking.' I point to the black coffee. In looks about as appetizing as a bowl of pickled gherkins.

'Yeah, I noticed that. What's going on?'

'I just thought that all the milk I take in coffee is wasted calories,' I begin, 'and I figured that if I cut it out then I'll save enough calories over the year to lose almost two stone.'

'How do you figure that?'

'Well, I drink something like ten cups of coffee a day, with at least two ounces of milk in each one. So if I cut out the milk – skimmed, of course – then I save . . . hold on.' I fish into my handbag for the calculations that I did this morning. 'About 240 calories a day. Over a week that works out to almost 1,700 calories, or just over 87,000 a year. Now, I read somewhere that to lose one pound of body fat you need to cut out about 3,500 calories. So, by cutting out milk, I will lost almost twenty-five pounds in twelve months without really noticing.' I sit back and take a sip of my drink. Sorry, I retract the final part of my statement. I'd rather drink the Thames. 'It's going to be a feature on Light As A Feather. How to lose weight without really noticing.'

'OK,' says Liz doubtfully. Maths was never her strong point. 'So a black coffee for you?'

'Yes, please. With two sugars.'

Twenty minutes later we are standing in front of a church hall, waiting for the members of Marjorie's Watch Your Weight Whittle Away class to come out. There's a big sign in the garden proclaiming 'Jesus Loves You'. If that were true then He would have given me the face and body of Uma Thurman. He really seems to love her. He even threw in a fantastic-looking husband and amazing career.

'Action stations,' mutters Liz as three women step through the big wooden door.

The women are clutching this week's diet sheets and discussing their various successes.

'I only lost a pound this week,' says one, 'but then I didn't have time to take off my nail varnish beforehand. I'm sure this must weigh at least another few ounces. What do you think, Lily?' She examines her manicured fingers.

'Oh, I don't know,' replies the one called Lily. She's short and dumpy, about sixty, and I can see a little apron dropping down underneath her raincoat. 'I lost two pounds this week.'

'How?'

'I took off my engagement ring.' She is wearing a rock the size of Gibraltar. Liz looks miserably at her own ring. It seems to have shrivelled away in shame. 'How did you do, Tessa?' She looks at the other woman in the group, who seems about forty.

'Stayed the same. I don't know why. I followed the diet sheet to the letter.'

'Did you eat the cakes I gave you?'

'I did, but you said they were fat free. They can't have added anything. I mean, fat free. That means no calories, doesn't it?'

Perfect candidate. I step forward. Liz hovers in the background.

'Excuse me, ladies. Can I have a moment of your time?' I paste on my best smile.

'You're not a Jehovah's Witness, are you?' asks Lily. 'We were told to watch out for them. Apparently they're targeting the churches in the area.'

'No, I'm not a Jehovah's Witness.' My old headmistress Sister

Mary Claude would be upset. She always told us that people could tell we were Catholics because we exuded it. 'I run a slimming website,' I begin, 'that offers free advice, slimming tips, a chat room which allows people to discuss their worries and concerns about losing weight—'

'And you run this?' Tessa looks me up and down incredulously.

'Well, I will do soon. It's not yet launched.'

'Is it one of those internet things?' asks Lily. 'I've read about them.' She turns to the others. 'It's where men look for wives. They chat for days to get to know each other, then he proposes, and the next thing it turns out she's from Thailand and can't speak a word of English.'

'So how does she chat to him on the internet if she can't speak English?' asks Tessa.

'Oh, they're clever these women. They buy a special, oh what's it called, a programme that translates as they write.'

'Are you sure?' Tessa sounds sceptical.

'Absolutely. Somebody in the chip shop was talking about it last week. And somebody got pregnant over the internet in America, you know. In one of those internet cafés. Apparently it you use it after some men it can happen. A bit like those girls when we were children who used to get pregnant from a toilet seat.' She shakes her head at the memory. 'I tell you, I ended up very constipated when I first heard that.' She looks at me. 'Anyway, dear, you were saying?'

I check my feet to make sure that I'm still connected to planet Earth.

'Yes, I'm about to launch a dieting website and—'

'When?' asks Tessa.

'On Monday,' butts in Liz. Is she out of her mind? 'There will be a limited service when it launches, enabling it to evolve according to your demands.' Evolve? Demands? She's interviewed too many management consultants.

'And *you* are going to run this?' Tessa looks at me again. 'What sort of qualifications do you have? I mean, how do we know that your advice works? It doesn't seem to have for—'

'I took it.' Liz cuts off the inevitable statement at the pass. 'And look at me.' She gestures to her body. 'Orla knows what she's doing, but she just hasn't done it yet. Like all of you, she's been busy with other things and one day looked in the mirror and thought, "Woah, what's that?"' Steady on, Liz. 'She'll start with everyone else, so that you can benefit from each other's experiences, and offer support as you go along. I mean, you all go to this slimming club today, but what happens tomorrow if you're desperate for a chunky Kit Kat?' Stop it, Liz. I'm getting hungry. 'Can you call Wendy? Or do you have to rely on self-discipline? This service is available any time you want it.'

'I'll only man the chat room for two hours,' I add, 'from noon, but anybody can sign in at any time and chat to another person in need of support.'

Tessa takes a leaflet from me. 'How much does it cost?' she asks.

'Nothing. All the details are here.' I hand a sheaf of leaflets out to the others. 'Take some for your friends. We can all do this together.' And at that minute I know we can.

'Orla has even got some ideas on how you can lose weight by giving up things you hardly even notice having.'

'Like sex?' asks Lily.

SLIMMING TIP TEN

To help brothers in their pursuit of thinness –
starve them

'Tonight, Matthew,' I mutter at my reflection in the mirror, 'I'm going to be Seductress Sally.' I pucker up my lips and apply my Simply Siren lipstick, take a clean tissue, blot, and re-apply. I check my eye make-up. Perhaps another coat of mascara to accentuate the wanton look.

I'm standing in the ladies at Christopher's, a restaurant in Covent Garden, and, appropriately, a former brothel. Sebastian is sitting at a table outside, probably wondering whether I eat enough roughage, the length of time I've spent in here. Tonight, exactly one week after he sent me home with a chaste peck on my cheek, things are going to change. Sebastian will not know what hit him. Tonight I am out to prove to Liz, once and for all, that he does not bat for the other team. Although he may need to call in the reserves after midnight.

I've followed all Liz's advice. I fluttered my eyelids for England – until the waitress asked me if the air-conditioning was affecting my contact lenses. I've flicked my hair coquettishly and lightly touched Sebastian's hand at every chance I've had. He seems to be enjoying the floorshow, although I nearly blew it when I flicked a hair into his Caesar salad.

I've actually noticed a change in our relationship this week. It seems to have moved up a gear. He's rung every day, even on Wednesday when he was at Wimbledon with clients. It sounds silly, but I can't help thinking that his parents' golden wedding anniversary had something to do with his change of attitude. Maybe seeing them together celebrating their marriage made him realize that he wants a grown up relationship too. And the coverage of Tony Younger definitely helped. He was on the phone Monday morning to find out if I was behind the stunt. Obviously, I lied and said yes.

I check my hair once more, breathe into my hands for any telltale signs of garlic, and sweep my hands over the back of my black chiffon skirt to make sure it is where it should be and not tucked into my knickers. Which are most definitely not big. Right. Here goes. I say a quick prayer to St Jude, patron saint of lost causes to alert him that he can have the night off. Sebastian is sipping a glass of champagne when I return. We've almost finished our second bottle.

'Sorry.' I take my seat. 'Queue in the ladies.'

'No problems, babe. Shall we order desserts?'

'Do you know what I'd really like for dessert?' I say, cupping my hands over his.

'Banoffee pie?' Wow. Playing dirty.

'Not exactly.' Although another night . . .

'Selection of cheeses, babe?' Foul.

'No. Not even a taste of Stilton,' I say firmly, stroking his hands gently with my fingers. 'What I'd *really* like is you!' I whisper. There. I'm a hussy. Sister Mary Claude would be shocked.

'Really?' Sebastian's eyes are twinkling.

'Yes,' I nod. Come on, man. Get the bill and let's get out of here. Do I have to do everything?

'And you're sure you wouldn't prefer the sorbet?' Red card.

'Absolutely,' I say, staring into his eyes as I drain my glass. 'But it was a close run thing.'

'Let's get going then, babe,' he says, pushing his chair back and standing up. 'Why don't you come to Sebastian?' he winks. Lasciviously.

'What about the bill?' I look around for our waitress.

'Already paid.' Oh my God. I'm a transparent hussy. One step below a desperate one. 'My treat. I've made some good trades over the past month,' he smiles, before whispering, 'but the best is yet to come.'

We walk down the stone staircase in silence and out into the busy street. Tourists are pouring out of the theatre across the road. *The Lion King* has just finished another performance. They mill around, programmes in hand, wondering what to do next, searching for the lady holding the umbrella in the air to direct them to their coaches.

'Come on,' says Sebastian, taking my hand. 'If we don't move fast, we'll never get a cab.' He pulls me down the road, onto the Strand and we stand waiting for a cab to come over Waterloo Bridge. How many Friday nights have I stood in the pouring rain in exactly the same place waiting for a cab to appear? Tonight a yellow light miraculously appears within minutes. It's a sign, I think. He's the *one*.

'Where to?' the driver asks.

'Goswell Road,' I reply. My place. Tonight I'm in the driving seat. I'm so glad that I gave fifty pounds to Finn to make himself scarce. We don't say anything, but I notice that Sebastian hasn't let my hand go.

'Are you sure?' he asks as the cab pulls up outside my door.

'Come on.' He pays the driver and follows me into the building.

Once inside the flat I'm not quite so certain. I feel nervous and shy. Luckily Finn's sleeping bag appears to be tucked away and, as far as I can see without conducting a detailed search of the living room, he hasn't left any boxers where they shouldn't be.

'Right,' I say breezily, heart racing. 'Drink?'

'I think I may have had enough,' says Sebastian as he settles himself into one of my leather armchairs. Why didn't I buy a sofa? Two chairs don't look quite such a bargain now. He smiles and pats his lap. No way. I'd squash him. Even if he does play rugby.

'Nonsense. I'll get another bottle.' I make my way into the kitchen.

'What about dessert?' Sebastian calls out. 'I thought you had some ideas.'

'I've got some Ben and Jerry's,' I tease.

71

'Really.' Sebastian appears in the doorframe. 'And what are we going to do with that?' The film *Nine and a Half Weeks* rushes through my mind. Panic rises. Is my bedroom a mess?

'I'll just get the bottle opener,' I say, pushing past him.

'Wouldn't it be here?' he gestures at the kitchen. Since when did men become logical?

'No, sorry. Can't keep it here. My brother is a terrible alcoholic. Have to hide it away, in the other room,' I blurt. 'Back in a moment.'

I dash through the lounge, across the little hallway, open my bedroom door, scan the floor quickly to check for errant clothes, glance at the bed to check it's made . . . and find Finn. Sitting cross-legged on my quilt reading a copy of *Slimming World*.

'Shh,' he whispers, one finger on his lips while he flaps his other hand in the air trying to calm me down. 'Shh. Do you want him to know I'm here?'

'*I* didn't want to know you were here,' I hiss.

'Sorry. I know you told me to go out, but I sort of figured that, judging by past experience, Sebastian wouldn't come back with you. And I kind of thought, what's the point in going out? And then I heard you at the door, panicked and hid in here. It's not as if you're planning to use this room, is it?'

I glare at him.

'Oh, sorry.' He sounds shocked. 'That's what you meant by coming back. I was thinking of when you brought your school-friends back and wanted me to make myself scarce. Like when you and Mairead Ryan wanted to play your Bucks Fizz album. Look' – he digs into the pocket in his jeans – 'here's the £50 back. It's only fair.' He smiles apologetically.

'And what am I meant to do with it? What am I meant to do now?' I hiss.

'I could hide under the bed?'

'I'm not having you underneath me while Sebastian's on top of me.'

'I found your ear plugs.' He lifts up a pair of airline freebies. 'I won't listen.'

'No,' I whisper emphatically.

'Orla,' Sebastian calls from the living room. 'A guy could die of thirst in here. Have you not found that bottle opener?'

'You keep your bottle opener in you bedroom?' asks Finn, incredulously. He opens the drawer of a bedroom cabinet and roots around. 'Where? In here?'

'No. It was an excuse, so I could check the room,' I spit. 'Stop looking through that drawer.' He closes it quickly. 'What am I going to do now? You've got me into this mess. Think.'

'If you don't come out in two minutes, I'm coming in,' shouts Sebastian. How often have I longed to hear those words? Now they're as unwelcome as a low calorie chocolate bar in my fridge.

'One minute,' I shout back. I turn to Finn. 'You keep dead quiet. Not even a mutter. I'm going to have to entertain him outside. I don't want you to move outside this room.'

'Will you be long?'

I glare at him. Please tell me we had different fathers. 'I'm warning you.' I leave the room to find Sebastian walking towards me. I can hear Sugababes playing on the stereo.

'I was just on my way to get you. I found a corkscrew, and *voilà* . . .' He holds up an open bottle of white wine and two glasses. 'Shall we take them through into the bedroom?'

'Woah. Down, boy,' I whisper. I hope I sound sexy and husky, and not like one of those people in the adverts for cough mixture. I put my hands up to his shoulders and push him back into the room, and he leans down to kiss me as he moves. 'What's the rush? Why not sit down and have a drink or two?' I point to a small Persian rug, just in front of the fireplace.

'I don't think this will fit us both,' he says doubtfully, looking at the manky carpet underneath.

'Live dangerously.' I kneel down, take the bottle and glasses, and start to pour the wine. He kneels in front of me and takes a sip from his glass. Then he leans over and kisses me. I can feel the chill from the wine on his lips.

'You don't know how much this means to me,' he mutters, pushing me down onto the rug. I don't like to argue, but I do

73

know. Let's just say I can feel it. He starts to slowly undo the buttons on my little cardigan, kissing my chest each time he frees one. Little tiny kisses that barely touch. He reaches my stomach and starts to gradually pop the button on my skirt waistband. I'm so enraptured that I can't move. He slowly unzips my skirt, starts to slowly slide it down over my hips. I'm in another world, exhilarated as I listen to the music. The all-girl band moans softly. I know how they feel.

'That's very clever,' mutters Sebastian as he finally detaches my skirt. 'The way you can throw your voice. It almost sounds like you're moaning in a different room.'

What? I open my eyes and sit bolt upright, pushing Sebastian away. I listen carefully to the music. The Sugababes aren't moaning, not even close. I'm not moaning. Definitely not close. The noise is coming from my bedroom. Finn. My bloody stupid brother is chanting. Sebastian looks at me.

'There's someone else in this flat, isn't there?'

'My brother,' I mutter. 'In the bedroom.' I reach out for my skirt and use it to hide my body, which suddenly feels out of place and out of shape.

'What is he doing there? Looking for the corkscrew?' Sebastian looks annoyed. 'And why is he making that racket?' Finn is now in full-blown chant mode. I hope he's praying for his life. I'm going to murder him.

'I'll find out.' I hastily put my skirt back on, wrap my cardigan around my chest, march to my bedroom, and fling open the door, to find Finn kneeling by my bed, eyes closed and ear plugs in place. I walk over, pull a plug out, and scream into his ear, 'What the hell are you doing?'

He jumps back in fright. 'Orla. Oh, no. Don't say it hasn't worked.'

'What hasn't worked?'

'My chant.'

'Did I not tell you to keep quiet?' I scream.

'Yes but—'

'But nothing. You arrive here uninvited, tell me you're moving in, and then proceed to ruin my life.'

74

'I didn't. I was chanting to improve your life.'

'How do you work that one out?'

'Well, I was desperate to go to the loo, so I started to chant quietly until the feeling went away. And then I thought that I was being selfish. So I changed the purpose of my chant. I was chanting for you. So that he wouldn't be gay. It worked, didn't it?' He asks. 'He didn't seem gay tonight, did he?'

'Not until you started chanting,' I shriek. 'I never said he was gay. Why are you interfering in my life when you can't even sort out your own?'

'I'm sorry.' He looks upset.

'Not half as sorry as I am that I allowed you to stay. I want you to leave tomorrow.'

Sebastian appears behind me. All the buttons on his shirt have been done back up and it's tucked neatly back into his trousers. Our moment, the long-awaited moment, has passed.

'What's going on?' he asks frostily.

'You must be Sebastian,' says Finn, jumping off the bed, hand extended. 'Good to meet you. I've heard so much about you.' I blush.

'And I've just heard you.' I realize that he doesn't just mean the chant. He's heard our entire conversation. Finn is blissfully unaware.

'I didn't know he was here until I popped in earlier,' I start to explain. 'He was meant to have gone out.' Sebastian ignores me. Finn carries on, oblivious to the tension.

'Yeah, sorry about that. It was meant to be an internal chant, but you know, like when the mood gets you, you get swept away with the emotion of it all.' My brother smiles sheepishly.

'Yeah,' Sebastian says, 'I think I know that feeling, but it's so fragile, isn't it? Doesn't take much to destroy it.'

'Exactly, man.' Finn looks surprised. He thinks he's met a soul mate.

'So you think I'm gay?' Sebastian asks Finn.

'Hey, no. I don't even know you. Liz thinks you're gay,' Finn replies, 'but I can tell her now that you're not. Don't worry.'

'So Liz thinks I'm gay, does she?' Sebastian turns to me. 'As she has never met me, how on earth could she have formed that opinion?'

'Finn's got it all wrong,' I bluff. 'He mistook you for somebody else.'

'Oh, somebody else you brought back here to prove they weren't gay,' snaps Sebastian. 'Well, I think it's time for me to go home. Three's a crowd and all that. unless that is something else you want to prove.' He stares at me, then holds his hand up in a sarcastic farewell, walks across the hallway, and lets himself out of the door.

'Don't go, Sebastian,' I call out as the door slams behind him. I spin round to face Finn. 'Tomorrow,' I scream at him. 'Tomorrow you're going. Now get out of my bedroom.' I push him aggressively out of the door and into the hallway. Then I bury my head in my pillow and start to cry.

SLIMMING TIP ELEVEN

Concentrate on the positive

'So you haven't heard anything from Sebastian since Friday?' Liz asks.

It's Sunday evening, and after nearly forty-eight hours of moping around and feeling sorry for myself, I called for reinforcements. There's nothing like a shared wallow. Unfortunately Liz arrived at the same time as my weekly curry. Talk about bad planning. Now I'm forced to share it. We're kneeling around the coffee table, dipping into the steaming tin foil containers.

'No,' I shrug, breaking off a piece of keema nan.

'Nothing at all? Not even a text message?'

'No means no. Surely all women know that?'

'Bad taste, Orla,' Liz reprimands me. 'And what about Finn?' She looks down at the last poppadom. Surely she wouldn't be so cruel as to deprive a friend in need?

'What about him?' I ask carefully. Watching.

'Where is he?' Her hands moves dangerously close.

'He's gone to mass.'

'Mass?' Liz looks up in surprise, forgetting her meal. 'I thought he was a Buddhist now.'

'He is, but he feels really guilty about what happened and says only the Catholics know how to do guilt properly. He's been gone most of the day.' I reach towards the poppadom, push my finger through its centre, and watch it shatter on the plate into several pieces. There. Now that's fairer. I pick the largest section up.

'So you're not going to throw him out any more?'

'I checked with the council. The bin men have a rule against it.' I shove a forkful of pilau rice into my mouth. 'Seriously though, where would he go?'

'Back to your mother's?'

'I don't hate him that much. Besides she wouldn't understand what all the fuss was about. She'd think it was great that he was here while I was entertaining a man friend. I mean' – I slip into my mother's accent – ' "you hear such terrible things about what happens after a few drinks". Finn's my personalized contraceptive. Even the Church can't argue against that one.'

'Why doesn't he get a flat of his own?'

'He hasn't any money and I'm not subsidizing him. No, I'll just have to wait until he gets a job.'

'Well, he's going to help out on Light As A Feather, isn't he?'

'I'm not paying him,' I say indignantly, 'and I'm not making any money out of it.'

'Are you ready for the launch tomorrow?' Liz's spoon hovers predatorily above the last bit of chicken tikka masala.

'As ready as I'll ever be. Are you sure it wouldn't be better to delay until we've advertised it a bit more?'

'Look, we've door-stepped all the slimming clubs in the City and told the members about it. My article, "How to keep your figure when all around are losing theirs", is in the magazine tomorrow. Let's strike when the iron is hot.' Good thinking. I pull the silver foil chicken tikka masala container towards me and empty its contents onto my plate. Liz looks bemused. 'Anyway, you don't want too many clients at the beginning. Let it build up slowly to allow you to adjust. It'll be fun, honest.'

'That's what you said about kickboxing.'

'Well, I thought it was,' Liz replies indignantly. 'Anyway, just think, if it all works out, you might even be able to leave your job at Browns Black. Become a dotcom millionaire.'

'Don't raise my hopes. Do you know what Tabitha did this week?'

'Apart from issuing a written warning?'

'Oh that. And I was just feeling better. No, she came running out of her office towards me shrieking after she discovered a blister on her finger and asked me what she should do because' – I pause for effect – 'I was used to dealing with bulges.'

Liz looks at me in horror. 'What a bitch! What did you say?'

' Nothing, what could I say? She didn't really want an answer, she was cackling so much at her own joke. Then all afternoon I could hear her on the phone to different friends, complaining about how she was now a "fat bird" because she had gained some weight on her finger. So I showed her my finger. I expect a second written warning will be issued next week.' I scrape the sag aloo onto my plate as well.

'What did Patti say?'

'She wasn't there. She had another "problem" with the fish at lunchtime. I wouldn't mind, but I heard her booking a table at a steak house.'

'I must say, you're being remarkably calm.'

'About Patti? She's only young. She'll learn.'

'About everything. Tabitha is a complete bitch to you, Patti leaves you to do all the work *and* drops you in it with City Hunk of the Week, your brother turns up uninvited to live with you, and your boyfriend does a bunk. I'd be going crazy.'

'Takes more than that to make me crazy,' I say. 'It would take at least somebody trying to finish off my keema nan.' Liz puts it back. Wise girl. 'I just don't know what to make of Sebastian.'

'Did you ring him?'

'Once or twice.' Liar, liar, pants on fire. 'I kept getting his answer phone.' Sixteen times.

'Did you leave a message?'

'Apart from asking him to call, no. Anyway, who am I kidding? If Sebastian really liked me, then Finn's chanting wouldn't have put him off. Would it?'

'You never know with men. It doesn't take much to put them off their stroke.' Liz sips a glass of wine. 'Jason is thrown off course by a draught, but that could just be a matter of size. How do you really feel?'

A bit sick after hearing about your love life.

'Like shit,' I reply. 'I expected him to be bigger than this. He didn't have to go storming out like an adolescent. I know it was embarrassing and we were really only starting out, but, I mean, nobody takes my brother seriously.'

'There's plenty more—'

'Fish in the sea? Pebbles on the beach?' I sigh at the inevitable platitude.

'Er no, pilau rice. Finish it off. I'm stuffed.' Liz pushes her plate back onto the coffee table and climbs back into the armchair, wine glass in hand. 'I never thought he was good enough for you.'

'You never met him. He was gorgeous.'

'Doesn't matter. He didn't sound right. From what you said. He just didn't do the things that boyfriends should do – and I'm not just talking about sex. You need somebody kind and decent. Listen, I'm meeting up with some candidates for City Hunk of the Week soon. Why don't you come along? It would do you good.'

'So would a plate of cabbage, but I'm not trying that either. No.'

'Oh go on. Be a devil.'

'What happens if Sebastian spots me? Out with a bunch of good-looking men?'

'I'd hope it would make him jealous.'

'Good point.' I push my empty plate away. 'I'll give it some thought. I can't say fairer than that.'

'Talking of good-looking men, I got a call from some Eastern European guy called Sven. Works at your bank. Wanted to know if you'd submitted his details for City Hunk of the Week.'

'No. He's such a publicity junkie. What did you say?'

'That I was wading through the pile of applications as we spoke, and that no doubt I'd soon come to his. Why didn't you send it in? What does he look like?'

'Like a photo-fit on *Crimewatch*.'

'Ah, come on. Does he have a good figure?'

'Seen better ones on a calculator.'

'I'm getting the sense you don't like him.' So intuitive.

'He's a pain. Sven's desperate to get into the newspapers. Whenever his counterparts at other banks get mentions, he has temper tantrums at my desk. The man never does anything interesting enough to get press coverage.'

'Well, send him in anyway. I bow to your opinion, obviously, but we'll keep them on record. He sounds a horror.' Liz glances at her watch. 'I've got to get going. I promised Jason that I'd collect a video on the way home and the shop shuts in half an hour.' She stands up. 'We'll see you tomorrow, about eleven? And don't worry tonight. You'll be fine. I know you can do this.' She takes my hands. 'But you must promise me one thing before I leave.'

'Yeah?'

'You'll cancel the standing order at the curry house.'

SLIMMING TIP TWELVE

Don't be afraid to talk to other people about your problems – even if it's just your brother

I can't believe it. In less than an hour Light As A Feather is officially going live. Me, Orla Kennedy, who has only ever lost pounds at the races, will offer advice and pearls of slimming wisdom on-line. I have to put Sebastian out of my head and my best foot forward. Everybody is helping.

Jason is just setting up my laptop on the coffee table. I've taken a day's holiday, but apparently he's got one of those 'twenty-four hour things'. I expect he'll become a martyr to them in the run-up to the wedding. Liz is officially interviewing potential candidates for her Hunk slot though actually she's making coffee in the kitchen. And Finn is in my bedroom doing something in my honour. I think it involves incense, otherwise that boy *has* got problems.

'Coffee up,' shouts Liz as she walks back into the room carrying a tray. She's brought a pot of coffee, four mugs and a plate of Danish pastries. 'Well, you're not starting for another hour, are you?' She smiles at me.

I nod towards the scales, placed strategically over the wobbly floorboard that knocks five pounds off your weight.

'You won't look when I weigh myself?'

'No, we promised.'

'Because I will be heavier than normal because of last night's curry.'

'I said, we promised.'

'And Jason, you won't check on my details and progress when you're maintaining the site?'

'Scout's honour.' He holds his hand up in the brigade's salute.

'I'm so nervous,' I admit, and point at a pile of slimming magazines and diet books at the side of the armchair. 'Go on, Liz. Ask me anything. Pick any one.'

'Orla, this is not your finals. Relax. I thought the whole idea of this website was that it only offered sensible advice. Come on now. Deep breaths. In . . . out . . . in. Just remember, sensible advice is your forté.'

The doorbell rings.

'Oh my God.' I start at the noise. 'Do you think it's one of the City slimming clubs? Come to warn me off their clients?'

It's Patti.

'Hi,' she smiles. 'I just wanted to come along to offer moral support. I know you must be nervous.' She nods at Liz and Jason.

'What did you say to Tabitha?' I check my watch. 'You haven't even eaten the fish yet.'

'I told her I was getting the morning after pill.'

Jason nearly chokes on his coffee.

'Well, she can hardly check, can she? And I used the wisdom teeth excuse weeks ago.' She looks around the room. 'Is your brother here?'

'In my bedroom. He's sending me positive energy.'

'I must just go and introduce myself. I've heard so much about him.' Patti grabs a Danish pastry and heads off to my bedroom.

Liz, Jason and I sit in silence for a while, interrupted only by the occasional giggles from the bedroom. At least somebody has fun in there. I jot down some welcoming words for the site, while Liz flicks through one of the pile of bridal magazines that she's brought round with her. Occasionally she lifts one up in front of her face, turning it to one side and then the next as she checks out a potential wedding dress. Then with a sigh and a disappointed shrug, she'll put it down again. The silence seems to go on for ages until, suddenly, Jason checks his watch.

'Orla, it's time. Finn. Patti. Come on. We're just about to launch.'

Everybody gathers around me as I kneel in front of the laptop.

'What do I do?'

'Hang on a minute.' Jason counts down. 'Five, four, three, two one . . . right. Light As A Feather is officially on-line.'

'Should have had some champagne,' says Patti. 'I normally have a glass in my hand by now.'

'Just type a message, Orla,' encourages Jason. 'Anything. The chances are others will log in over the next few minutes so don't worry if there isn't an immediate response.' He crouches beside me.

'Here goes.' I start typing. Nothing too clever or over-the-top. Just a polite welcome to all my clients. Clients. Wow. How cool is that? Butterflies fill my stomach as I finish my message.

Orla>
Hi there. My name is Orla Kennedy, and I'm here to welcome you all to Light As A Feather. If you have taken the time to log on then I know that we all share a common goal. We are all here to lose weight. I'm afraid that I'm not about to publish some revolutionary diet, although like you I have probably tried them all. Who can forget the after effects of the grapefruit only diet? Certainly not my stomach. But let's be honest. We secretly know that there is no quick fix way to lose weight. It's going to be a tough and slow slog, but we can do it together. We'll support each other and work together to achieve our goals.

'Eat your heart out, Tony Blair,' whispers Liz.

'Too much?' I whisper back.

'Not if you were accepting an Oscar,' giggles Patti.

'No, fine as it is.' Liz smiles supportively.

'Girls, why are you whispering? They can't hear you,' interrupts Jason. 'I think it's great, Orla. Don't worry. But should you have put your name up there? What if Tabitha hears about it from someone? You're not allowed to moonlight, are you?'

'Shit.' I didn't mean to do that. I was going to use a pseudonym. 'Can we do anything to take it off now?'

'Sorry. It's gone up in real time.' He considers the matter. 'Just don't mention where you work. Be vague about your career.'

'Orla!' Liz suddenly screams. 'Somebody has just signed on. Look, her name is Tessa.'

'Oh please, don't let it be Two Tons. I think she'll be too far gone to save,' says Patti. I ignore her.

Tessa>
Hi there. I feel a little strange. Like you can see me.

Orla>
I know.

Tessa>
What do we do now?

Orla>
Well, let's start with why you want to lose weight.

Tessa>
My son is getting bullied at school by the other children. They say his mummy is ugly and fat.

'God, I wish I'd brought the tissues,' interrupts Patti. I glare at her for spoiling my concentration. 'Look,' she points at the screen. 'Two more people have joined the room.' She nudges Finn, who has his eyes closed. He's deep in meditative contemplation. Or some other guff.

Bella>
Hello, I'm Bella.

Lily>
Hello. Lily.

Orla>
Hi there and welcome. I'm Orla. I was just talking to Tessa who wants to lose weight to stop her child getting bullied at school.

Bella>
Hi, Tessa. I know exactly what you mean. My five-year-old is getting bullied by his school friends too and he's really upset that I won't enter the parents' race at his sports day. But I couldn't. I'd worry that I'd have a heart attack, even if it is just an egg and spoon race.

'You don't have to eat it,' mutters Patti. I glare again at her. 'Sorry.'

Orla>
Is that why you want to lose weight, Lily?

Lily>
Are you that nice lady that I met outside the slimming club?

Orla>
Yes, I think so. Why do you want to lose weight?

Lily>
My daughter says I've let myself go since I remarried. But it's not my fault. My husband has an ice cream van and he makes such lovely desserts. I'm just trying to show my support for him.

Orla>
So you've put on some weight since the wedding?

Lily>
I think so. I keep bumping into pieces of furniture.

Orla>
I'm sorry?

Lily>
Well, my belly seems to get in the way and it never did before.

Bella>
I have the same problem with my bust. When I go to restaurants, it rests on the table, and the waiters have difficulty placing plates down. They always seem to catch it, although I think one or two do it deliberately .;-)

Oh my God. I forgot. Internet *aficionados* have another language. 'What does that mean?' I ask Jason.

'Wink, wink, nudge, nudge.'

Orla>
Men!

Bella>
I know, but then I feel embarrassed because it seems to work like one of those little pelican bibs that children used to wear. It catches everything that drops. It's like I have a Picasso print stamped across my chest. What can I say? (o) (o)

'I am a well-endowed female,' translates Jason, blushing.

Lily>
I know what you mean. My daughter Trixie says that if my husband ever wants to see my bust, I'll have to raise my skirt.

Jason coughs in embarrassment.

Orla>
Well, I think we all have valid reasons for losing weight. I want to look good in a bridesmaid's dress next summer.

Cecilia has just logged on.

Cecilia>
I don't know what I'm doing here.

Orla>
You want to lose weight, like the rest of us.

Cecilia>
Actually I'm not fat. I'm only doing this because my husband spotted one of your flyers and suggested it.

Orla>
OK. Well, thank you for joining us. By the way, what was the last item of clothing that you bought?

Cecilia>
What's that got to do with anything?

Bella>
Oh come on.

Cecilia>
A pair of shoes.

Orla>
And before that?

Cecilia>
A pair of Jimmy Choo sandals.

Orla>
And before that?

Cecilia>
A pair of mules.

Orla>
You're in denial. You must be overweight. Your subconscious is refusing to allow you to go into a boutique and buy anything because it will not be in the size you want it to be. Don't you see? Your shoes remain the same size. There's no embarrassing moment when you go into the communal changing room. Plus they're likely to be a small size that you think of as 'normal'. So you keep buying them. It gets over the natural female desire to shop and yet does not embarrass you.

'Wow,' mutters Liz. 'You're good.

Orla>
The main thing now is to recognise that. Accept you are overweight, and do something about it. Your husband wouldn't have suggested you joined this site just to be nasty, would he?

Cecilia>
I don't know. He's a City banker.

'Enough said,' says Patti.

Orla>
I'm sure he loves you whatever size you are.

Cecilia>
But he won't let me in any family photographs at the moment. He's very image conscious. I blame it on his background. He was so poor when he was younger that he now can't help wanting life's little luxuries.

After spending the next five minutes cajoling and encouraging Cecilia, she finally admits that she has a weight problem although she's adamant that it won't be as bad as the rest of us. I explain to them all about inputting their vital statistics, and we discuss our objectives for the week. To exercise at least three times for twenty minutes and to keep our daily calorie intake below fifteen hundred. We each go off to our respective scales, then input our personal data. I'm surprised to find that my weight is a few pounds less than I'd expected; must be all the chasing around last week. I'm just about to sign off when a new entrant logs on.

Mary>
Am I too late, Orla dear?

Orla>
Sorry?

Mary>
It's me. Your mother. And Marcella is here. We're using Finn's computer. Hold on a minute, she wants to type something . . . hello there, Orla, Marcella here. Isn't this fun? How's London? Your mammy said that you were getting involved in the old chat show business.

Orla>
Marcella, I'm doing it now. Chatting on-line.

Mary>
Oh my goodness, Orla, are you really? Can other people hear me? Hello? Anybody there?

Cecilia> Bella> Lily> Tessa>
Hello.

Mary>
Oh my. Hello, girls. That's a nice name, Cecilia. Are you named after St Cecilia, patroness of music?

Cecilia>
No. My grandmother.

Mary>
Wonderful story, you know. They tried to suffocate her, then they cut off her head. Your cousin is named after her too, Orla. You know, Eileen's daughter.

Could this get any worse? Liz, Patti and Jason are giggling. 'Do you want me to unplug her?' Jason asks. 'The emergency power surge line?' Finn looks as horrified as I am.

'Better not. She'll only keep on about it for weeks.'

Orla>
Mammy. It's lovely to hear from you, but we've really haven't got much time. The supervised chat room closes shortly and we all need to get on.

Mary>
I was only just going to wish you all luck. Is Finn there with you? Is he getting enough sleep? You know how cranky he is on less than eight hours.

Orla>
Well, you all have the information and diet sheets for the coming week. I want to wish us the very best of luck.

Lily>
Thank you. I can still eat cakes, can't I?

Bella>
TUVM, or thank you very much if you didn't understand that.

Mary>
Do you see that, Marcella? Bella's doing that language that they spoke about on Gloria Hunniford. What do I write back? Hold on, Bella, Marcella's just showing me. I:/.

'Your mother's just written "I am constipated",' points out Jason. 'Are you sure that I can't pull the plug?' I shake my head.

'And she goes on about me eating enough fibre,' mutters Finn.

Bella>
:[

'Real downer,' translates Jason.

Orla>
OK girls, before my mother gets onto her varicose veins, let's sign off. I look forward to chatting to you all, same time and place next week. Let's hope we all have good news to relay. Don't forget, if you have any problems, you can contact me on the e-mail address at the bottom of the site. Ciao.

Cecilia> Bella> Lily> Tessa>
Ciao.

Mary>
What's that mean, Marcella? Look it up quickly . . .

Get dumped

It is a fortnight since Finn ruined my life. Sebastian hasn't called. Not once. Not even when I've been out; twice I've checked that my answer machine is working, and buttons one, four and seven all look distinctly worn on my touchtone phone. Each time the mobile rings, my spirits rise, only to come crashing down to earth with a thump when it isn't him on the other end. The phone now serves to mock me. Each ring emphasizing just how easily accessible I am if somebody truly wanted to contact me.

Liz has tried to buck my spirits, uttering those standard platitudes, but while I may have fallen off this bicycle I don't think that I'm quite ready to get back in the saddle. It all seems like a distant dream now. Orla Kennedy holding hands with Sebastian. Kissing him. Enjoying the intimacy of a relationship, such as it was. And, if I'm being really truthful, enjoying the incredulous glances of other women who couldn't quite understand what he was doing with me. I can tell them now. Nothing.

A few people at work have guessed that something is wrong. Not Tabitha, obviously. She's too wrapped up in her own little world. But Harry, who fills the chocolate machines on each floor, is worried. He came to see me yesterday, wondering why I hadn't called him to restock this floor's machine. We normally chat at least twice a week. We even exchanged Christmas cards last year. Lauren, who pushes around the food trolleys at breakfast and elevenses, is also concerned. She even jokingly put her hand on my forehead yesterday, testing for a fever after I turned down the offer of two egg muffins for the price of one. (They're always a bit cold and the eggs congealed, but that's the way I've grown to love them.)

Strangely, Light As A Feather almost eases my heartache. Thirty-two people have enrolled in five days, and for two hours each day I feel wanted as I offer slimming tips and listen to dieting problems. Between us we've lost forty-one pounds and three of those are mine. A broken heart – the greatest diet known to man. I've just signed off today's session. Patti isn't back from lunch yet. She's chaperoning Tony Younger, who is meeting a young female journalist from the *Financial Times*. Patti is there to make sure that Tony doesn't say anything he shouldn't. I just hope he does the same for her.

Of course, I should have gone. It is the first time I've given Patti any responsibility since she sent out that awful press release on Tony Younger's appointment. It is just ironic that it should be him she's chaperoning. But I can't face him. Tony still blames me for the City Hunk of the Week débâcle, and has shunned me several times in the bank's foyer and canteen. I don't blame him, and even though the whole catastrophe wasn't really my fault, I feel guilty. A deep, Catholic guilt. Tony seems such a nice, genuine guy. I really connected with him over drinks in Corney & Barrow. I doubt he'd have wanted me at today's lunch with Patti, of whose role in his embarrassment he is blissfully unaware. Besides I needed to be here to monitor the chat room.

My phone rings. Sebastian? My heart races as I pick up the receiver.

'Browns Black. Orla Kennedy speaking.' A little shake in my voice.

'Orla?' It's Finn. I should have realized. Since when did God do anything for me? I bet Sebastian has re-filed my entry in his little black book. Under 'Steer clear. Weird brother. Think of genes'. He's concerned. 'Are you all right? You sound like you're out of breath.'

'What is it, Finn? I'm busy. I've got three press releases to get out before I leave tonight.' Actually it's one, but that doesn't make me sound like a high-powered executive.

'I've had a bit of an accident.'

'Are you OK? What were you doing?' What will my mother say? I should be watching him at all times.

'I'm fine. Honest. It's nothing serious, but could you pick up some vacuum bags on your way home?'

'Vacuum bags?' Not plasters? Paracetamol? Ice? (Well, you need a stiff drink after a trauma.)

'Yeah, for the vacuum cleaner.' And then God created man, and it all went horribly wrong.

'I realized that, Finn. But *why* do you need them?'

'Well, it was for Light As A Feather.'

'What was?'

'Lots of the clients have said how they'd love a series of exercises that they could print off and follow.' And then God created the mind of man. But got distracted.

'How many?'

'Em, two. Cecilia and Amy. She's new. Hasn't been in the chat room during the monitored sessions, but she was in there yesterday when I was checking out the site. Seems very nice, actually. You'd like her.'

'Vacuum bags,' I prompt. 'Can we speed this up? Some of us are working.'

'Oh yeah. Anyway, I thought it wasn't a bad idea, but I didn't want to bother you with it, so I bought this book called Flex Your Muscles With Empty Bottles that shows how to exercise using things in the house. I thought I could draw little matchstick men showing how to do them, which could be posted on the site.'

'Vacuum bags?'

'It got a bit messy.'

'How?'

'I was just coming to that.' He pauses. Why can't Finn just confess outright? Why the drama? He was like this when he was eight and pulled the leg off my Barbie. He told me she'd been in a hit and run, and that Action Man had been at the wheel. 'Well, I thought I'd better try them out first. See they worked. So I tried an exercise using baked bean tins as dumb-bells. The beans can even be low calorie. Press-ups using a chair are good. But I got a bit carried away . . .'

'And?'

'I improvised on the stepping. I mean, you haven't got any stairs in your flat, and I thought lots of people might have that problem, so I looked around for something to step on.'

'And?'

'It didn't work. Who would have thought there were so many cornflakes in a box? They should mention it on the packet.'

'What?'

'That it doesn't take the weight of a grown up. Somebody could have an accident.' I think it was my mother. 'So could you bring in the vacuum bags? And check your e-mails. Amy said she would e-mail you.'

'Can't you get the bags?'

'Well, I could, but I spent the last of my money on the exercise book. By the way, sis, can I claim that back through petty cash?'

'What petty cash?' I explode.

'You really need to relax, Orla. When you look in the mirror, does a smiling face look back? No. That's why I turned to Buddhism, you know, because life had too many problems.' And I'm talking to mine. 'I could teach you to chant when you get home, if you like?'

'Or I could teach you to pack. Goodbye, Finn.' I slam the phone down and get back to working on the press release. Privately I think it's a waste of time. How many journalists will be interested in a stock market listing for a Bulgarian knitting needle manufacturer? I can't even see the *Financial Times* writing about this one and everyone knows how desperate they get to fill their pages. Still, it's what I get paid for. I'm trying to think of some knitting needle jokes when Sven appears. It's Friday, dress down day, but he's wearing a three-piece, pinstripe suit, discreet navy tie, and white shirt. A flamboyant yellow silk handkerchief flutters in his breast pocket.

'Sven. Going somewhere nice?'

'One never knows when the photographers might want to take a picture. It is best to always be ready,' he replies sharply, glancing not so subtly at my faded floral dress. 'Don't you think?' I nod slowly. 'I mean, look at this.' He thrusts a broadsheet newspaper into my hands. 'See that article?' He stabs at a small piece in the paper's diary where all the amusing anecdotes are written up. 'That's my cousin.' I glance at the picture of a man sitting in the middle of a trading room, surrounded by all his colleagues, having his head shaved.

'He seems nice,' I say, doubtfully. But hardly normal. Shaving with an audience.

'He's in the newspaper.'

'He is.' The knitting needle factory suddenly seems exciting. I shift the papers around on my desk as if I'm itching to get on. But Sven doesn't take the hint. I read the accompanying article to get rid of him. His cousin shaved his head for charity.

'Why? Why is *he* in there? Why can't I get in there?' he screams, slapping the newspaper with the back of his hand. I pointedly look at his full head of hair. 'My cousin gets into a newspaper for a stupid childish prank and I can't get any press coverage.'

'Are you doing any charity events?' I ask. 'Like your cousin?'

'Charity? I'm an investment banker, for God's sake,' Sven yells. 'I've a reputation to keep up. Have you seen the deals that I'm working on? They're ground-breaking.' I prefer the word boring. He lifts up the press release I'm working on. 'Have you looked at this properly? Knitting needles. I'm securitising knitting needles. How many people can do that?' Well, if my mother only had the pattern. 'It's fascinating stuff. The newspapers should be queuing up to interview me. You're the press officer. Organize it. I want a front-page piece. Soon.'

Deep breath. Word this next sentence carefully. And slowly. Very slowly.

'I can't dictate what journalists write,' I answer. 'Nobody

can. I present them with the facts and they make their own decision. But, if you want my personal opinion, the deals that you work on fail to attract attention because they're too esoteric. Now, if you want to do a massive ground-breaking deal for a *British* company, like Marks and Spencer, say, the *British* newspapers will probably cover it.'

'Who asked you for your opinion? I told you what I want. I'm warning you, Orla.' He stabs his finger at me. 'If I don't get some publicity soon, I'm going to get you fired.'

'Well, I'm doing my best,' I reply calmly. 'And I can only hope that we both benefit from it. Now, if you'll excuse me, I have work to do.' I turn back to my press release.

'I don't make idle promises,' mutters Sven before he turns on his heel and storms off. Then I start to shake. I've just hammered another nail into my career coffin. There is no way that I can get press coverage for a knitting needle deal. Not even in *Cable Stitch Weekly*. Not even if I call in a few favours. But I know why he's so desperate for media attention. It boosts his profile. Which boosts his market value. Which boosts his bonus. QED. A simple equation that even I, who failed maths GCSE twice, can solve. I suddenly feel depressed and desperate. All resolve disappears as I reach into my desk drawer for my secret comfort stash. I rifle through the chocolate bars, all soft and squishy from the heat, and pull out the biggest. Little waves of excitement pass through me as I start to unwrap it.

'What are you doing?' I start at Patti's voice. 'A Mars a day help you work, rest and *weigh*.'

'Patti. What are you doing here?'

'Wrong question. What are you doing *there*?'

'I was feeling depressed.'

'No excuse. You told me to stop you whenever you weakened.' She steps forward. Hand outstretched. 'Give it up.'

'But . . .' I clutch the bar a little tighter. 'I need it.'

'No, you don't.' She thrusts her hand at me. 'Hand it over.' I pass it across. Feeling like a naughty schoolboy caught with a catapult and a pile of sucked-on pieces of tissue for ammunition.

'You're going to eat it,' I accuse.

'Well, it's open now and it would be a shame to waste it.' She bites into the bar, right in front of me. 'Believe me. I'm only doing this for your own good. It gives me no pleasure at all.' She pushes a finger to her lips, catching a dripping string of toffee, then licks it. Eyes closed. 'So, how did today's session go? Any new clients?'

'One, but I don't think she'll be back.'

'Why?'

'I don't think I was really her scene. She said that she wanted to incorporate more exercise into her life. So I asked how she travelled to work, then suggested she got off the bus one stop early.'

'Sound advice.'

'Apparently her journey is only one stop.'

'Ah.'

'Then I suggested using stairs instead of lifts.'

'Also good advice.'

'How was I to know that she had just installed a stair lift at home? She thought I was winding her up. Don't think she'll be back. Speaking of which, why are you back from lunch so early? Has the restaurant lost its licence?'

'Funny. Actually Tony doesn't drink at lunch and nor did Trish, the journalist we met, so I decided to abstain. Wouldn't want people to think I was an alcoholic, would I?' Too late.

I smile. 'Was lunch good? Did Trish get everything she wanted?'

'Think so – and more besides. She got Tony's mobile number.'

'Oh?'

'In case she needs to call him after hours. She promised not to use it unless it was an emergency.' Like when she has an empty bar stool beside her. God, Orla. Listen to yourself. Anybody would think you were jealous. You're mourning over Sebastian. Remember? 'Actually I think she quite fancied him, and I must say today he was looking pretty good. He's put on a bit of weight since he joined. Not much, but that gaunt, starved look seems to have gone.'

'Did he mention me?'

'No, but I think he's got over the City Hunk of the Week fiasco. Trish asked him about it and I held my breath, waited for him to explode. Honest, Orla, I would have admitted that it was my fault, if he had.' Yeah, right. 'But he laughed it off. Right in front of me. Said he'd been really upset at first, but has had so many favourable comments about it, calling him a good sport and stuff, that he kind of doesn't mind any more. Although he did tell me walking back that he asked for his desk to be moved. Apparently the analyst sitting beside him was using Tony's photo for extra-curricular activities. You know the guy I mean. Was off last year with repetitive strain injury.' She screws the Mars bar wrapper into a tiny ball and tosses it into a waste paper bin under my desk.

'So, has he forgiven me?'

'Didn't say. Sorry.' She shifts uncomfortably. 'By the way, I met Darren when we were out. You remember. Sebastian's colleague?'

'Of course I remember. Did he say anything?'

'About Sebastian?' Her face crumples up with concern.

'No,' I shriek. 'About the Argentinean economic crisis. Of course about Sebastian. Has he mentioned me?'

'Darren didn't actually say and I didn't like to ask too many questions.' Patti smiles apologetically. Her cheeks glow from the little red patches that have suddenly appeared. I can tell that she wishes she hadn't mentioned anything about her encounter. Tough. I want details. And I want them *now*. 'I was playing Miss Corporate,' she shrugs. 'Didn't think it was appropriate to discuss personal matters in front of journalists.' *Now*. Now she wants to play the game correctly. 'He did say that Sebastian had been a bit out of sorts recently.'

'About me?'

'No.' Patti looks embarrassed. 'Sorry, didn't mean to raise your hopes. Apparently he was due some big pay-out, a special trade or something? Anyway, it fell through, and he had banked on it for some sort of holiday. Sorry.' I can't help it. Tears well up in my eyes. The end of our relationship has not had the slightest impact on him. I was well down the list of his priorities. 'He's a rat, Orla. He doesn't deserve you. Honest.' She keeps talking, but the words fade in and out. Like a radio that isn't completely tuned in. I've heard this speech so many times. It doesn't matter who is saying it. I know the words almost by heart. Yeah. Absolutely nothing wrong with me. Complete mystery why I don't have a boyfriend. Yeah. Of course. It will happen. When I least expect it. I'll meet some-one. Obviously. Might even know him now. Just hasn't happened yet. Silly to worry. Let it all out though. Amazing what a good cry can do. This shoulder's available any time. Day or night. But just not on a Saturday. Because you never know what might happen that night. 'Anyway, better get on. As I got back from lunch early, thought you wouldn't mind if I left around four today. Got a big weekend planned.' She sits down at her desk and looks over at me. 'What was Sven hassling you about?' Back to business. Orla's distress over in Patti's short-attention-span world.

'Something and nothing, really,' I reply quietly. 'He wants to see his name in the newspapers more. Says he'll get me fired if I don't manage it.'

'Sven couldn't fire a water pistol,' she says indignantly. 'Relax. I'm sure something will come up that gets his name in print. In fact, I'm positive. It'll just take some time.' Patti takes her seat, switches on her computer and starts working. 'Have a little faith.'

I'm working with my mother.

SLIMMING TIP FOURTEEN

Always read your mail carefully

To   Orla@Lightasafeather.co.uk
From Amy@Hotmail.com
Spoke to your brother Finn. He said it would be OK to e-mail you directly. I went into the chat room to try it out, but I don't think it's really my scene. I wouldn't know what to say. But wanted you to know that I love it. Honestly. I've picked up all kinds of useful tips on losing weight. So thank you.
A grateful slimmer

Another satisfied customer. I can feel a blush spreading over my face. People are actually listening to my advice. And following it. Even Liz, my best friend, doesn't always do that. Mind you, I did tell her early on in her relationship with Jason that he wasn't the settling down type. How wrong was that? Just as well I haven't started a Lonely Hearts chat room. Amy sounds nice. Pity she's too shy to enter the chat room. I've found that people really do share their dieting secrets. How else would I know that eating Maltesers before standing on the scales really doesn't seem to alter the reading? I nervously type out a reply. It's after lunch, and I don't want anybody sneaking up on me and seeing what I'm doing.

To   Amy@Hotmail.com
From Orla@Lightasafeather.co.uk
Thanks for the kind e-mail. Glad the advice is helping. But you shouldn't be embarrassed to join the chat room. We're all in the

same boat. We all want to lose weight. And if we row together, I'm
sure that we can throw the excess load overboard.
Orla.

I look again at the e-mail I have just sent. I really am reading too many American self-help books. Amy will think I'm weird. I am just about to send another one apologising when a little sealed envelope appears at the top of my screen. I glance over at Patti. She appears engrossed in an analyst's report, but I know that she's photocopied an article from *Marie Claire* and slipped it inside. I check Tabitha. She's in her office. I double click on the envelope.

To   Orla@Lightasafeather.co.uk
From Amy@Hotmail.com
Your support is much appreciated. You must get hundreds of
people e-mailing you. I still think that I'd feel a bit odd in the chat
room. Like I really shouldn't be there. I have so much to lose, you
see.

Flattery will get you everywhere. I wonder how much she has to lose. How much is really embarrassing? Four stone? Five stone? No. I bet Amy is huge. Like one of those American women on Oprah. The massive ones who somehow always seem to have men chasing after them. Even though they can't run very far. I always look at them and think: how? I know it's bitchy, and they probably have lovely personalities, but *how?* Listen to me. Jealous cow. I'm doing the exact thing that I resent other people doing. Judging the book by the cover.

To   Amy@Hotmail.com
From Orla@Lightasafeather.co.uk
We all do. The chat room makes us all realize we're not alone. That
we all share the same concerns and fears. Take me, for instance. I
normally hate entering a room where I don't know anybody. The
first thing anybody ever notices, you see, is the wrapping. In my
case, it's bubble wrapping. But in the chat room it doesn't matter.

Nobody can see me. I can say what I want, discuss my deepest anxieties about my size, and know that nobody will judge me. Because they can't see me.

Good, Orla. Nice and sympathetic. Not judgemental. Encouraging. Sharing experiences, and admitting inner fears. Yep, really have read too many American self-help books.

To   Orla@Lightasafeather.co.uk
From Amy@Hotmail.com
But you sound so confident in the chat room. I could never imagine you feeling anxious. I see you as some high-powered executive. Not like me. I mean, I work in the City, but I'm a sort of researcher for one of the banks. Boring old numbers person.

I briefly wonder what bank Amy works in, but decide not to ask. I'm being deliberately vague about my career when any client of Light As A Feather asks, to prevent any gossip getting back to Tabitha, so it would be a bit rich of me to pry into Amy's business. Besides I think the anonymity helps everybody open up a bit more. Her e-mail continues.

Bet you've got real plans for Light As A Feather. I saw in your flyers that there were plans for future services. Are you doing deals with restaurants, gyms etc?

Deals? What sort of deals? Like a supermarket offering two items for the price of one? How would that work on a chat room? I want to ask Amy what she means, but she thinks I'm a high-powered executive. What a joke.

I mean, you've probably thought of this already, but what about Mario's in the Broadgate Circle. Near Liverpool Street station. The Italian delicatessen? I'm sure people would love to have diet plans using the stuff in his shop. It must be on the way home for most people in the City. I know I'd be keen. My calorie book lists all of food at M&S, which is a bit pointless really because it's all on the packets anyway, but I'd love to know how many calories are in Mario's homemade lasagne. Or even the tiramisu, which, before you lecture, I know I shouldn't have when I'm on a diet, but if I had the calories for it, then I'd be able to incorporate it into my weekly menu without worrying.

Why didn't I think of that? Amy is quite right. Mario's would be perfect. It's like a little bit of Italy in EC1. Huge Parma hams hang from hooks over the glass counter, which is covered with bottles of olive oils of all different sizes, infused with multiple herbs. Shelves crammed with a variety of pastas. And a chilled cabinet packed with homemade lasagnes, cannelloni, and meatballs. All available to heat up at home. If I could just get the recipes . . .

To   Amy@Hotmail.com
From Orla@Lightasafeather.co.uk
Your're right. I have a few deals up my sleeve, but I don't want to spoil anything by announcing them too early. Just keep tuning in to see. And I really don't lecture. Mario's tiramisu is delicious, and the only way to successfully lose weight and keep it off is not to feel deprived. A little of what you fancy does you good.

To   Orla@Lightasafeather.co.uk
From Amy@Hotmail.com
Thanks for that. I expected you to explode about the calories in cream. And I'll definitely keep tuning in. Better get on now though. The boss is hovering. Have a nice weekend.

I glance across at Patti. She's struggling to keep her eyes open. I spot her blink firmly once, twice, three times, trying to shrug off the somniferous effects of lunchtime drinking. Only Browns Black's chairman is allowed to take a post-lunch siesta.

'Patti,' I yell over. 'Mind the phones. I'm just popping out to get a proper coffee. Can I get you one? You look like you need it.'

'No thanks.' She checks her watch. 'You won't be too long? I did want to leave at four. Remember?'

I grab my jacket and bag and dash out of the bank to Mario's. I am halfway there before I realize what I am doing. I'm rushing. Like a slim person. No dawdling along the pavements. How long have I been doing this? I've never noticed it before.

Mario is clearing away some blackened jacket potatoes when I arrive. He is big and fat, with a big white linen apron stretched right around his circumference. A little waxed moustache dances under his nose.

'Orla,' he smiles, lifting the potatoes towards me. 'You like a potato? Any filling you want. On the house.'

'Mario,' I say, staring indignantly at the offering. 'I've seen bigger walnuts. I'm not here to buy, although I'll take a cappuccino. I've actually got a business proposition for you.'

'Orla, I told you before.' He shakes his head. The rolls of fat around his chin tremble with the movement. His moustache wobbles. 'I no like credit. I no give credit. Mario, he prefer cash. In hand. Now.' He holds his palm out towards me. I look blankly at it. 'The coffee, it is seventy-five pence.'

'Oh.' I place some coins in his hand and watch as he froths up a stainless steel jug of cold milk. 'Sorry,' I suddenly remember, 'could you make that skimmed?' He tuts before lifting a different jug. 'I've started a dieting website,' I explain. 'Did you just snort?' I demand, piqued.

'Just tickle in my throat,' he lies.

'Well, I suppose it is quite funny,' I admit. 'But it's not as stupid as it sounds. It's targeted at City people and I want to promote this delicatessen on it.' He nods. As if he understands what I mean. 'I want to write some diet plans for busy City people and it would be great to incorporate your food. You know, so they can pick it up on the way home. I just need the recipes to work out the calories.'

'But,' he splutters, 'they are family secrets.'

'Obviously I would pay you some sort of fee.'

'They are here.' He reaches under his counter and pulls out

an Italian cookbook. 'What?' He shrugs at my incredulous look. 'My mother, she help out the author.'

We chat for another ten minutes. I'll work out a diet plan using Mario's food, and he will sell the complete week's eating schedule. Light As A Feather will get a small fee for each package he sells and Mario will leave flyers for the site around the delicatessen.

'I have idea,' he suddenly pipes up. 'I could deliver food. As long as not too far.'

'Brilliant. I'll look up the A to Z and work out some postcode boundaries.'

Mario looks blank.

'Areas where you will deliver.'

'Oh, *si*.' He ducks under the counter, pulls up two glasses and a bottle of grappa. 'A toast? To our business relationship.'

'Thanks, but can I pass on the grappa?' Mario looks disappointed. 'But I'll have a piece of tiramisu if you're offering. With extra cream.' Well, as I recommend to my clients, one should not deprive oneself.

SLIMMING TIP FIFTEEN

Put feet into mouth and swallow

Monday morning. Nine o'clock. Patti is already hard at work, reading through all the weekend's newspapers to check for any mention of Browns Black. Her desk is strewn with supplements, thick broadsheets, and a pile of tabloids. She is the picture of concentration, her tongue just poking out of the side of her mouth. She holds a pair of scissors in one hand, ready to cut out the relevant articles, and a paintbrush sticks out of a plastic pot filled with paste. Put her in a wobbly, low-budget set and she could pass as Blue Peter presenter. I can't be one hundred per cent sure, but I'd bet last year's bonus that none of that forest of paper on her desk contains any mention of Sven's knitting needle transaction. I predict he'll be visiting me later, ready to let rip.

I turn on my computer and quickly, before Tabitha arrives, check out Light As A Feather. The chat room is empty, but I have an e-mail.

To   Orla@Lightasafeather.co.uk
From Amy@Hotmail.com
Check out the Sunday Times *supplement. Page twenty-eight. Think you might find it interesting.*
A
PS Did not weaken over the weekend

I walk over to Patti and pick up the *Sunday Times*, flicking through the sections.

'What are we looking for?'

'There's something on page twenty-eight that someone said I might find interesting.' I drag my finger through a list of advertisements. What did Amy mean? Is it one of these?

'This?' asks Patti.

'What?' I glance at what she's indicating. 'Do I look like I need a moustache clipper?' I bark.

'No, but I was thinking of Christmas. Something for Tabitha. To show we care.'

'She'd show us the door. Now if you're not going to help . . .' I grab the open supplement with both hands, and am about to walk away, when she tugs on the paper.

'Wait. Is this it?'

I set the section back down. Patti is pointing at a small advertisement, hidden in the bottom left corner of the page, and edged in a big black border. I'd thought it was a death notice.

' "Due to the cancellation of a major order," ' Patti reads out, ' "Undetectable Undergarments has a five hundred garment surplus of 'Pull Your Tummies In Tightly Knickers'. The knickers, which are made of a fine Egyptian cotton, edged with broderie anglaise and in a range of pretty colours, contain Undetectable Undergarments' specially patented lycra, designed to pull in bulging bellies, sagging seats and whittle a full two inches off the wearer's waist." '

'Yeah, but the trouble with those sorts of knickers is that the excess weight has to go somewhere,' I say dismissively. 'You probably find that wearing these you can't get your jackets on, because the fat's been pushed up around the shoulders.' I'm about to walk back to my desk, disappointed, when Patti continues.

' "This unique lycra restrains the excess weight within the body of the knickers, preventing unsightly tyres above the waist. The panties are completely discreet. Your little secret. 'Pull Your Tummies In Tightly Knickers' are not available in g-string model." ' Patti looks at me. 'But why would you want five hundred pairs of knickers? There's only seven days in a week.'

'It's not for me,' I hiss. 'It's for Light As A Feather. I could sell them through the site.'

'That's a really good idea.' She looks at me in surprise.

'I know.'

'But you don't have five hundred customers. What happens if you can't sell them all?' Now. Now she has to become all-logical.

'I could give them away as Christmas presents,' I say doubt-fully.

'Hmm. Pull Your Tummies In Tightly Knickers: when you care to send the very best.'

'I don't bloody know, do I?' I snap. 'I'm just trying to think of some ways to expand the site.' I walk back to my desk with the supplement and dial the Yorkshire number.

'Undetectable Undergarments. How can I help you?' The receptionist sounds like she's talking through her nose.

'I'm ringing about the advertisement.'

'Are you calling about Bounce Free Booby Bras, Pert Posterior Pantyhose, Pull Your Tummy In Tightly Knickers, or graduate recruitment?' She drones.

'Well, they all sound very nice,' I say hesitantly, 'but I was really wondering about the knickers.'

'Hold the line please.' The theme to *Bodyguard* plays down the phone. Irony. Don't you just love it?

'Surplus Sundries. Justin speaking. How can I help you?' Justin sounds like Dale Winton in tight trousers. Or Pull Your Tummy In Tightly Knickers.

'I was interested in your knickers pile.'

'A wonderful choice if I may say so, madam. An order from one of the country's most respected department stores, I'm sure you know who I mean, which they just cancelled without warning. Poof. Can you imagine?'

'Er, no.'

'Well, it took us by surprise, I can tell you. Left us really in the lurch. I wouldn't mind, but they'd advertised these knick-ers in their latest catalogues. Women up and down the country will be waiting for them. Where will they go now? Bellies from

Land's End to John o'Groats will be hanging out.' I glance down nervously at mine and breathe in deeply. 'The quality of the order is wonderful though, madam. I've checked them all out personally.'

'Oh right.'

'It's a dirty job, but somebody's got to do it, eh?' He giggles. I think I'm right about the knickers. 'Are you in retailing yourself, madam?'

'Not really.'

'Say no more. Is it an early Christmas present for a loved one? Perhaps a great aunt?'

'Not exactly.' I explain briefly about the site and how I hope to sell the knickers through it.

'What an interesting idea. Can I just take down some particulars?' I hear the pages of a notebook being flicked in the background. 'Unfortunately, I must tell you before we start, there are now only four hundred and ninety nine pairs left. Unforeseen circumstances, you do understand, although I can now assure you that the knickers will fit a forty-inch waist, thirty-two inch inside leg.'

'Oh good,' I say uncertainly. 'How much are you selling the knickers for?'

'Two and a half thousand pounds, madam.'

'Sorry?'

'Oh, you're quite right. Less one pair. Hold on a mo.' I can hear him tapping on a desk calculator. 'Two thousand, four hundred and ninety-five pounds. That sounds better, doesn't it?'

'It's a bit more than I expected to pay, actually.'

'Madam. These are top of the range knickers. They sell for fifteen pounds a pair. I know I shouldn't discuss clients, but' – he lowers his voice into a conspiratorial whisper – 'if Kate Moss hadn't discovered these, I doubt she'd ever have got work on the catwalk. Terrible pot belly, you know. Between you and me, I think it's digestive problems.'

'I never thought she ever had any problems with her figure.'

'That's why we're called Undetectable Undergarments,' he

giggles. 'But, I should point out, you never see her do nude, do you?'

'Well, I'm really sorry. I think I've been wasting your time. I haven't got two and a half thousand pounds spare at the moment.' I'm just about to hang up when I have a brainwave. 'What do you usually do for new suppliers?'

'You mean like an introductory offer?'

'Yes.'

'We send samples so they can test demand,' replies Justin, 'and we occasionally offer concessions.'

'OK, so let's pretend I'm a new supplier. Why don't you send me out fifty pairs of knickers as a sample.'

'*Fifty?*'

'Representing ten per cent of the stock,' I add, 'and I'll send you two hundred pounds as a deposit to hold the rest. If I'm successful with the fifty pairs, then I'll take them all.' And find the money somewhere.

'Well, we have had rather a lot of demand for this order.' Justin sounds doubtful. 'I've only just put the phone down on a rather charming Egyptian gentleman. Says he has a big shop in London.'

'Yes, but I'm the first person to put down an order? A firm order?'

'That's right.'

'And we're talking about a new medium to sell your product through.'

'Eh?'

'Is anyone else selling your products through the internet?' I repeat.

'No.' Justin pauses, then takes a deep breath. 'Oh get me. I'm so daring. Let's do it. When I get your cheque, I'll send out the fifty pairs. I'll hold the stock for three weeks. Now, can I tempt you with Pert Posterior Pantyhose?'

'No, I think I'll just stick with the knickers. Thanks, Justin. I'll put the cheque in the post today with all my details. Patti,' I shout out as I replace the receiver and fold up the newspaper. 'Guess what. I've just bought fifty pairs of knickers.'

'Washing machine broken?' I start at the male voice and turn towards Patti. She's busy shaking her head in embarrassment for me. Tony Younger is standing in front of her desk, staring at me and *laughing*. 'Or is it your birthday?'

SLIMMING TIP SIXTEEN

Learn to be assertive

Two hours later and it's nearly time to sign on with the Monday crew at Light As A Feather. Tony disappeared moments after humiliating me. Apparently he has just completed some major report on the internet and was looking for press coverage. He has obviously decided that I'm not to be trusted, so has enlisted Patti's help. Glad he caught her before lunch.

Patti was a bit embarrassed about it all. And a little excited. It's the first time that anybody within Browns Black has approached her directly to work on their behalf. She is taking it quite seriously. After Tony left, she went to the press department's stationery cupboard and took out an unused A4 sized feint-lined writing pad and a new pen. She has written Promotion of Tony Younger in large black letters on the cover of the pad.

The phone rings. It's Liz.

'Hi there. Sorry we didn't get to see you at the weekend. Did you have a good one?'

'Yeah, didn't do much. Got a video out. You?'

'Went to see Jason's parents. His father has a brother who does wedding videos and he wants us to hire him. Keep it in the family and all that.' She sighs.

'Sounds OK. Why don't you sound excited?'

'Well, on the way home, Jason told me that the last time his uncle did a family wedding video, he got so carried away with the emotion of it all that he forgot to change the tape. His cousin has a lovely video of everybody arriving at the church, but none of the vows.'

'Ah.'

'The last scene apparently has her arriving at the church, smiling at the video camera, then spitting her chewing gum out. Oh well, it's still eleven months away. Perhaps he'll retire by then.' She pauses. 'Speaking of our wedding, how's the diet going?'

'Shh.' I try to silence her. 'Don't want everybody to know.'

'Nobody in this office knows you, Orla,' she says, a little wearily.

'OK, then.' I drop my voice. 'I've lost seven pounds since Light As A Feather launched.'

'Wow!' she screeches. 'That's amazing.'

'That's water,' I concede. 'It'll start slowing down now.' I've been quite excited seeing the weight drop so quickly. I'll be quite disappointed when it settles down to a pound or two a week. I suddenly remember my big news. 'By the way, I'm branching out. I'm going to sell knickers.'

'Well,' Liz sounds confused. 'If that's your ambition in life, em, good for you. But isn't public relations a better long-term career?'

I explain about the Pull Your Tummy In Tightly Knickers, and how I, Orla Kennedy, haggled. I was like a real business-woman. Determined to get my deal at any cost.

'They sound fantastic,' Liz finally says. 'Discount for friends and family?'

'Certainly not. A girl's got to make a living. If I sell the full five hundred, sorry four hundred and ninety-five, at fifteen pounds, I'll clear almost five thousand pounds.'

'*If*,' reiterates Liz. 'Well, I'll take five pairs. One for each day of the week.'

'What about Saturday and Sunday?'

'Orla, I'm newly engaged.' She giggles. 'And I'm sure my mum and her friends will take a few pairs, but you really need some advertising. If I can think of some way to get them in the magazine, I will. But how will you raise the rest of the money? I'd offer to help, but the wedding and all that . . .' Her voice tails off.

'I don't know. I'll think about it. But if it works out, at least I'll be able to give Jason some money for his work.'

'That reminds me. Jason said that he checked out the site last night and thinks that you have about one hundred and twenty people regularly checking in, whether for the chat room or for dieting information. That's not bad going.'

'No, it isn't.'

'And the other thing.' Liz sounds a little sheepish. 'If Jason asks you, I'm out with you tonight. Right?'

'Tonight? I can't make it. I'm meant to be . . .'

'We're not really going out. I've just got to see someone, and I don't want Jason knowing about it.'

'Oh.'

'Don't sound like that. It's nothing sinister. Just a potential candidate for City Hunk of the Week, and Jason will only get jealous.'

'Well . . .'

'Oh come on,' Liz pleads. 'I'm meeting some more on Thursday. Why don't you come along?'

'I don't know.' I glance at my watch. Two minutes to noon. 'Liz, I've got to go. I'll call you later, and yes, I'll cover it with Jason. 'Bye.'

I replace the handset, feeling mildly uncomfortable about Liz's request. She wouldn't lie to me. It is all perfectly innocent, isn't it? Come on, Orla. You know how crazy about Jason she is. It's probably for his own good. I put the doubts to the back of my mind, as I log on to Light As A Feather. Cecilia is already in the chat room.

Orla>
Hello there. Welcome to week three.

Cecilia>
Guess what. I've lost four pounds. Can you believe it?

Orla>
Congratulations. A round of applause for Cecilia.

Cecilia>
Thanks. I was expecting it to be a real struggle this week. Had to go to a couple of client dinners with my husband.

Orla>
Did you use the Light As A Feather calorie counter?

Cecilia>
Yes. It was a shock to find out that a bottle of wine contains more than seven hundred calories. They should write that on the label somewhere.

Orla>
So, you cut out alcohol?

Cecilia>
Why would I do that? You said we shouldn't deprive ourselves.

Orla>
That's right. So you limited your intake?

Cecilia>
Yeah. Kept to my two bottles a day, and limited all food. Actually I didn't eat anything else.

Orla>
Nothing?

Cecilia>
No, that's not strictly true. Ate a few sticks of celery. Read they're negative calories.

Orla>
But that's not exactly balanced.

Cecilia>
Darling, nor am I after two bottles. Anyway I think of wine as one of those meal replacement drinks. I have a bottle instead of a meal. Don't worry. I never eat breakfast.

Orla>
What about vitamins?

Cecilia>
I bought a few bottles of pills from the health food shop.

Bella>
It doesn't sound very healthy.

Cecilia>
But it works. Shall I give you my plan, Orla, so you can post it up on the site?

Orla>
No thanks. What about you, Bella? How did you manage this week?

Bella>
Stayed the same. But I'm not bothered.

Orla>
Oh?

Bella>
Well, it's my lunar cycle. The full moon plays havoc with it.<:-o

I check the date. It's not April 1.

Orla>
Lunar cycle?

Bella>
Yes, Marjorie at my slimming club told me I was a martyr to it. Next week I'll probably be back on track, when it's out of my system.

Lily>
Are we too late? Tessa is here with me.

Orla>
How did you both do?

Lily>
I put on four pounds; Tessa put on three.

Orla>
But you both stuck to the diet plan?

Lily>
Yes.

Orla>
You didn't eat anything that wasn't on it?

Lily>
No, dear, nothing apart from Larry's fat free desserts.

Orla>
Fat free desserts?

Lily>
Yes, dear. Shall I get you some? They're on special offer at the moment. Buy one, get one free. Tessa's just over collecting her order.

Orla>
How many did you eat?

Lily>
I don't know, dear, but it doesn't matter. They're fat free; they have no calories.

Orla>
Look, ladies, are you all taking the piss today?

Finn>
Can I stop you there? Please, no foul language in the chat room.

Orla>
Piss off, Finn.

Finn>
But I'm the site monitor . . .

Orla>
I said FOAD. Now, ladies, can't you just follow the plan? I did this week and I lost two pounds. Cecilia, your diet might be fun, but it is totally unbalanced and nutritionally deficient. Bella, Marjorie was having you on. There is no link between the full moon and weight loss. Lily and Tessa. Really. They may be fat free but those desserts will be packed full of sugar. That's why they taste so great.

Cecilia>
Spoilsport.

Bella>
And I thought Marjorie cared.

Lily>
Even the Black Forest Gâteau?

Orla>
So, shall we all stick to the diet plan next week?

Cecilia> Bella> Lily>
OK.

Orla>
Now, were there any more problems last week?

Cecilia>
My husband said we could be arrested using this site.

Orla>
What?

Cecilia>
He said we should be using metric measurements, and that otherwise the Weights and Measurement inspector would complain.

Orla>
He's having you on, but if you want to work in kilogrammes, be my guest. How much weight did you lose this week?

Cecilia>
Four pounds.

Orla>
OK, One point eight kilogrammes.

Cecilia>
I prefer it in pounds.

I explain about the new link-up with Mario's and the knickers that will become available later this week.

Lily>
Will there be a thermal option?

Orla>
I don't think so, but these knickers will work wonders. Kate Moss wears them.

Lily>
Is she the girl in Eastenders?

Mary>
Are we too late? Hello, girls. Marcella says hello too. We got waylaid. I typed in the wrong address, and we ended up in something called Feather Light. Sounds amazing. Ordered three for your father's bed.

Slimming tip seventeen

Ignore feng shui

'Finn.' I pull the quilt off my brother. He's wearing striped flannel pyjamas that our mother sent over last week as part of a large package of goodies. There was nothing in it for me. He tries to snuggle himself into his airbed. Ignoring me. His face pushing itself into the cushions.

'Go away, Orla. It's early yet.' He wriggles around, squeezing himself further into the cushions, like a small toddler with a tea towel over their head thinking they're invisible because you can't see their face. If he pushes in any more he won't be able to breathe.

'Finn. Where is everything? Finn.' I shake him and whip out the cushions. His face jerks upwards with the effort. His sleep-filled eyes wide with shock. 'Once again for the hard of hearing.' I put my mouth right up to his ear and shout. Enunciating carefully. 'Where. Is. Everything?'

Finn sits bolt upright, his hair tousled, and begins to rub his eyes with the palms of his hands. He inhales deeply, then pulls his hands away from his face, and looks sleepily at me. 'Is something wrong?' What? Apart from having an idiot as a brother?

'Where's my jam? Where's the low-fat spread? Where's the bread? And where's the bloody bread knife? 'Cause I'm going to murder you. It's nearly nine, I've been searching for ages, and I'm going to be late. The bloody alarm didn't go off. We must have had a power cut during the night.'

'Oh sorry. I forgot to plug it back in.' He takes advantage of

121

my surprise to tug the quilt back. I keep the cushions out of reach.

'Back in?' I look at him confused. 'Why on earth did you unplug it?'

'I was vacuuming your bedroom.'

'I don't know whether to be grateful or strangle you,' I admit, staring at him, 'but that doesn't explain where everything else is.'

'I've feng shuied you.' He smiles. As if he's done me a huge favour and is just waiting for a grateful pat on the head. Like an obedient King Charles spaniel. All dribbly.

'You've what?' Keep calm, Orla. There is obviously a perfectly logical explanation for this.

'Feng shui. Your chi energy was being repelled.' He shakes his head, considering the dangers that could befall me, adding, 'It was raging like a rapid, and it needs to become reflective like a lake. I started in the kitchen. Your sink needs to move as well. The water flows the wrong way; it's directing finances away from the house.'

Go crazy, Orla. You were wrong. It's not logical.

'The only thing directing finances away from the house is you,' I shout. 'But where're the bloody breakfast things? I haven't got time to listen to this psychobabble.'

He explains where the knife and jam are.

'And the bread? Low-fat spread?'

'Wheat is the enemy of modern man,' he starts. 'It overloads one's system. Our bodies are not designed to eat it.'

'What?'

'I threw the bread out.'

'What?'

'And the low-fat spread,' he shrugs. 'It's merely chemicals and e numbers. There's no nutritional value to it. I was doing it for you.' His voice becomes high-pitched. Pleading. 'Your body should be a temple.'

'You what? Are you an idiot? Don't answer that,' I yell. 'What am I meant to eat for breakfast?'

'I stewed some organic apples yesterday. They're in the

fridge, and there's some porridge oats in the cupboard over the microwave.' He stands up, wrapping the quilt around his waist. 'I could make some for you.'

'Who do you think I am? Goldi-bloody-locks?' I grab my coat and keys, and march towards the door. 'When I get home this evening I want those cupboards restocked and everything back in its usual place. Do you hear me?' He nods. 'Right, and I also want a giant pack of Honey Nut Cheerios.'

'But I didn't throw those out,' Finn argues. 'There weren't any in the cupboard.'

'Precisely. I'd run out.' I slam the door, screaming over my shoulder, 'Don't even think about asking me to pay for them.' I start marching to work, constantly glancing over my left shoulder for an empty cab to cut the journey time. My karma is obviously all out of sync because I don't spot one until I'm walking up the steps to Browns Black twenty minutes later. See? Perfectly feng shuied kitchen cabinets, and what bloody use are they on a busy London street?

'Morning,' I mutter at the receptionist as I flash my security pass at her.

'Morning, Orla. Lovely day. Ooh.'

'What?' I stop.

'Looks like somebody was in a hurry this morning.'

She nods at my feet. I look down. I'm wearing two different shoes. One black. One brown. Perfect. It's going to be one of those days. And I'm not even pre-menstrual.

'Feng shui,' I growl at her.

'Is that the new shop on Bond Street?'

I march off without answering, catch the lift to my floor, and walk to my desk. Avoiding wide-open spaces where people have a good view of my shoes.

'Patti,' I nod, sitting down.

'Guess what?' She bounds over to me like a bunny rabbit in the Easter Parade.

'What?' Can't a girl get any breakfast before she's accosted?

'I got some great coverage for Tony Younger's report on the internet. Look.' She shoves a copy of the *Daily Telegraph* in front of me. 'It's the lead story on page twenty-nine. And it doesn't even mention City Hunk of the Week. Speaking of which, Liz just rang to check you are on for tomorrow night. To go interviewing with her.' Patti winks at me.

'No.' I put my hand up. Pre-empting the inevitable. 'You're not coming. So don't even think about asking. Anyway I haven't yet made up my mind.'

'Spoilsport. And I'm a good judge of six packs.'

'Are we talking beer?'

'Ha ha. Orla's cracked a joke.' Where did respect for elders go? She taps her finger on the newspaper. 'Good, isn't it? And there's a piece in the *Guardian*, the *Financial Times* and even the *Mirror*. But the *Mirror* did unfortunately mention City Hunk of the Week.'

'Ah well, someone was bound to.' I glance down at the article. Skim reading. 'This looks good, Patti. Really good. Well done.' It does. She blushes with pride. I nod towards Tabitha's office. 'Has she seen it?' Patti nods. 'Said anything?'

'Not yet.'

I look across at Tabitha's office. She's talking to somebody.

'Who's in there with her?'

'Oh.' Patti screws up her face in disgust. 'That awful guy, Sven. He's been in about ten minutes. He was looking for you, then marched in to Tabitha.'

'Where did you say I was?'

'Having breakfast with a journalist from the *Financial Times*. It's OK,' she adds, as I look uneasy. 'I've rung him. He'll cover for you if they call. What? We've shared a few bottles in the past. Helped each other out.'

I nod in an I-believe-you-thousands-wouldn't sort of way. Suddenly Tabitha's office door opens and she calls out.

'Orla, could you come in, please?'

Tabitha is wearing a skin-tight, black polo neck, a leather mini skirt that my mother would call a pelmet, and long black boots that cling to her trim calves and end just under her shapely knees. She may be a bitch, but she looks hot. Sven looks like he's died and gone to heaven. And then I walk in. I'm

124

wearing a black baggy jumper that was lying on a chair under a pile of un-ironed clothes, a long suede skirt that sags around my seat, and one black and one brown shoe. Could life get any better?

'Tabitha,' I nod. 'Sven, good morning.' He quickly glances at my outfit. I can tell he doesn't like my footwear.

'Orla, Sven has come down here to complain about you.' Tabitha looks irritated. Listening to Sven for ten minutes does that to people.

'Sorry?' I glare at him.

'He says that you don't get enough press coverage for his deals, and I think he's right.' Tabitha stares at me. 'I've just done a search of our press cuttings database and there's nothing, *nothing*, about Sven or his work.' She pulls out a copy of today's *Daily Telegraph*. 'Can you explain why Patti was able to get so much coverage for Tony Younger's research report, when you can't even get a line about Sven's groundbreaking work?' She puts her hands on her hips. 'Can you?'

Sven smiles at me. A nasty, malevolent, sneering smile. All Finn's calming words fly from my mind. I just want to rip Sven's bloody self-important head off. He repels my chi energy.

'Have you read about any of his deals, Tabitha?' I enquire, sarcastically.

She looks flustered. 'Well, I've been very busy,' she bluffs.

'Shall I tell you about last week's? Sven is doing a deal involving a knitting needle factory. Still awake?'

'There's no call for such an attitude,' snaps Sven. 'Knitting is the new sex. The sex of the twenty-first century.' Wow. Mrs Sven is lucky. A quick purl one, knit two, and I bet he casts off for the evening.

'Of course it is, Sven. Orla. This is *not* a joke.' Tabitha waggles a perfectly manicured finger at me. 'This is a serious matter. A managing director of this bank has made a complaint against you. A formal complaint.'

'Tabitha,' I butt in. 'I can't make journalists write things, you know that. I can only give them the information. It helps if that information is interesting. Tony Younger's report *was* interesting. It was about the internet.'

'Pah. Internet!' explodes Sven. 'How long will that last? It's a fad. Here today. Gone tomorrow. Knitting has been around for centuries. People will always need jumpers. Can't you explain that to the journalists?'

'I tried, Sven, I really did, but nobody was interested in an obscure, European knitting needle factory.' I turn to him and shake my head sympathetically. 'Nor could I whip up enthusiasm about your deals for *kapok* producers in Portugal or zip manufacturers in Iceland. You work in a niche market. And people just aren't interested. I'm sorry.'

'She presents them all wrong,' he shouts at Tabitha, pointing at me. 'Where would men be without zips? Think about it. I'm working on essential services, which are every bit as important as gas and electricity, yet it is those companies that always get mentioned. This woman is just not trying hard enough.'

'I've tried bloody hard,' I interrupt indignantly. 'I even asked journalists who owed me favours, but I still couldn't get these deals in the papers.'

'You haven't. She didn't even manage to get me into City Hunk of the Week, and I heard that your best friend makes the selections.' Even Tabitha looks surprised at that one. 'How useless is she?'

'Orla.' Tabitha turns to me. 'Is this job too demanding for you?'

'No,' I snap.

'Well, it seems to me that a recent graduate recruit is making a better show of it than you at this moment in time.' She points at the paper on her desk. 'Sven deserves coverage. He is a valued member of this team. A managing director. I want to see headlines shouting about him. Do you hear me?' I nod. Sven preens himself as she turns back to him. 'I think I might hire our public relations adviser for a few extra hours this week. I'm sure he'll think of a clever way to promote your work within the newspapers.' She looks at me. 'Still here? Haven't you calls to make? I want results. Move.'

I march back to my desk. Seething. As I leave Tabitha's office, I hear her muttering something to Sven about the necessary employment of minorities. People with disabilities. Like weight.

Patti looks over. Anxious. A huge bouquet of flowers lies on top of her desk.

'Where did you get them from?' I ask, looking at the selection of burgundy and yellow gerberas, hand-tied with a silken thread.

'Tony Younger just dropped them off,' she says coyly. 'For all my efforts this morning.'

'Oh, that's all I bloody need,' I explode. 'The graduate trainee is getting bouquets while I'm getting briquettes. My life sucks.'

'So everything's not all right?'

'Bloody Sven and his stupid deals,' I rant. 'That man is an idiot if he thinks that the British press will write about his deals.' I sink my head into my hands. 'My days here are numbered. I can feel it.'

'Why not get coverage in foreign newspapers?'

'Eh?'

'He didn't specify which country, did he? Ring the local Bratislava papers. Or try the ones in Reykjavik. Can't see that many City investment banks do work in those areas, so make him a local hero there. Then perhaps he'll go travelling a bit more often and keep out of our hair.'

'Patti.'

'Yes?'

'You're a bloody genius.'

'Well,' she smiles, 'I learned everything I know from you. You're just so overwhelmed by his impossible demands that you can't see the wood for the trees. Now, can I go to lunch yet?'

'It's only eleven thirty.'

'I need to see a man from the *Financial Times*,' she replies.

'Better make sure that company credit card is well used.'

'I will.' She grabs her bag and jacket. 'See you later.'

She skips off. Patti may be young and naïve when it comes to the lunchtime drinking, but I reckon that one day she'll be a top public relations executive. She seems to have impressed Tony Younger. I glance again at the flowers. Patti is the sort of career woman that Tabitha can only dream of being. I glance over to her office. Sven has left. I still feel angry that Tabitha upbraided me in front of him. Perhaps it's the lack of breakfast, but I suddenly decide to have it out with her. Complain about her lack of support for me, a member of her department, in the face of unwarranted criticism.

I march over to her office. The door is open, but Tabitha is on the phone. Talking to her best friend, Samantha. About some dinner she was at last night. She glances over at me and beckons me to take a chair. 'This won't take long,' she mouths. Her eyes hard and cold.

'Samantha, darling, I meant to tell you the funniest thing. Your old flame *Donkey* was there last night.' I sit upright. Surely not. 'In Circus. Yes.' She bursts into fits of giggles. 'Of course, I asked if England had scored a hat-trick recently.' No. No. This is not happening to me. Samantha dated Sebastian? My Sebastian? I want to leave the room, to shut out this story, but my legs won't move. I have to hear it through. Tabitha glances at me. 'Sorry,' she mouths again, 'girl talk. One minute.' She holds up a finger. 'Yes, he asked after you. Of course, darling, but wait till you hear this funny story. Remember how he hated fat girls? What did he call them? Oh, that's right. Porkers. Ha, ha, ha. Well, his boss found out and bet him that he couldn't date a porker for a month. Five thousand pounds. Well, you know Seb and a bet. He said he bumped into one in some wine bar or other off Moorgate, and started seeing her. Nothing serious or anything. He said it was as if she couldn't quite believe her luck. Anyway he won the money, then his boss upped the stake. Ten thousand pounds if he'd poke the porker.' I sit there. Feeling sick. My legs are shaking. I feel disconnected. Disorientated. I want to stand, but I have to hear the story's ending. 'No, of course not, dear. He couldn't go through with it. Said it was made much easier in the end by the porker's brother. Some nutcase or other. Made a lot of noise. Sebastian used it as an excuse and walked out. Lost the second bet though. Damned shame. He was planning a holiday to Bali on the proceeds.'

I will myself to stand. I can't say anything, but I don't think I've ever hated anybody as much as I hate Tabitha at this moment. The bitch. The witch. She knew it was me. I'm nothing but a laughing stock to her. Somebody who does all her work and takes all her shit. I take a step forward. Tabitha starts. 'Sorry,' she whispers, 'this call is taking longer than I thought. Catch up with you later.' I walk out of the office like a person learning to use their legs again. Dead weights dragging me down. Tears pour down my face. Mascara stings my eyes. I take four paces outside her office and then I run. Blindly towards the lifts. Towards the open air. Towards oblivion. I rush forward, head down, and collide with somebody. I look up, frantically wiping the tears away. It's Tony Younger.

SLIMMING TIP EIGHTEEN

Alcohol can be good for you

'Orla.' Tony looks at me. Horrified. 'What's the matter?'

'Nothing,' I gasp out. My body shaking from the effort.

'It doesn't look like nothing.' He grabs my forearms with his hands, trying to calm me. To stop the shaking. 'Has something happened?' Men. So intuitive.

'Forget it.' I try to wriggle my arms free. 'I'm all right.'

'You don't look all right. Honest.' His face is full of concern.

'Well, I am.' But as I say the words, Tabitha's conversation fast-forwards through my mind. *Donkey. Porker. Bet.* And the tears start to fall again.

'Look, you're not fine. Come on, let's get you out of here. Away from nosey parkers.' He calls the lift behind me. 'Alcohol or coffee?'

'Alcohol,' I gasp.

'Right.' He pushes me into the lift, watches me in silence as we descend to ground floor, out through the bank's lobby and into the street. A bicycle messenger, clad in lycra, pulls up in front of us and looks at me before rushing into the bank with an urgent package for some over-important investment banker who just can't wait for the Royal Mail. Or whatever it's called these days. I wipe my eyes with the back of my hand and study the streak of black mascara left behind. 'Follow me,' orders Tony. I follow him left, right, left and into a side street that I didn't know existed. That's the thing about the City; it's filled with surprises. 'Good distance from the office,' Tony winks as he pulls open the wooden door. 'Nobody will know us here.'

He leads me down the stairs and pushes me into a little glass cubicle, its table already set for lunch for four. I notice that he's in shirt sleeves, all rolled up like a busy executive, and that his red tie with little green leaves is loose around his neck.

'Crawl into there,' he orders. 'Gin and tonic?' A nod. 'Slimline?' A shrug. 'Double?' Vigorous nodding.

Minutes later he returns, places the long hi-ball glass in front of me, and settles down on the opposite side. He's got a tomato juice.

'So, what's wrong? Did the knickers not fit?' I glare at him. 'Sorry,' he mutters, looking sheepish. 'Lame joke.'

'Nothing.' I gulp my drink thirstily.

'That's what you said earlier.'

'*Nothing* I want to share.' Oh yes. Admit to the world that Donkey dated Porker for four weeks for five thousand pounds. Even hookers get better rates than that. I'm cheaper than a prostitute. A tawdry joke for Sebastian and his friends. I try to change the subject. 'Your flowers to Patti were very nice.'

'Are you crying because you didn't get any?' He smiles at me and I blush. 'She did a great job and I think people should be told these things. I was actually thinking of getting a drink to celebrate the coverage that she got for me.' Rub it in, why don't you? A failure in romance. A failure in work. 'So, it was my luck that I ran into you.'

'I thought you didn't drink at lunchtime,' I remember.

'Only on special occasions.' He holds up his glass. 'Bloody Mary. No smell of vodka.'

'Oh for God's sake. What is it with men? Why can't they say what they really think?' I suddenly erupt. 'She did well and I did lousily with your appointment. Is that it? Just say it.'

'So it's man trouble?' he says quietly.

'Can we change the subject?'

'All right. I'm also glad I caught up with you because I owe you an apology.' I look at him. 'I think maybe I overreacted when I arrived, with the hunk thing and all that. I still think it was bloody unprofessional of you, but perhaps it didn't reflect as badly as I feared on me.'

131

'I'm glad.'

'I actually got a few fan letters. Emmie loved it.'

Oh.

'So that's me opening up. I did try to apologize before, but you scuttled off every time I spotted you before I could say anything.' He takes a long drink. 'I won't tell anybody what you say, if that's what's worrying you.'

'It's Tabitha,' I finally say. 'She's a bitch. There.' I shrug my shoulders. 'Saying that makes *me* sound like a bitch. You probably think I'm jealous of her. Men always think that when women describe other women as bitches.' I adopt a childish voice, a sing-song style like the playground bully uses when she's taunting her victims. 'You're just jealous because she's thin and beautiful, and you're fat.' I suddenly feel silly. 'Well, anyway, that's not what it's about.'

'I didn't imagine for one moment that it was,' responded Tony graciously. 'Particularly as, while Tabitha is undoubtedly thin, she is most certainly not beautiful.' He looks at me strangely. 'Women, you never see what you've got. You're always looking in the mirror, but you never *really* look properly.'

'Well, anyway . . .' I interrupt, feeling slightly awkward. 'It wasn't about that.'

'So what did she do? And don't say nothing.' He smiles. A nice, open, friendly smile. So I tell him. Not everything. Obviously. I can't tell Tony that somebody was willing to take money to sleep with me. That he viewed me as such a joke that it took a bet for him to want to make love to me. Not a bottle of wine. Or soft music. Or desire. But *money*. And, in the end, even that wasn't enough. Ten thousand pounds couldn't persuade him. I was still too repellent. Finn was right. My chi is repelling. But I tell Tony that a man dated me for four weeks for a joke. A juvenile bet with his boss. A man that I really liked, whom I thought liked me. He listens until the end. Never interrupting.

'Well, if you don't mind me saying it, he sounds more like an ass than a donkey,' he finally says.

'Funny,' I sigh.

'No, I don't mean it that way. If he can't see beyond a bet to see *you* then he really is an ass.'

'Amazing the compliments you can get with a sobbing fit,' I reply. 'I might try this more often.'

'That's not why I'm saying it.' He sounds irritated. 'Look, it might sound like a cliché, but he just doesn't deserve you. Lots of men would love to be going out with you.'

'Yeah, right. They're forming an orderly queue outside as we speak.'

'This man *is* a prize idiot. Stop feeling so sorry for yourself. It's truly horrible what he did, but that just means he is truly horrible. You're better off without him. Think of it as a lucky escape.'

'You think I'm silly.'

'No.' He shakes his head. 'No, I don't. I can't imagine how hurt and upset you must be feeling, but I definitely would *not* give Tabitha the satisfaction of any clue to it. Walk tall when you go back. Walk proud. You're above it. Oh, and you'd better clean that black stuff off your face. You look like an urchin.' He laughs, spotting my empty glass. 'Another?'

I look at my watch. Got to sign on for Light As A Feather in ten minutes.

'Better not. I've got to get back.' I stand up. 'Thanks, Tony.'

'No problem. Any time.' He smiles. A kind, generous smile. 'You do know that?'

I do. But I won't be back. Tony has been fantastic, but I've opened up too much. Tomorrow I won't be able to look him in the eye. Humiliation and embarrassment, those old adversaries of mine, will kick in. And I'll end up pretending that I'm too busy if he calls for a chat, ducking down side streets to avoid bumping into him, and leaving Patti to deal with all his publicity requirements.

'You've been brilliant. 'Bye.' I lean forward and plant a small kiss on his forehead thinking what a very lucky girl Emmie is.

SLIMMING TIP NINETEEN

Accentuate your curves with alcohol

Liz is a great friend. Couldn't ask for anyone better. Honestly. But today she's being a pain-in-the-butt friend. The sort of friend who won't take no for an answer because they're doing it all for your own good. And so it is tonight. Liz is adamant that I should accompany her to assess contenders for City Hunk of the Week. No excuses accepted. And the words heartache, heartbreak or not-in-the-mood are as banned from the conversation as that naughty one beginning with 'f' in my mother's house.

Liz is meeting the three potential hunks in The Avenue on St James's Street, a road that runs from Pall Mall to Piccadilly. She calls it a dirty job, but is glad that *she* got to do it. And she claims it will help my healing process. It makes me sound like a leper.

I went through the motions yesterday afternoon. Ask me if anything happened, and I really couldn't tell you. I remember only one thing. Tabitha had a smirk on her face each time she walked past. What I'd give to wipe it off. Oh, and I sent a text message to Sebastian. Patti helped me with the language. I'm not sure exactly what it said, but she assured me it was something along the lines of 'I hope you live a long and happy life'. Just used fewer letters.

I run home first to change before meeting Liz, and push open my front door to find Finn sitting at the laptop. He looks embarrassed, as if I've caught him doing something. And then I spot it. A huge box. In the middle of the floor. Where the coffee table should be.

'Finn,' I explode, pointing at it. 'If that's another feng shui moment, I'm not in the mood. Move it. Now.'

'It's nothing to do with me,' he replies indignantly. 'All I did was sign for it. It's from Undetectable Undergarments.'

My knickers.

I rush over, rip up the brown tape along the top seam, and throw the box open. Inside is an array of cotton ball pink, white and pale blue knickers in different sizes and styles. I pull out a few. They look good. I stretch one pair out as far as it will go and watch it spring back into shape within seconds.

'Are they knickers for women or elephants?' Finn suddenly asks. That's not very Buddhist-like, is it?

'Get on with your . . . what *is* it you're doing?' I snap.

'Just checking the site,' he says quickly. 'You had forty-five visitors today. That's the most ever in one day and' – he checks his notes – 'eighteen clicked on the Pull Your Tummy In Tight Knickers advert. I think you'll get some orders.'

'Great. It's probably the sandwich bag advertising.'

'Eh?'

'Mario was getting some new bags printed up and said he'd put a plug for Light As A Feather on them.'

'Won't that put people off their lunch?'

'No, because we decided on the line: "Mario's sandwiches can aid weight loss as part of a calorie controlled diet. See Lightasafeather.co.uk for details." Clever, huh?'

I dive into my bedroom with a pair of knickers from the box, and search through my wardrobe. Eventually I settle on the silk, two-piece outfit that I wore for my final date with Sebastian. The skirt's cut on the bias, so it looks quite slimming. I redo my make-up with extra bright lipstick, and check my reflection. These knickers do seem to work. The skirt definitely seems to be loose on my waist. I stand sideways and check my reflection; my stomach is definitely looking flatter. A shiver of excitement runs up my spine. Orla Kennedy is looking thinner.

Liz is at the bar when I arrive. She's sitting bolt upright on a stool, with her legs angled to one side like the fashionistas in the front row at the Milan collection. And she's drinking a Manhattan. A *Manhattan*. I look at her in surprise when she says it. What the hell is that?

'The girls on *Sex in the City* always drink it. It gives an air of sophistication, don't you think?' She pushes the glass forward. 'Go on. Taste it. It's all right. Sort of sweet really.'

I take a sip. It's like something Finn used to make me drink when we were children playing witches and wizards. 'Thanks, I'll stick to chardonnay.' I signal to the barman. 'So.' I settle back on the stool. 'How will we recognize them?'

She looks at me. In despair. 'Do you see many hunks in here?' She gestures around the bar. Pointedly. There are five men sitting in the armchairs nearby. One has a dog collar, and a glass of water in front of him. Actually, I'm giving him the benefit of the doubt because of his career. It could be neat gin. Two look like extras from the *X Files*, and the others look like they came here by bus. Using their pensioner passes. 'I think we'll spot them. Couple of ground rules though. One, no mention of Sebastian. Two, no mention of diets. Three, no mention of weddings.'

'But—'

'I said no mention.' She pushes her hand out towards me in a halt sign. Her ring, which, just a few weeks ago, she couldn't take her eyes off, is missing. 'If I tell them I'm engaged, it might inhibit them.' I nod, feeling uncomfortable. Like I'm being disloyal to Jason.

'Can I just tell you about my knickers?' I whisper. The barman slides my drink over. He looks at me strangely. 'I'm wearing them now.'

'I should hope so.'

'No,' I snap. 'The new ones from Undetectable Undergarments. Can you notice a difference?' I slip from the stool and stand in front of Liz. 'And look,' I prod my rib cage (well, the flesh surrounding it; my rib cage hasn't been seen since I was two weeks old), 'there are no extra rolls. These knickers are good.'

'Glad to hear it, although I think you've lost weight anyway.'

136

I blush with pride, waiting for a second compliment when Liz suddenly hisses, 'Now get back on that stool, I think we're go.'

I turn around to watch three beautiful men walking through the glass door. One of the waitresses even stops to look. Liz lifts her arm and waves. They smile, revealing three rings of Colgate confidence, and walk over.

'Hi,' says the tallest one. Green eyes, blonde crew cut, Hugo Boss suit. 'I'm Joe, this is Pete.' Dark, blue eyes and exceptionally wide shoulders. 'And this is Alex.' Dark, brown eyes with tiny little ringlets. Latin looking. 'Are you Liz?' She nods and introduces me. 'So what happens now?'

'We order a drink,' interrupts Pete. 'Two bottles of Moët,' he tells the barman, 'and leave a couple on ice.' Liz pushes her Manhattan well away and awaits the champagne flute. Such fickle affections. Pete grabs the stool next to mine and turns to me. 'Orla. That's an unusual name. Where does it come from?'

'I'm Irish.'

'And tell me, is it true what they say about Irish girls?'

'Well, that rather depends on what they say.' Oh my God. Listen to me. I'm flirting with an Adonis. And me with a broken heart. Must be the scarlet lipstick I'm wearing.

'Touché. So how do you know Liz? Do you work on the magazine with her? Are you on the selection panel?' He winks at me. 'What do I do to get chosen?'

'Sorry, not involved in any of that,' I reply, accepting a chilled glass of champagne from the waiter. I look across at Liz, who is throwing her head back and flicking her hair for all it is worth. Still, at least she's put her notebook on the table to project a modicum of professionalism. 'I'm just here to make up numbers. Liz is your woman.'

'Ooh, I don't know.' Wow. Return flirt. I drop my eyes and take a sip of champagne, licking my lips as I slowly pull away the glass. Advantage, Orla. 'It's not as if I really want to be selected to take my shirt off and pose in a financial magazine,' he whispers. 'Would you?' I shake my head, blushing. 'I just came along because my friends egged me on. We've got a bet going.' He nods in their direction. Suddenly I lose the urge to flirt. What's the point? They're all the same. 'Actually,' he continues conspiratorially, 'I can't be bothered. Bit childish and all that.' I nod. Knowingly. 'Anyway, tell me about yourself. What do you do?'

'I work in the City, at Browns Black.' I'm back in neutral mode. Switched off the flirt button. Content to have a nice chat with a good-looking guy without anybody getting the wrong idea or getting disappointed. 'In the press office.'

'There's been a couple of rumours about Browns Black recently.' He scrunches up his nose as he tries to remember. 'Black hole or something?'

'Yeah, I've heard about them. The bank's standard response is no comment, but I can't really see there being anything in them. My boss has looked into it and she says not.'

'Oh, right.'

I suddenly feel boring. Pete's stopped flirting too. I look across at Liz. She's got a tape measure in her hand and is busy measuring the biceps on Joe. He was obviously expecting this. Underneath his beautifully cut jacket is a shirt without sleeves. Custom made. Its shoulder seam scoops around the top of his bicep.

Pete looks over. 'Our Joe's a bodybuilder,' he explains. 'He enters competitions. They don't usually look as primed as that, but he was preparing for today. Last night he drank two bottles of wine to dehydrate his body, and show his muscles off to perfection.'

'Last night I drank two bottles of wine, but my muscles look nothing like that.'

'They look fine as they are.' He smiles at me. 'Sometimes when Joe's up for an important contest, he drinks a bottle of whisky the night before to really dehydrate.'

'Does it work?'

'Don't know. He's never managed to make it to the contests.' He grins. 'So, don't you want to go over there and feel them too?'

'Felt one. Felt them all.'

'A woman of the world?'

'No, a woman who can't be bothered moving off this stool.' I tip my glass towards him as he refills it with champagne.

'Not like your friend then? It seems this is her ideal job.' Liz really does look as if she's having a good time. Alex is now being measured up. When she stretches the tape measure around his chest, she's forced to move really close to his body to snap the two ends together. Chests touching. Just a few days ago we were discussing silk versus satin. 'I suppose it will be my turn next.' He smiles. 'Don't worry, I've practised my speech.'

'Eh?'

'You know, when I grow up I want to be kind to animals, help small children, and end world poverty.'

'Right. That always reminds me of that story, which my friend Richard swears is true, where the American consulate in some Eastern European country is asked by a journalist what he wants for Christmas.'

'Never heard it.'

'He's embarrassed to ask for anything too big or expensive. And on Christmas Day he opens his newspaper to find this article, where the German foreign minister asks for world peace, the Russian president calls for an end to nuclear arms, the Irish president prays for the end of Third World starvation and there, right at the bottom, is the American consulate's request: a box of jellied sweets.'

'No!' He almost sprays his champagne over me.

'Well, that's the story.' I sip a bit more, looking over at Liz. She smiles, before beckoning Pete over for his 'interview'. I stay put, emptying the rest of the bottle into my glass. I watch the three men flirt with Liz as she jots down their particulars. She's really enjoying herself. Loving her job. I feel a small twinge of jealousy. Tomorrow she'll wake up beside Jason, eager to get to work. Tomorrow I'll wake up alone, walk past a snoring lodger on my way to a job where I'm not appreciated and a boss that I loathe. Spot the difference. I down the drink and suddenly feel lonely. It's time to go home. I grab my bag and walk over towards Liz.

'Liz.' I tap her arm gently and speak quietly to her. 'I'm going to get off now. I've had enough.'

'But—'

'No, I really have. It's been fun but it's time to go.'

'Really?' She looks upset. 'Is it my fault? Did I not include you enough?'

'It's nobody's fault,' I say gently. 'I'm just feeling a bit contemplative. I want to go home. I'll call tomorrow.' I throw my hand up in a wave to the trio of hunks. ' 'Bye then. It's been nice meeting you. Good luck.'

They smile back. I'm just walking out the glass door when I feel a tap on my shoulder. I turn. It's Pete.

'I just wondered . . .' He looks sheepish. 'Can I call you?'

I look at him. He's gorgeous. I can see Liz winking at me and mouthing, 'Go for it' in the background. I feel all excited. A gorgeous man is asking *me* out. But then I find myself shaking my head. He's gorgeous, but admit it, Orla. The conversation dried up within twenty minutes. 'I'm sorry,' I hear myself say. 'I'm not really ready for anything at the moment.' I smile at him and walk out of the door to hail a cab.

But it's not true. As the black cab pulls up, I realize that I am ready for something. I'm ready for change. A life change.

SLIMMING TIP TWENTY

All you need is motivation – and a hangover

Liz stirs a stick of celery around a Bloody Mary on the wooden table in front of her. Her hair is pulled back into a tight ponytail and she's wearing what she calls an 'out of the flat in two minutes' outfit. Stretch black bootleg trousers, thin black polo neck, camel suede jacket. Sunglasses sit atop her head.

'God, I need this,' she says before taking her first sip. 'It is a double, isn't it?' I nod. 'With extra Tabasco sauce?' Another nod. 'It might just save me.'

It's eleven, the morning after the night before. I never really understand what that statement means. Morning is always after the night before. The morning before the night after just doesn't make sense. I woke bright and early, missed Finn's irritating chants, and was in the office before eight. I felt like a slim person bursting with energy as I sorted out my desk. Getting organized. Getting ready to change my life. The only trouble is, I haven't worked out how.

Liz called almost as soon as I arrived. She was desperate for a hair of the dog, and I think if I'd agreed to go with her, she'd have gone to one of the early morning pubs in Smithfield, home of the meat market, where butchers can get a pint of Guinness long before opening time. I told her I was too busy, but agreed to meet now. We're sitting in the Pavilion in the middle of Finsbury Circus Gardens. It's a wooden shed, a quaint building that wouldn't look out of place in the middle of Sussex. It looks tiny from the outside, but inside stretches out like Doctor Who's Tardis. Liz is facing in – the glare from the sun hurts her eyes – and I'm looking out at three old dears in white shirts, comfortable shoes, and sensible cardigans playing bowls on the lawn outside. The Pavilion doubles as the clubhouse for the City of London bowling club.

'I can't stay too long,' I say sipping on my fizzy water. 'Tabitha's meeting with Giles, and I don't like to leave Patti in charge. You never know what she might do.'

'She's all right. You need to give her more credit,' mutters Liz. 'Anyway, I didn't come here to talk about Patti. Why did you run off last night?'

'I didn't.'

'You did. It was really embarrassing for me. Left there like that with three men.'

'It wasn't a date, Liz,' I point out reasonably. 'It was a professional meeting. They were all there to audition for the City Hunk of the Week slot. If you couldn't cope with three men at the same time, you shouldn't have booked a trio.'

'It wasn't really my fault,' she sulks. 'They insisted. Claimed there was safety in numbers.' She takes a large sip of Bloody Mary.

'Well, do your interviews during office hours if you're worried.'

'I'm not really,' she concedes. 'And an office environment doesn't really work. They need to unwind, relax, feel they can open up to me.'

'Hence no engagement ring?'

'I'm not going to do anything,' she protests. 'It just seems to make it easier for them if they think I'm single. They seem to tell me more.'

'What does Jason say about it?'

'Why tell him? It would only worry him. Make him jump to the wrong conclusions. *Like you*,' she adds pointedly. 'Honestly, I'm doing this for you too, you know.'

'Me?' I say puzzled. 'How can you be doing this for me? It's kind, but I never told you to find me a date.'

'Never mind. I'm getting another drink. Want one?' I shake my head, and wait for Liz to fetch a second Bloody Mary.

142

Another double. With extra Tabasco. And two sticks of celery. 'So why did you scuttle off so quickly last night? I thought you were getting on so well with Pete. I mean, he asked you for your number, didn't he?' I nod. 'So?'

'I didn't give it.'

'Why? He's gorgeous. Fun, good-looking, great body, nice personality, money . . . am I missing something?' She sips her drink. 'Did he have bad breath?'

'No, he didn't have bad breath.'

'I hate that in a man. Always make Jason floss before he goes to bed. So, what was wrong?'

'Nothing.' I shake my head. 'I just didn't fancy him. Simple as that. Looks aren't everything, you know.'

'And there you've been for the past months bleating on about how good-looking Sebastian was, how you couldn't believe that he fancied you—'

'But he didn't, did he?' I interrupt.

'You don't know that.'

'That's not usually the way that blokes behave when they fancy someone. Look, Liz, there was nothing wrong with Pete. And there's nothing wrong with me. In fact, things couldn't be better. I don't know . . .' I pause, considering my words as I watch one of the women bend and carefully aim the bowling ball down the lawn. 'I fooled myself for so long that I was having a relationship with Sebastian – and I wasn't. I was so amazed that he would look at me that it blinded me to everything else. But he didn't treat me as a girlfriend, did he? I thought a couple of calls a week was all right, but it wasn't. It wasn't a relationship; it was my dream world taking over from reality. And why was that?'

'I don't know.' I can tell what Liz is thinking. This is way too heavy for a girl with a raging hangover. But hey, she asked.

'Because reality sucks. Because my life was lacking something.'

'Eh?' Liz sinks her head into her hands and rubs her eyes. Hoping she'll clear her head. And understand what the hell it is that I'm talking about.

'Finn's got Buddhism, you've got Jason, Patti's got alcohol and my mother's got the phone.' I pause. 'What have I got?'

'You've got me.'

'That's not what I mean. I'm talking of a purpose.'

'You mean a man?'

'No,' I exclaim. 'I don't mean a man. I don't need a man. Not at the moment. I need something else.'

'A vibrator?'

'Liz. Are you going to take me seriously?'

'Sorry.' She looks sheepish.

'I'm talking about a rationale.'

'What about Light As A Feather?'

'Maybe. But just running the chat room in my lunch hour, and operating the site on a shoestring isn't really what I want either. Last night I made up my mind that things are going to change in Orla Kennedy's life. She just has to work out how.' I glance at my watch. 'Anyway, are you going to finish that quickly? I've got to be back at my desk in quarter of an hour. My dieting public awaits. And after the chat room closes guess what I'm off to do?'

'Don't know.'

'I've signed up for a twirling class.'

'Spinning,' she corrects.

'Doesn't matter, it will have the same effect whatever it's called. Your friend Orla Kennedy is going to start going to the gym. To coin a phrase, today is the first day of the rest of my life.'

SLIMMING TIP TWENTY-ONE

Less is never more

My mother is first to kick off the session.

Mary >
Orla, darling. These knickers are simply wonderful. Marcella hasn't taken them off since she got them. Honestly, we'll be burying her in them. :->>

I don't' know which is worse: my mother making jokes, or my mother using text code. Either way, these are worrying signs. Next she'll be laughing at Ali G. :->> It's the first Monday since the Undetectable Undergarments delivery, and this is the first feedback I've had from the general public. And my mother.

Cecilia >
A big smile back to you. I love them too. I had to go to a black tie dinner with my husband on Saturday and my dress was a bit tight. Put on the knickers and it looked wonderful. Even he couldn't ignore it. Can I buy a few more pairs? In different colours?

Mary >
Marcella would like another five pairs. She's going to raffle them for the St Vincent de Paul's Christmas appeal. I just hope the nuns don't buy all the tickets. They won all the cuddly toys last year.

Lily >
Do they do any with a bit more of a leg? Sort of midway between the knee and the crotch?

Tessa >
I'd like another couple of pairs and some for a few of the mothers at my son's school. They all were admiring them at my son's open day. He had painted a picture of me wearing them.

Bella >
Do you do anything that works the same way on busts?

Orla >
So, I'm making a wild guess here, you all liked the knickers?

Mary >
They're wonderful, dear. And, you wouldn't believe it. I got this call last night, late it was, and somebody asked what knickers I was wearing. Isn't that a coincidence? Well, I had to tell him. I gave him the site's address, in case he wants to order some.

Orla >
Mum, he sounds like a weirdo.

Mary >
Really, dear? How can you tell? I thought he was from Limerick.

Orla >
So, girls, how did you all do this week?

Cecilia >
Well, I did remember to balance my diet more and lost two pounds. I only had one bottle a day and lots of extra celery.

Lily >
I lost a pound, but Larry was a bit upset that I wouldn't eat his desserts. He says he likes my love grips.

Bella >
Handles, Lily. I definitely feel more energetic. Those exercises you posted up on the site really helped me. I might even volunteer for the egg and spoon next year.

Orla >
Tessa?

Tessa >
Pass.

Orla >
Come on. You're among friends. Remember.

Tessa >
I put on three pounds.

Orla >
Why?

Tessa >
Because my son comes home in tears every night about the bullies, and when he goes to bed, I end up in tears too. So I comfort eat.

Orla >
But . . .

Tessa >
But nothing. It's all very well for you to offer advice and comfort, but you can't stop me feeling lonely and sad. Can you? And it's going to get worse. With the dark winter nights. I can't go out when my boy's in bed. I know you say that a little of what you fancy is all right, but I don't want a little bit of chocolate. I want the whole sodding bar.

Orla >
When you feel like that, you should check into the chat room.

Even as I say the words, I know how empty they are. Loneliness can't be alleviated on-line. It doesn't clear up with :->> or a 'big smile' written down. It needs a human touch.

Cecilia >
I'm often in there. Have great chats with your brother, Orla. He's sorting out my skandhas.

I'll sort out his skandhas one of these days.

Mary >
Finn? Is he all right? Where is he?

Orla >
He's fine, Mum. He's busy at home sorting through the last few pairs of knickers. He seems to enjoy it.

Mary >
You will order some more?

Orla >
Yes. Honestly. Promise. Look, Tessa, it may seem like it's only words, but I really do care. We're all in this together, and I know we can all do it. I've even started going to the gym since this site launched, and it's all thanks to you guys. Just having your support makes me want to do something to prove I'm worth it.

Tessa >
What this service really needs is a fact-to-face aspect to it. Like banks. You know, they may offer telephone and internet services but, in the end, some people still want to go into branches.

I don't like to mention the slimming club that I first met her outside. If face-to-face were really what she wanted then surely she'd still be going there. I thought people like the anonymity of a chat room. That they liked to be able to chat about their weight problems without people eyeing them up and thinking, 'Twelve stone? *And* the rest.'

Mary >
Marcella and I had a really funny experience yesterday, didn't we, dear? She's nodding, girls. We decided to swim the web and found this really funny little chat room. It was filled with all these men, but they were a bit muddled. They thought we were young girls, didn't they, dear? She's nodding again. They kept asking us what schools we went to and whether we liked Britney Spears. Well, they

always repeat on me unless I boil them for ten minutes so I said no.
Tessa, dear, what you need is a grandchild.

Tessa >
My son is eight.

Mary >
Any other children?

Orla >
Look, Mum, I think that's enough prying for one day. See you all
here the same time next week. And Tessa, think about using this
site at other times. It's here for you.

Cecilia >
You never told us how much you lost.

Orla >
Three pounds. Thanks for asking. 'Bye.

Patti is reading over my shoulder as I sign off. She didn't
have a lunch with a journalist today, but has spent the past
couple of hours on the phone. Talking quietly into the
receiver, with surreptitious glances in my direction to check
I wasn't listening in. She also spent a while feeding a lengthy
document into the fax machine, sending it out into the great
beyond. She hasn't told me what she was doing, and I
haven't asked. As long as it's nothing to do with hunks, I
don't care.

'I didn't like to say anything before, just in case you were
offended, but it really does look like you've lost weight now,'
she says. 'It's gone around your chin.' She cups both hands
around her chin and pushes up. Emphasizing the point. 'So it
can't just be the knickers!'

'No,' I admit shyly. 'It isn't just the knickers. Everything is
getting a bit loose on me.'

'Well, it shows, and your skin is really glowing at the
moment. You're so lucky that you never get spots.' She points
to one on her chin. 'It looks like I'm growing another nose. By

the way, when are you going to get some Pert Posterior Pantyhose? I'm dying to try some out.'

'The million dollar question,' I admit, 'or more precisely, the two thousand three hundred pound question and whatever else the tights and bra stock costs. I just don't have the money.'

'What about Finn?'

And I thought she was becoming more sensible in her old age.

'I'm supporting Finn,' I point out. 'He has nothing in his bank balance. And even less in his head.'

'Oh, don't be bitchy. I thought he was lovely when I met him around your house. He really looks up to you. What about Liz?'

'All her money is being saved for her wedding. And anyway, if anything I should be offering money to Jason, for all the work he has put into the site.'

'Your mum?'

'It just wouldn't be worth the hassle.'

'So you've got this great business idea, which people seem to love, and you're going to do nothing about it.' I nod. 'How many pairs of knickers do you have left?'

'Four. They're all size eight.' I look at her. 'You can have them for a tenner.'

'I bet Richard Branson didn't get where he is today by giving away knickers. What sort of a businesswoman are you?' Patti grabs her bag. 'I'll take them, but I'll pay full price.' She opens her purse and looks inside. 'But can I give you half today, and the rest when we're paid?' She hands me three ten-pound notes. Patti's right. I can't give up. I promised my clients.

I dial Mario's number.

'Orla, is good to hear from you. I was going to call.'

'Oh yes?'

'Yes, you never guess. Today I had order for food from Seattle. Is that near Shepherd's Bush? Do I deliver there?'

Seattle? Where Frasier lives? But this is meant to be a service for City workers. What would people in Seattle be tuning in for? They have their own dieting websites, don't they?

150

Imagine, somebody in Seattle is listening to me! Maybe losing weight with my advice. Oh God, I hope it's working. Americans always sue for things that don't do what they say on the packet, don't they?

'No, Mario. You don't deliver there.'

'Is pity. She wanted eight weeks of food. She go on holiday and want to put Italian food in freezer for husband. Is big order.'

'Is also impossible. So how many orders have you taken since the service was launched?'

'An extra five hundred pounds so far. So you get fifty. Is good, yes?'

'Very good. Thanks. See you tomorrow.' I hang up the phone. Fifty pounds and all the money I've made from selling the knickers so far makes about seven hundred and fifty pounds. Not enough to become a regular supplier for Undetectable Undergarments. I ring Justin.

'Orla, good to hear from you. And are the ladies in London delighted with their knickers?'

'They are. Bellies in Balham are *so* last year. That's what I'm calling about. I'd like to take the rest of the stock. Do you ever offer credit to your suppliers?'

'Richard Branson never got where he is today by offering credit on knickers now, did he?' Justin snaps.

'I suppose.'

'I'm really sorry,' he sighs, 'but we have two leading London department stores just crying out for this stock. Honestly, I'm wiping away a little tear at your troubles' – he sniffs – 'see, there it goes, but I really can't let you have these knickers on credit.'

'But I was the first person to put in a firm order,' I say. 'Doesn't that count for anything?'

'I thought we'd been very obliging. If I remember rightly – my mind, you know, old age – the knickers are being held for you for another week?'

'Yes, a week tomorrow.'

'Well, just because I like your voice, I'll give you another two days, and if you come up with the money by then, I'll have a special deal for the Pert Posterior Pantyhose and Bounce Free Booby Bras. Now,' he simpers, 'can't say fairer than that, can I?'

'No,' I admit reluctantly. A special deal? How am I going to get the money for that if I can't get the money for the knickers?

'It's so lovely doing business with a lady,' says Justin. 'And now, if you don't mind, I've got to rush. Our designers have been working on a new prototype and we're having a demonstration at three.'

'Oh?'

'Yes, top secret.' He hesitates. 'But seeing as it's you. Hold on.' I can hear him get up and close the door behind him. 'Right, it's a special bikini that holds everything in and makes the wearer look like she's got a washboard stomach. Revolutionary stuff. Made out of material that astronauts have worn on the moon. I'm just working on a new brand name at the moment. I was thinking Bung Away Your Bits Bikini. What do you reckon?'

'Definitely catchy.'

'Oh!' He turns giddy on me. 'You're an angel. I'll give you three extra days. Ciao.'

I hang up. Disappointed. And those bikinis sound brilliant. I could sell hundreds, I'm sure. Patti is busy with whatever it is she's doing, and Tabitha is having a meeting with the chairman. I check my voicemail. No urgent journalist enquiries. I check my e-mail.

To   Orla@Lightasafeather.co.uk
From Amy@Hotmail.com
I know I'm a bit late, but can I order a few pairs of knickers from you?
A x

To   Amy@Hotmail.com
From Orla@Lightasafeather.co.uk
I'm afraid the stock has run out and I can't afford to buy any more.
O x

To   Orla@Lightasafeather.co.uk
From Amy@Hotmail.com
Have you thought of borrowing some money?
A x

To   Amy@Hotmail.com
From Orla@Lightasafeather.co.uk
I've got a mortgage, a car loan and a credit card that's so embarrassed about its debt profile that it wouldn't work last week in Safeway. What bank would lend to me?

To   Orla@Lightasafeather.co.uk
From Amy@Hotmail.net
Not you. But it might to Light As A Feather. OK, so it's a dotcom, but it's not lost any money so far so that puts it ahead of thousands of others. It's also got a loyal client base and the potential for solid sales. It's not a fad. There will always be fat people. You just need to put together a business proposal. Say what you expect to make from the site over the next three years, how many clients etc.

To   Amy@Hotmail.com
From Orla@Lightasafeather.co.uk
Eh?

To   Orla@Lightasafeather.co.uk
From Amy@Hotmail.com
It's simple. They're as in the dark as you are, and in three years who is going to check? Just put down some numbers (make them sound realistic and achievable) and have a go. Actually, thinking about it, I probably wouldn't go to the high street banks, but what about a specialist lender, like a venture capitalist or something, who lends to new businesses starting up? I've heard of a company called Abacus Ventures, which would be right up your street. I'm sure they'll be in Yellow Pages.
A x

A huge pile of Yellow Pages rests on top of the filing cabinets in the corner of the department. Patti and I never use them. It seems so much easier to dial for Directory Enquiries, but I can't actually ring up and just ask for venture capitalist, London. I take down a book, dust off the cover and open it up at the relevant heading. 'Abacus Ventures: We make the numbers add up.' I dial.

SLIMMING TIP TWENTY-TWO

Find a distraction in life

The pretty receptionist smiles as I approach the desk. My heels click on the marble floor.

'Can I help you?' The little bow at her neck shakes as she talks.

I try to keep the nervousness out of my voice. 'I have an appointment with Mike Littlechild, head of new business. At ten thirty.'

'And your name is?' She smiles again, grabbing a large pencil.

'Orla Kennedy.'

'Thank you.' She jots it down on a large pad in front of her, taps out an extension number on an elaborate switchboard, talks into the handset, then looks up. 'He'll be right down. Please take a seat.'

She points to a selection of chrome and black leather arm-chairs (the mainstay of all City receptions), arranged in front of a waterfall. I don't sit down. I stare at the water, which cascades down a marble wall, hitting sculptures of gulls in flight, before gathering in a pool at the base. The head of a black marble trout peeps up through the water, causing ripples in its surface. Finn would marvel at this, delighted that Abacus Ventures has a water feature in its reception. I just can't believe its bad taste.

'Gross, isn't it?' I turn at the voice. A short, stocky man is standing in front of me. Right hand extended. 'Mike Little-child. Abacus Ventures.'

'Orla Kennedy. Light As A Feather.'

I blush at the irony. But Mike Littlechild just politely smiles.

Like he hasn't noticed anything untoward in what I've just said. He's got a nice smile, plump pink lips, and a little dimple. Green eyes twinkle behind his metal spectacles. I inadvertently glance at his left hand. There's a wedding band on his second finger. Blast.

'It's the trouble with buying property from other banks.' He nods at the waterfall. 'They move to Canary Wharf and we're left with their bad taste.'

'So it's not a feng shui feature?'

'Pul-ease!' he exclaims. He turns to the receptionist. 'Hannah, which meeting room are we in?'

'The Trafalgar Room on four.'

Mike leads the way. The Trafalgar Room is filled with mock Chippendale furniture. Delicately carved chairs with tapestry seats surround a large mahogany table in the middle of the Trafalgar Room. He moves over to the sideboard where two chrome thermal jugs stand. Bone china crockery is set beside an enormous plate of foil wrapped biscuits.

'Coffee? Tea?'

'Tea, please.'

He pours and sets the cup in front of me, then places the plate of biscuits on the table between us. An invisible force starts to pull my hand towards the plate before Mike pipes up, 'Oops sorry, shouldn't tempt you' and drags them away. Be firm, Orla. You need the sugar. To calm *your* nerves. To keep your hypoglycaemic levels steady. I reach out and grab two mid-flight, just as he pulls the plate off the table.

'Right.' He settles himself. 'I like your business plan.' He pats the document in front of him that I delivered two days ago. On Tuesday. Just one day after calling, following a night of absolute chaos. 'Really like it. Your idea is new and original and, no pun intended, the dieting industry is a growing one. But I'm slightly concerned by your predictions for client growth.' He glances down at the figure. 'Ten thousand regular users by the end of next year. And you currently have?'

'Two hundred and twenty-two.'

Including me, Patti, Patti's flatmate and her boyfriend, her flatmate's colleagues, her flatmate's boyfriend's sister, my mum, their mums, Marcella, the twelve members of St Vincent de Paul's fund-raising committee in Clontarf, Liz, her colleagues, Jason, Finn, and a few misguided Buddhists who believed Finn when he said it was a new religious site. We've all spent the past three days logging in and out of the chat room at regular intervals. It's been chaotic. One day it took ten minutes just for everybody to say their names.

'That's quite a leap. Is it not a little over ambitious?' He pushes his glasses back up the bridge of his nose with his forefinger and looks at me.

I'm ready for this question. I practised the answer with Patti last night, using terminology from my old economics A-level, her 'how to bluff at maths' textbook and a few bits of banking spin that I've picked up along the way. Amy also offered some suggestions. I lift up my leather briefcase (borrowed from Jason who bought it for an interview, used once), and withdraw a leather presentation pack (borrowed from Liz who got it at a conference she attended, never used).

'I think you'll see from these pages here that these projections are realistic.'

Exhibit A: Bar chart. In colour.

'We have a time scale along the horizontal axis, denoting the months from launch until the end of next year. The vertical axis demonstrates the number of clients. You'll see here' – I point at the first month in the bottom left hand corner – 'the number of clients that initially signed on, and here' – I point at the next month – 'the current levels. Now if we extrapolate that growth rate across the time span' – I run my finger along the bottom line – 'then we see an exponential growth rate. Of course' – I smile, dazzling him with my science – 'I have also considered a differential coefficient of plus or minus one, plus a stochastic shock variable for, say, the introduction of compulsory new weight guidelines by the government.' I roll my eyes upwards. 'Tony Blair likes to control everything. I've also introduced an upwards bias to the numbers as a result of an accelerated and aggressive advertising programme. Now if we take these all into account then I think you'll agree that this' – I point at the final prediction – 'looks infinitely achievable, wouldn't you say?'

Mike Littlechild looks at me, utterly bewildered, which doesn't surprise me in the slightest because I've just recited gobbledegook. I know it's gobbledegook because it made total sense last night after a couple of bottles of wine with Patti.

'Have you taken into account an economic slowdown?' he finally says.

'Exhibit B.' I pull out another bar chart. Again in colour. 'I've assumed that households would tighten their belts, again no pun intended.' I smile and carry on. 'In an economic slowdown, people will want to save that five pounds a week they spend on slimming clubs, and instead look for free advice. In such an environment, I believe that my initial projections might prove to be an underestimate. As you can see, I've shifted the differential coefficient by two to incorporate my assessment.'

Note to self (1): On return to office, find out what a differential coefficient is.

Note to self (2): On return to office, apply for job as investment banker because *you're hot, baby*.

'Hmm.' Mike Littlechild is doing exactly what I do in such circumstances. Pretending he knows exactly what the other person is talking about when he hasn't actually got a clue. It's the contemplative nodding that gives away his ignorance. 'And what about underwear sales?'

'Exhibit C. We have managed to sell fifty pairs of knickers in less than a week. Directly extrapolating from that suggests minimum sales of two and a half thousand pairs per year. However, if we boost advertising—'

'Sorry,' Mike interrupts. 'What advertising do you have at the moment?'

'Flyers and sandwich bags. It's all detailed.' I point at the business plan in front of him.

'Oh.'

'Of course, we were constrained by a limited budget, but if we boost advertising,' I repeat, 'then I believe we could sell ten, maybe twenty, thousand pairs of knickers per annum. And I'm not even thinking of Pert Posterior Pantyhose, at five pounds a pair, or Bounce Free Booby Bras at twenty pounds. I mean, every woman I know has a part of her body that she isn't happy with. Light As A Feather has the underwear to help.'

'And the stock is readily available?'

'Well, yes.'

'You hesitated. Why?'

I explain about Undetectable Undergarments' deadline.

'Light As A Feather needs some working capital to acquire the remaining stock and establish a regular order line with the company.'

'Any plans for further link-ups with other products?'

'Mario has a sister who runs a delicatessen in Canary Wharf. I thought I might approach her.'

'How well has this venture with Mario's done?' I produce another chart. A pie chart – it seemed appropriate. 'Have you thought of a nationwide link-up?'

'Mario only has one branch. He has a cousin in Birmingham. I could approach him?' I look uncertain.

'I'm not talking about Mario. There are other chains of delicatessens across the country. Any other ideas?'

'I had thought of approaching a few gyms. Beauty salons? To boost the clients along the way.'

'Good idea. Now, any ideas for manning the chat room for extended periods.'

'I can't,' I admit, reluctantly. 'I've got a day job.'

'Such a pity. My wife logged on a few times recently and she says you offer good sensible advice. That you empathize with the slimmer.'

'Thanks. I try.'

'We need to exploit that. "Orla Kennedy really cares". That sort of thing.'

'I do. I really do,' I gush. Work it, Orla. Work it.

'How much working capital are you looking for?'

'About,' I stammer. Amy advised me to aim high. 'Twenty thousand pounds.'

'Per week?'

I almost choke on my tea.

'It would be a short-term funding requirement,' I bluff.

'Right, well I can get the cheque drawn up and biked to you this afternoon. Payable to Light As A Feather?' I'd prefer Orla Kennedy. 'We also normally like to take a stake in the businesses we invest me.'

'Oh?'

'Something small. It's a sign of our commitment to your business, and also acts as surety just in case you decide to abscond with the money or run the business to the ground.'

'Oh?'

'Say twenty per cent to begin with and as shareholder, we have the rights to insist on certain changes.'

'Oh?'

'Yes. Firstly I think we have to extend the hours you monitor the chat room.'

'I can't do more than I already am,' I protest.

'I was thinking an evening service to begin with, but eventually I'd like a round the clock service. Like The Samaritans.'

'I . . . I really don't think I can manage that. I mean, I need to sleep sometime.'

'I know that.' He looks at me like I'm an idiot. 'We're taking a stake, not your soul. No, what I'm thinking is that we can set up a training programme for Orla Kennedys. We're going to clone you, girl. Whenever a client visits the chat room, "Orla Kennedy" is there to offer support and comfort. And I think we should consider a nationwide roll-out. Stop being so parochial. Weight is a national problem. We need a major advertising campaign. I'm thinking radio interviews, television appearances, newspaper interviews.'

Radio? TV? Newspapers? Me?

'But . . . but my boss.'

Finally Mike stops and looks at me. 'Orla, I think you should forget your boss.' He checks the details in front of him. 'Although you haven't said where you actually work. Trying

160

to keep it all separate, are you?' I nod. 'I understand. Look Abacus Ventures *believes* in your company. You should too, or we'll have to reconsider our proposal. You can't give the commitment to Light As A Feather that we *require* if you're holding down another job. Abacus Ventures can make your figures work, but only with one hundred per cent effort from you.' He stabs his forefinger towards me, before rolling it into a big nought with his thumb. 'And a differential coefficient of zero.'

'I know that, and I'm very grateful, honest, but—'

'Go back and resign. Light As A Feather could change your life. Don't you want that opportunity?' Change my life? Of course I want such an opportunity. But twenty thousand pounds doesn't sound like I can order the caviar. 'Right, I'll go away and draw up some strategic plans, using your facts and figures.' Mike stands.

'You're only joking about me resigning, aren't you?' I say. 'I know we've spoken about a twenty thousand pound loan, but that isn't going to change my life, is it? It just buys the stock. It doesn't pay for staff.'

'Didn't I make it clear?' Mike looks at me in surprise. 'That's a sign of our commitment, a small down payment for the stake, if you like, but we're looking at a funding programme worth around' – he looks down at his notes – 'half a million pounds to begin with. We value this company at two and a half million pounds.'

'Half a million pounds?' I scream. 'Two and a half million pounds?'

'Yes.' He looks at me carefully. 'We'll draw up plans to extend the funds within weeks. Your business proposal just needs some finessing around the edges.' He grabs my hand and shakes it vigorously. 'Congratulations. We think you're onto a winner, and if it doesn't work out then you're not the business-woman we think you are.' I doubt I'm the businesswoman anybody thinks I am, but just nod sagely. Scared to open my mouth in case the words 'Are you mad? This is just another drunken idea from me and Liz' come out. 'So can we agree another meeting on Monday morning? Say nine?' I nod again. 'Then I can put some flesh onto the bones of our roll-out programme. See you then.'

I walk slowly back to Browns Black. My legs feel shaky. Very shaky. Should I resign today? No, better wait until Monday when I see the plans and have a cheque in my bank account. I get back to my desk in a daze, throw down my briefcase and leather presentation folder and sink into my chair. Shaking my head in disbelief. This is my purpose. My life *is* going to change.

'Patti,' I call over to my colleague, without looking over. 'I've got it. I can buy as many pairs of knickers as I want.'

'Isn't it great to have an ambition?' replies a man's voice.

I look over. Tony Younger is standing by Patti's desk while she buries her head in her hands.

SLIMMING TIP TWENTY-THREE

Shock therapy can aid the slimming process

Four hours later I recover the power of speech. Like those people who lose their memory after a shock, but find it is miraculously restored after another one, mine returns when my mother calls and asks a totally outrageous question.

'Orla,' she exclaims, without waiting for an answer. 'Has Finn got a girlfriend?'

'What?' Finn with a girlfriend. That's more startling than me getting half a million pounds. And much more embarrassing than Tony Younger wondering about my knickers.

'Does he have a girlfriend?' she repeats.

'I don't think so.' I choose my words carefully, trying to keep the incredulity out of my voice. Don't want my mother to know she's borne a son who is totally unattractive to the opposite sex. She's getting old. The news might cause a heart attack. 'Why do you ask?'

'Because he phoned up yesterday and asked me to send his suit over. The navy blue one that he bought in Arnott's sale three years ago. Lovely material it is. One hundred per cent wool, fitted him perfectly when I took the trousers up six inches. Express Delivery, he said. I ask you. Eighteen pounds forty-three it cost and I'm a pensioner, you know.'

'But why do you think he's got a date? Maybe he just missed the suit. Fancied getting dressed up once in a while.'

'Because the only time he ever wore the suit before was when he had that date two years back with Mary Maloney. From down the road. Do you remember that?'

'When he got so drunk he threw up in her handbag?'

'We only had her word for that,' my mother snaps. 'Finn denied it. Anyway, I've seen the sort of bag that girl carries around. Tiny. Don't fit anything in them. Just big enough for a lipstick. How does she manage for hankies?' She pauses. 'Personally I never thought she was good enough for Finn. And I was right.' My mother's voice drops. 'She's with child now. And I hear there are *no* wedding plans. In my day—'

'Mum,' I cut in. 'What did Finn say that he wanted the suit for?'

'A meeting of some sort, apparently. Tonight. Somewhere posh.'

'Finn? Somewhere posh?'

'That's what he said. Oh, Orla, you are looking after him, aren't you? He's such a sensitive boy. I wouldn't like to see him get hurt by some streetwise London girl.' I wouldn't wish him on any streetwise London girl.

'Mum, you're jumping to conclusions. He's probably got a special meeting of the Buddhist society.'

'If that's what it is, he can send me a cheque for postage,' she retorts. 'It's bad enough that he's turned from the one true faith, without expecting me to support another. I thought it'd be just a phase. Like when your cousin dyed her ponytail pink.'

'Calm down, Mum,' I sigh. 'Look, I'll find out what's going on and get back to you. By the way, I raised half a million pounds for Light As A Feather today.'

'That's nice, dear,' she says. 'Could you just find out what sort of family she's from? Now if they were Irish . . .'

''Bye, Mum.' I hang up. Patti is looking at me. Laughing at the side of the conversation that she overheard. 'My mother is convinced Finn has a girlfriend.'

'Why?' Patti seems surprised.

'Oh, something to do with asking her to send over his suit.' I pause, reflecting. 'He has been acting a bit strange recently, rather secretive, hanging up the phone when I walk into the room and hiding his e-mails from me as I walk past.'

'Probably your imagination,' soothes Patti. She walks over to my desk, leans right in so nobody else can hear her, and adds, 'What's that I heard you tell your mother about half a million pounds?'

'I know. It's amazing, isn't it?' I explain all about my meeting with Mike Littlechild and his plan for Light As A Feather. Rolling out nationwide. Cloning Orla Kennedys across the globe.

'So, are you going to resign?'

'Steady on.' I put a hand up to caution her. 'I haven't got the money yet. Let's wait and see.'

'But you can't carry on working if you're being cloned.'

'Why not? Maybe I'll send a clone in to deal with Tabitha.'

'Let's celebrate,' Patti suddenly says. 'Tonight. I'm sure Browns Black would love to pay to celebrate your good fortune. And I'll think of somewhere for us to go.' Patti wanders back to her desk and pulls a restaurant guidebook out of the drawer. I can see she doesn't plan to do any more work today. Thank goodness Tabitha is at an off-site meeting.

I dial Liz's number and tell her my news.

'That's really great. I'm so proud of you. Wait till I tell Jason,' she bellows down the phone. 'Let's celebrate.'

'Great minds and all that. That's just what I was going to suggest.'

'Tomorrow?' Oh, that wasn't what I was going to suggest.

'Tonight's better. Before the initial euphoria dies down.' And besides, now I've got the taste for celebration in my mouth. I'm salivating at the thought of champagne.

'I'm so sorry, Orla, but I can't tonight. Any other night, but I've got a business appointment.' She sounds disappointed.

'Not another hunk interview?' I say sulkily. I thought we always said men came second.

'No, honestly, something far more serious. It's taken at least a week to get this meeting together. Damn. I can't believe my bad luck.'

'Anyone I know?'

'Shouldn't think so.'

'Well, if you're going to blow me out for it, what's the meeting about?'

'Oh, can't say at the moment.' She hesitates. 'Nothing that exciting, but still, well, don't want to rock the boat. Just in case it doesn't come off. If it was any other night, Orla, you know I'd be out celebrating like a shot.'

'Never mind,' I say. 'We'll do something tomorrow.' I replace the handset. It takes a few minutes before I realize that Liz was being rather cagey about whom she was meeting. A sense of unease grips me. Liz wouldn't be having an affair, would she?

Three hours later Patti and I are sitting in the Rivoli Bar at The Ritz. My worries pushed firmly to the back of my mind. A bowl of homemade crisps lies on the table in front of us beside two chilled glasses of champagne. The bottle is resting in a silver ice bucket, within inches of Patti's side. She had insisted that the waiter leave the bottle where she could see it. 'You just never know,' she'd stage whispered to me. 'If he wants to take it away, then he can mark the label in front of me to show where the champagne was when he last poured.' It was left where she wanted but, though his expression was imperceptible, I sensed the waiter had another place he'd quite like to put it.

'So, how are you feeling?' Patti asks after we've clinked glasses for the sixth time.

'A bit spaced out, really,' I admit. 'I can't quite believe it all. I e-mailed Amy before I came out to thank her for prodding me into action.'

'Should have asked her along for the celebration,' replies Patti.

'I did, but she already had tickets for the cinema. Some foreign film with subtitles. I'd never heard of it.' I shake my head.

'Sounds fascinating,' says Patti, pulling a face. 'Now don't you be getting all silly. You know, saying that you can't do it. Crediting Amy when it was you who went and got the funds. I mean, she only suggested venture capitalists. Trouble with you,' she adds, sinking back into her tapestry-covered banquette, 'is that you have no confidence in yourself.'

You're a bloody graduate trainee, Patti, remember your place.

'I do,' I protest.

'Well, not enough,' she continues. 'Everybody in the bank knows that Tabitha is useless, and that you do all the work.'

'What?' I almost choke on my champagne as I sit bolt upright. Shocked. 'I haven't said that. Why do they think that? Tabitha will go ballistic if she finds out.'

'Relax. Who's going to tell her? Besides, I know you haven't said anything.'

'Well, who has?'

'Me.' Suddenly I see this graduate trainee with a long career ahead of her. And me with a long career behind me.

'What?'

'I tell them. Anyway, why are you so worried? You're going to be leaving soon, aren't you?' Good point. I relax and slump back into my comfortable chair. 'I even told them that Tabitha didn't come up with the new advertising slogan, although quite a lot of people had already heard about your bust-up, and that she wanted, "Browns Black: A big fish. Come fry with us".'

I cringe at the memory of the fish advertising campaign. Tabitha had spent the whole week working on it, and then when she announced it, I had fallen about laughing. Thought she was winding me up. Testing out irony. The joke was on me. My reaction went down about as well as a Wonderbra in a convent. She upbraided me in front of everybody on the floor. Told me that I didn't understand the play on words. That I was destined to always be a gofer rather than a getter. I couldn't let that go. I told her it was an advertising campaign for a local chippie, and even then it was marginal. A cliché. She challenged me to come up with a better idea. There. On the spot. So I did. 'Browns Black: All shades of advice.' The look on her face was of utter contempt. But it got even worse. The chairman was walking past, saw the commotion, and arrived just in time for my slogan. For once he had his hearing aid turned on. He liked it. Clapped at it, in fact. The scowl turned into a smirk, and there, in front of everybody, Tabitha stole my idea. Took full credit. Told the chairman that inspiration had hit in the DIY store when she was selecting paints. (Actually I think she nearly lost it there. Even the chairman couldn't see Tabitha in a DIY store and he's half blind. She'd have been better off saying the manicurist.)

'So everybody knows that I came up with that slogan?' I ask, pleased at the revelation.

'Well . . .' Patti fills her mouth with crisps to muffle the next sentence. 'I say we came up with it together. But,' she adds quickly, seeing my expression, 'that you were the main inspiration.'

'Pity you don't take credit for the City Hunk of the Week fiasco,' I snap. Patti has the grace to blush and look awkward.

'Actually, I have,' she says quietly.

'What do you mean?'

'I told Tony Younger that it was my idea.'

'What?' I look at her in surprise. 'Why? After all this time?'

'I was talking to Fi, a friend, and she said it wasn't fair on you.' She looks sheepishly at me.

'When? Why hasn't he said anything to me?' I say indignantly. 'He was quick enough to shout at me in front of everybody. Why hasn't he bloody well come over and apologized?'

'I thought he had apologized.'

'How do you know?' I snap, remembering his apology the day of Tabitha's revelation.

'He told me when I confessed,' she says, 'but he admitted it could have been finessed. I said he wasn't to blame you because you were just protecting me, and he was going to come over and say something but—'

'When was he going to say something?' I demand. 'How long has he known?'

'Since this morning,' concedes Patti. 'I was just telling him when you came back from your meeting and raved on about knickers. I think you threw him off course. Anyway, that's all far more exciting.' She changes the subject. 'What will you do with the half million? I saw some great boots in LK Bennett;

they'd look fantastic with a long black skirt. And there's a brilliant satin jacket in Karen Millen. Mind you' – she sips her drink, cash registers ringing up before her eyes – 'with that sort of money, you could buy anything. Gucci or Armani, say? Actually it's late night opening at Harvey Nicks. We could drink up and pop along, if you like.'

'Whoa. Slow down. It's not for me to go shopping. The money is an investment in my business.' Get me. *My business*. Next I'll be waffling about underlying trends and price earnings ratios.

'Yes, but you'll need new clothes for your personal appearances. You can't go on breakfast television wearing that old skirt.'

'Why not?' I look down at my favourite black skirt, stroking it gently.

'Because the shine from it will reflect badly on the camera lens,' Patti snaps. 'Besides, it looks too big on you these days. I seriously think you've dropped a dress size.'

I shake my head modestly. 'You're just saying that because you want a share of my money.' I smile to show that I'm joking, but inside I'm glowing. Life is looking up. I'm losing weight and my career at Browns Black is nearly over. The waiter walks by, glaring at Patti. She holds his gaze and watches him stroll around the bar room.

'Oh my God,' she says suddenly.

'What?'

'Don't look now.' She nods discreetly over my right shoulder towards a seat, hidden by large pillars. I start to turn.

'Stop. I said don't look. You'll never guess who's over there. Enjoying an intimate drink. Our very own Tabitha and Sven.'

'Oh?' I shrug my shoulders. 'It's probably nothing. Discussing his media image?'

Patti raises her eyebrows. 'With her tongue in his ear?'

Laughter can burn up many calories

Patti can't stop giggling. She's sitting at her desk, but every few seconds her shoulders shake up and down as another fit hits her. I watch her privately re-living the moment that she spied on Sven and Tabitha. Leaning dangerously low to one side on her chair, opening her eyes wider in pretend shock at their indiscretion, then throwing her hands over her mouth in an attempt to stop any word popping out. All in her little fantasy world. Patti should be on the stage.

'Patti,' I say quietly, disturbing the third performance. 'What are you doing?'

'I'm practising for when I tell people.' She smiles at me. 'Got to get the mood exactly right. You know, build up to the moment. Make them feel they were there in The Ritz. Sitting where I was.' She winks. 'Obviously there will be some artistic licence.' She checks around that we're still alone. 'I might have Tabitha's breast flopping out or something. Perhaps the left one. I've always thought that one looks a little smaller than her right one.'

'Patti!' I shriek. 'You can't do that. What if she finds out?'

'Oh yeah. As if you care,' she shrugs. Her tone becomes belligerent. 'You're going to resign.'

I feel slightly awkward about Patti knowing my situation. It's not that I think she'll use it against me, but it just doesn't help. I can hardly ask her to be loyal to the bank when I'm planning to leave. And it sort of negates my right to insist that she works hard. I will, in all likelihood, not be here when her probation runs out, and not involved in the decision on whether she becomes a full employee or whether the press department sends her somewhere else to learn the ropes. The boys on the trading floor have been crying out for a graduate trainee. They have nobody to fetch breakfast. 'Just be careful, Patti. When you put your mind to it, you are really good at this job, but sometimes you skate just too close to the edge. All right?'

'Yeah, whatever.' Patti's excited for me, but I realize that she'll miss me. We've grown close, despite the age difference. I feel rather maternal towards her. And I think that she likes and respects me. 'Hey,' she says, 'should I have his flies open?'

'No.'

'God, Orla. Sometimes you're so provincial.' What was that again about respect? Suddenly Patti pulls herself upright. 'Oh my God, Orla,' she hisses from the side of her mouth, 'Sven is coming over.'

'No!' I turn to see Sven approaching us. He is wearing a black three-piece suit, a spotted red tie with matching handkerchief sticking out of the breast pocket, and a plain white shirt. In his hand, he's carrying a folder. 'Just act normal,' I hiss back at Patti. What am I saying? I'd have better luck asking my mother to disconnect her phone.

'Sven.' I smile at him as he reaches my cluttered desk. 'How can we help you today?'

'Is Tabitha around?' he asks. Patti tries to stifle a snigger. Sven turns to her. 'Is everything all right?'

'Sorry,' Patti replies. 'Sneeze. Sort of a cold.' She points to her chest. 'Get a bit clogged up here. Tabitha sometimes has exactly the same problem. Needs a bit of rubbing.' She smiles at him. 'With Vick.'

'Quite,' he replies, not at all sure what she means. 'Where is she?' He points at Tabitha's empty office. A pashmina is draped on the back of her chair, as if she's just popped out and is poised to return, but Patti and I know that Tabitha hasn't yet been seen at work this morning.

'We're not sure,' says Patti. 'She had an important off-site meeting yesterday, top secret and all that, and we're not sure if it overran into this morning. You know how these senior executives can be. Totally dedicated to their work, at the complete expense of their personal life.' She smiles. Once again.

'Right.' Sven looks slightly confused. 'Well, she asked for this.' He hands Patti the folder. 'Would you tell her that I've answered all the questions and have left all my numbers for any follow-up interviews.' He turns to me. 'If one needs something to be done, then one really needs to deal with the people at the top.' He jerks his thumb over his shoulder towards Tabitha's office. 'I just ask her once and she provides me with the most wonderful coverage.'

'So we saw,' mutters Patti.

Sven shoots a look at her. Not quite hearing what she said. He turns back to me. 'Quite frankly, the piece on me in the *Reykjavik Bugle* that you organized was nothing compared to this. That' – he points at the folder in Patti's hands – 'will be one of the biggest articles on any City banker.' He turns on his heel and marches off.

As soon as he is out of sight, Patti opens the folder and lifts out the first page. 'Oh my God,' she laughs. 'You have got to see this. It's his presentation for City Hunk of the Week. Listen . . .' She tries to imitate Sven's foreign accent, hissing out every s and rolling every r, as she reads, ' "Am I attractive to women? I think so. I appreciate all women, as any female employee of Browns Black will tell you. I am always courteous and respectful to them, whether they are the receptionist at the front entrance or a senior executive in the corporate finance division." '

'So it's just us that he's always rude to,' I interrupt.

'Wait.' Patti continues. ' "How do I keep my body in such good shape? I enjoy all vigorous activities" ' – she winks at me knowingly – ' "but in truth this body is a gift from God. I don't have to work too hard to keep it in shape." Is he serious?' She looks at me in horror. 'He's going to be a laughing stock. And listen to this bit. ' "What qualities do I most admire? Honesty, integrity and humility." Liz's having a laugh, isn't she?'

'Only one way to find out,' I press a button on my phone that speed-dials Liz. 'It's Orla. How was your meeting last night?'

'Oh fine. Got quite a lot of stuff for my article.'

'And it's out this week?'

'No, it's something that I'm working on. A longer piece. More investigative.'

'Well, Sven's going to be delighted.'

'What do you mean?' She sounds confused.

'We've seen his responses to the City Hunk of the Week queries.' Patti looks over and giggles. 'When did you decide to use him?'

'Oh that.' The penny suddenly drops for Liz. 'Tabitha rang earlier in the week and said she thought he'd be ideal.'

'You never said.'

'Didn't I? Must have slipped my mind. Sorry.'

'I told you ages ago that he wanted to be Hunk. I thought you agreed that he wasn't suitable material.' I must admit to feeling miffed. Liz knew how much Sven's appearance could have helped me, yet she had refused his request. Even when he had rung up personally. But now Tabitha rings and suddenly he gets a spread. 'Anyway, I thought you had all his details. Why did you want him to answer all those questions?'

'Just something I was wondering about. Maybe changing the format before it become too staid.' She changes the subject. 'So did you celebrate last night?'

'We certainly did,' I concede, 'and Patti saw things that nobody as young as her should ever see. Tabitha's tongue in Sven's ear.'

'Oh my God!' Liz shrieks. 'This just gets better and better.'

'Liz.' I suddenly remember my responsibilities as press officer. 'That was off the record.'

'You didn't say so beforehand . . .' Ah. The journalist's get-out-of-jail card. You must state that something is off the record before you say it or they can argue that it is actually all on the record. And so can be reported.

'Come on, I wouldn't have told you if you weren't my friend.'

173

'You're such a spoilsport . . .'

'Please.'

'Well . . .' She appears to consider the matter. 'I won't use it now, but you never know. There might come a day when this comes in very handy. Very handy indeed. Got to run.' Liz hangs up, just as I spot Tony Younger advancing towards me. He is holding a giant bouquet of flame-coloured, long-stemmed roses. Patti spots him too and shouts over.

'Tony, are you still having trouble with that girl from the *Mirror*? I could tell her to stop asking you out for drinks, if you want?'

He looks slightly embarrassed as he nods his assent.

'Orla,' he says as he arrives at my desk. 'For you.' He thrusts the flowers into my hands. 'By way of an apology. I gather I was wrong. Patti explained everything and what can I say? I was out of order.' He shrugs his shoulders and shakes his head. 'I feel truly embarrassed about the things I said to you. Anyway' – he looks over my shoulder to Tabitha's office – 'I'd better go now. Someone's looking and I don't want to get anybody else into trouble. See you around.'

He walks off as I read the card: 'With sincere apologies, an ungrateful hunk.'

SLIMMING TIP TWENTY-FIVE

Underwear can help

The doorbell rings. An irritating, extended ring that cuts through the peace of the morning. I open one eye and look at the illuminated dial of the alarm clock beside my bed. I open the other one in shock when I see the numbers zero, eight, zero, zero. In a straight line. Who on earth rings my doorbell this early on a Saturday morning? I sit up, trying to wake myself.

'Finn?' I shout out. 'Are you expecting anybody?'

'No,' comes the muffled sound of my brother. I can tell that his face is buried into his pillow.

'Then it's probably bloody Jehovah's Witnesses. Lift the intercom and tell them we're not interested,' I nestle into my previous position and try to go back to sleep when the bell rings again.

'Finn,' I shout, 'move your arse.' Ah, the trials of being a lodger who pays no rent. You swiftly transform into an unpaid skivvy, although food and non-alcoholic drinks are thrown in. Sometimes at.

'Hold on, hold on.' I can hear him shuffling to the intercom, then chatting to the mystery caller. 'It's a delivery,' he informs me. 'From Undetectable Undergarments. Shall I accept it?'

'Yes!' I scream, jumping out of bed and searching for my dressing gown. I find it where I dropped it yesterday morning. On the floor. After another trip around the room I discover one mule under my pillow and the other on the windowsill. A vague memory of my arrival home on Thursday night after celebrating with Patti starts to surface, but embarrassment rises, pushing it firmly back into blackout land. The land where all past transgressions are totally forgiven.

Finn is lifting a huge box into the lounge when I emerge from the bedroom. God bless Justin. I sent a cheque immediately on receiving Abacus Ventures' for twenty thousand pounds on Thursday, and he had promised to send the knickers out then and there. Before receipt.

'It is just so nice doing business with you,' he had gushed on the phone when I called. 'You're such a professional. I was saying only the other day to my, em, friend, shall we say, Peter, that your chat room is amazing. The knickers it has shifted! As I said to him, there aren't many start-ups that perform quite so well. I know I said we had two top London department stores crying out for this stock, but I've got to admit, my conscience has been pricking me ever since. I was lying. They're just interested in the younger audience. They're not interested in Mrs Higgins with the 46 FF bust. No, she's a niche market. They target the young girls who only want implant gels and push-up bras. They're not interested in our Bounce Free Booby Bras. They want to bounce. Some of these girls I see walking about the Yorkshire Dales, well, they ought to be ashamed of themselves. Your clientele just seems remarkably like our clientele.'

'Actually I was thinking of taking some of your Bounce Free Booby Bras to try out on our customers,' I admitted. 'I have one or two who really wish to reduce—'

'Say no more. I know exactly what you mean,' he interrupted. 'As for the knickers, well, the youngsters want gusset free, crotch free, and buttock free. I just refuse. I couldn't even ask our seamstresses to make them. I mean, two or three of them have heart conditions. Can you imagine what it would do to them to see a string turned into a pair of knickers? I tell you, our company insurance wouldn't cover it. But you know the trouble, Orla. Real people who would love our products just don't get to hear about them.'

'Actually, I might be able to do something about that. I'm

176

going to be doing a whole host of publicity for the chat room. I'll definitely be mentioning Undetectable Undergarments.'

'Oh, if you were here at this moment, I'd give you a great big kiss. I can see our Pull Your Tummy In Tightly Knickers will be going places with you. Shall I also send down our minimum order of Pert Posterior Pantyhose?'

'As a trial?'

'Absolutely. A sign of my faith in you. Anyway, got to go now. We've got another demonstration of the Bung Away Your Bits Bikini. Between you and me' – he pulls the phone close to his mouth – 'not all the bits were bunged away the last time. It didn't look so much like a washboard stomach, as a corrugated cardboard one. But Rome wasn't built in a day. Speak soon. 'Bye.'

Finn is on his knees, busy tearing the brown masking tape from the box cover, and dipping into the contents. He pulls out a few pairs of knickers. All different colours.

'How many of these have you ordered?' he asks as I hand him a mug of tea.

'About five hundred knickers, less what I ordered the last time, some bras and pairs of tights.' I look inside the box. It is crammed full. Immediately I feel panicked. Can I do this? Can I really sell all these? Should I not just forget about this silly idea and concentrate on being a better press officer at Browns Black? As soon as I ponder the question, I've got the answer. No. I'm fed up with pandering to egotistical investment bankers who think that anybody earning less than a quarter of a million pounds a year is unimportant. Fed up with listening to them threaten me when some newspaper dares to question the rationale behind one of their deals. And, most of all, I am fed up with Tabitha receiving a six-figure salary and expecting Patti and I to do all the grunge work, while she networks and strategizes. If Abacus Ventures has faith in me then I should too. Amy said as much yesterday in her e-mail. 'Believe in yourself. I do.' Brought a tear to my eye, but that could also have been something to do with the alcohol still coursing through my veins from the previous night's celebrating.

As Finn's busy unpacking the box, I remember my mother's comments about his suit. He hasn't mentioned anything and I haven't actually seen it in the flat. He's been living out of his rucksack since he arrived. I've seen the same three T-shirts, two sweatshirts, and two pairs of jeans in rotation. I'm not sure about his underwear, but I'm praying he might have more than just the one pair. If he has got his suit, I'd love to see him wearing it, if only to get a break from the rest of his wardrobe. The trouble with Finn, though, is that you never ask him anything directly; he is a master at evading questions. But I know how to get the answers. I've had years of practice.

'So, Finn, what do you think of all my news from Abacus Ventures?'

'If it makes you happy, Orla, then I'm happy for you.' He smiles, leans back against a chair leg, and takes a sip of his tea.

'Isn't making money against all your new principles?'

'Making money? No, but if I thought you were being greedy, then that would be a different matter. Greed is one of the Three Poisons that cause bad Karma.' He frowns at me. 'The only way to deal with greed is to give away everything.'

'Right,' I say doubtfully. 'Would that also include my Lulu Guinness handbag?'

'Orla, you're always mocking me. I thought you were asking for advice.' He looks a bit irritated, puts down his mug, and returns to dragging everything out of the box.

'I am, honestly,' I say, pulling a 46 DD Bounce Free Booby Bra out of its box. If no one on Light As A Feather fits this I might hang it over my bedroom door and keep my toiletries in it. 'What about my public appearances? What should I wear?' He looks at me as if I'm mad. 'OK then, what would you wear for a really important meeting?' Nicely put, Orla.

'Probably my jeans,' he replies without looking up.

'Jeans?' I exclaim. 'Haven't you got something posher to wear?'

'Orla, what we wear doesn't matter,' says Finn, delving further into the box, pulling out a pile of Pert Posterior

Pantyhose in American tan. Great. They'll really sell well. 'You're too obsessed with material goods.'

'Haven't you anything posher to wear for a pressing engagement?' I prompt. Come on, Finn. Who have you been meeting? Spill the beans. Is it a girlfriend? I stare at him intently. He is lying. Surely that's against his precepts?

'What important meetings would I ever have? Anyway, Orla,' he adds, delving a bit further into the case, and staring at a piece of paper that he's just pulled out, 'more urgently, where are we going to store all this underwear? You might have to think about getting warehouse space somewhere?'

'Don't be silly. It's only one box. Can't we store it here?' I look around my cramped lounge, which currently moonlights as an office and a bedroom. What difference is another function going to make? It's not as if it affects my council tax.

Finn shakes his head.

'This piece of paper here,' he says, waving it in front of me, 'says this is the first of six boxes. This is just to be getting us on with. The others arrive Monday. Orla, you're in business.'

SLIMMING TIP TWENTY-SIX

Trust nobody

'Orla, great to see you again.' Mike Littlechild shakes my right hand as I try to push myself out of the sunken leather chair with the other. 'We've all been working flat out on Light As A Feather these past few days.'

'All?' I repeat as I finally manage to scramble out of the chair without revealing my brand new Pull Your Tummy In Tightly Knickers. I'm also wearing Pert Posterior Pantyhose. My stomach feels all taut like a trampoline. I swear if somebody dropped a pound coin on me, it would bounce.

'Yeah, the team. Everybody at Abacus Ventures is very excited about this project. You'll be meeting them all shortly. Our A-team,' he smiles.

'A-team?' I repeat again, glancing quickly at my outfit. Damn. My shoes could do with a polish. As we walk across the foyer to the lifts, I surreptitiously try to shine them on my new tights. Around the back of my calves. I stop when I realize the receptionist is looking at me, and indicating to one of the security guards to check out my funny walk.

'Yes,' continues Mike. 'And one surprise. I can't wait to see your reaction.' He winks at me. 'But I'm saying no more until we get there.'

A large display easel stands in the corner of the room. It holds one of my bar charts, blown up large, and with some even more inventive projections if my eyes serve me right. How many customers are they predicting? Where I had ten thousand, and laughed at its unlikelihood, the chart now says fifteen thousand. Even I, without a shred of financial expertise in my body, know that such a prediction is about as likely as Princess Anne posing in *Playboy*.

The large meeting table is set for six people, with coffee cups and glasses. A collection of bottled waters and pots of hot drinks are placed in the middle. Two large plates of Danish pastries and croissants look appetizing, while another plate of Ryvita looks like something I'd use to sand my living room floor. 'We didn't know what you'd prefer,' admits Mike. Have a guess, man. Five of the places are laid out with leather edged blotting pads, notebooks, and pencils. These guys mean business. There's a knock at the door.

'Ah, here comes the team.' I fix a smile as Mike introduces Felicity (very posh, blonde hair in a chignon, a nose that could cut toast), Matthew (bald, red braces with dollar signs embroidered on them) – and Giles Heppelthwaite-Jones.

I freeze as Giles extends his podgy clammy hand to greet me. What if he tells Tabitha? I'm not ready for her to find out just yet. Not until I have the money in the bank and a rock solid business to walk away to. Then I plan to tell her to stick her job where the Sven doesn't shine.

'Enchanted, my dear. Can't tell you how thrilled I am to be here.' He offers a tiny bow. 'What a great business mind lurks inside that pretty little head of yours.' Pretty little head? Is he having me on? I stare at Giles, trying to make sense of the situation. Is this the surprise? I glance over at Mike, but he seems unaware of my confusion. Then the penny drops. Giles doesn't recognize me. I'm just the girl at Browns Black who takes his coat and fetches him coffee. He has actually never noticed me before. I'm a non-entity in his life.

'We're so lucky to have Giles on board,' gushes Mike. 'He's one of the top City public relations executives. Can get anything into the financial pages, can't you Giles?'

'Well, one doesn't like to boast,' preens Giles, fluttering his hand in an it's-no-trouble sort of way. 'But they do say that I'm the only PR man that all the editors of those pages take calls from. The *only* one.' Felicity's rosebud mouth opens in a huge 'gosh' shape.

'He'll definitely put Light As A Feather on the map. Actually' – Mike smiles at Giles in a sickeningly adulatory manner – 'he is the adviser to Browns Black. The top investment bank. In fact, and I know Giles won't mind me saying this, he devised their latest advertising campaign. Didn't you, Giles?'

What? How many other people claim credit for it? Next my mother will be telling her friends at coffee mornings that she did it. I look at Giles in amazement at his audacity.

'Well,' Giles shrugs in an if-you-insist-on-me-admitting-it fashion. 'It came to me in a DIY store. "Browns Black",' – he thrusts his hand out with each word, '"many shades of advice".'

'I thought it was "all shades of advice",' I say carefully.

'Details, my dear. Details.' Giles waves his hand in the air dismissively. 'Now tell me, Orla. Such an unusual name. Is it French?'

I look carefully around the room, just checking to see that this isn't an almighty wind-up. Waiting for a man with a camera to jump out and say, 'Fooled you!' but they all seem immune to my bewilderment.

'Irish,' I reply. Listening for any muffled sniggering.

'Well, I was right.' He looks me up and down before turning to Mike. 'Anthea is going to be just perfect for this. Absolutely perfect.'

We are just taking our seats when there's a tap on the door. Giles jumps up from his seat and rushes to the door, which flings open just as he arrives to reveal an absolutely stunning six foot blonde. She's wearing a tight black pencil skirt and a cashmere twin set, with the cardigan thrown casually over her shoulders. Perfectly pedicured toes stick out from the flimsiest pair of sandals that I have ever seen. But it's her legs that I can't get over. They're tiny. Absolutely tiny. Her calves? I've eaten larger chicken drumsticks. If I were ever out camping, I'd want this woman with me. Rub her legs together and start a fire.

'Anthea, darling.' A torrent of air kissing is going on between

Giles and Anthea. 'Let me introduce you to the gang.' He places his arm protectively on the base of her neck, and the Abacus Ventures' gang spring forward to shake hands. Then Giles, Mike and Anthea approach me.

'Orla,' smiles Giles. 'Meet Orla Kennedy.'

'Sorry? You just called her Anthea,' I correct him.

'No, Orla. I *mean* Orla Kennedy. Isn't this fantastic?'

'You've lost me.' Slight understatement. If they dropped me into the middle of the Sahara Desert without a map, I probably wouldn't feel quite as lost.

'This' – Giles presents Anthea – 'is your body double.'

'Is she a stunt girl?'

'Is she a stunt girl,' repeats Giles, guffawing. 'This girl's got a great sense of humour.' He turns to Mike, thrusting his thumb back at me. 'No, darling. This beautiful young lady here is going to be the face of Light As A Feather.'

'The face?'

Calvin Klein has Kate Moss; Light As A Feather has Anthea. Yes, she's going to be you. Aren't you thrilled?'

This is the surprise? That they'd thought I'd be *pleased* about? I look at them in horror. It really is true. Men just don't understand women. Dinner and chocolates, that's a surprise. Meeting a skinny girl? That's just humiliating.

'I haven't a clue about what is going on,' I finally concede. 'Mike?' I turn to him. 'Could you explain?'

'It's quite simple, actually,' he begins. 'Giles believes, and we're quite, em, we're . . .' He fumbles for the word, flapping his hands around as he tries to grab it.

'Bowing to my superior knowledge of public relations,' prompts Giles. 'My experience of building media images. Tom. Cameron. Had a hand in all of them.'

'Yes, that's right,' continues Mike, 'and Giles here feels, well, we all do, that perhaps you're not quite the right image for the major publicity campaign planned for Light As A Feather.'

'So you mean that Anthea will be the model in all advertisements?' I ask.

'Not exactly,' Giles smiles at me. 'Orla, you're beautiful.

Honestly. I love what's going on with your hair, and Anthea would die for your eyelashes, but, quite frankly, television adds a stone to people. Fourteen pounds. And I don't feel, no disrespect intended, that we can put you on the little screen.'

'Sorry?'

'Anthea will be the public face of Light As A Feather. I mean, let's be honest, you don't promote Alcoholics Anonymous with a large bottle of gin, do you? No. Anthea will become Orla Kennedy for all public appearances. A woman who has slimmed down using her own advice. What better figurehead than a success story?'

'I'm a success story,' I blurt out. 'I've lost over a stone. By eating sensibly and exercising a bit more.'

'Jolly good, dear, keep it up.' Anthea looks at me. 'Only another twenty to go. And then, what will you be? Ten stone?' She smiles. I hate her. I wish she were on a camping trip with me. I'd bloody leave her on the fire.

'Such a sense of humour,' gushes Giles. 'Do you see, Mike? Anthea's going to be absolutely perfect on telly. Go on, Anthea. Show them how you give good' – he throws his fingers up into inverted commas – 'advice.'

Anthea smiles at her small audience, adopts a little-girl-lost look and says in a very friendly, I-care-about-you manner, 'Breakfast is the most important meal of the day. Personally I prefer a bowl of fresh fruit, with perhaps a little fromage frais, but that's just me.' She points coyly to herself, before adding, 'And at just under two hundred calories, it's packed with vital vitamins for everyday health.'

'Bravo!' Giles bursts into a round of applause. 'She knows the calorie content of anything.'

'So do I,' I protest.

'I know, but I look like I do,' replies Anthea.

'You can't do this,' I protest to Mike.

'Actually we can.' He rifles through a document on the desk and passes it over. 'Check out page eight, third subclause, fifth line down. It's there in black and white. We have the right to make management changes.'

184

'Anthea will be running Light As A Feather?' I shriek.

'No, no, no . . . heavens no,' Giles laughs. 'She's got far more important things to do with her day. She'll just do publicity. You'll still do the chat rooms. Have you visited them yet, darling?' he asks Anthea. 'They are so interesting. Full of people with nothing better to do in their lunch hours. Never see them down The Ivy, would you?'

'So I just carry on as normal?' I ask in confusion.' I'm not involved in any of the big marketing campaigns?'

'We might use you for radio though,' interrupts Giles. 'On those days when Anthea can't make it.'

'She's got a face for radio,' sneers Anthea. Felicity sniggers.

'Can you imagine, Mike,' Giles says, 'Anthea in Hold Your Belly In Tight Kickers? It'll be a sensation. People clamouring to buy them, to get a washboard stomach like this.' He thumbs at Anthea's perfectly flat belly. 'Little knowing that this young woman has spent hours, nay months, in the gym to achieve this perfection.'

'But—' I start.

Anthea butts in. 'Giles, will I be topless? You know my views on nudity.' She plants her hands onto her hips.

'Of course, darling. Only if the part absolutely warrants it.'

'Or if the money's right,' Anthea adds.

'Wait,' I cut in. 'That's deception. I can't allow this. Those knickers are brilliant; they sell without false publicity. I'll tell people.'

'Orla,' Mike interrupts. His voice hard and businesslike. 'If you'd like to turn to page nine, fourth subclause, second bullet point, you'll see that Abacus Ventures must insist on complete confidentiality about this agreement. I mean, if it ever got out that Anthea isn't who we say she is, then it could be the end for Light As A Feather. The agreement doesn't leave this room. We're investing half a million pounds; it gives us certain rights.'

'So when does the publicity campaign begin?' I ask frostily.

'Wednesday morning. "Orla Kennedy" is booked onto *Welcome To The Day* with presenters Stephen and Suzy,' smiles

Giles. 'It's a great slot. Nine in the morning. She's going to be interviewed about how she "lost" ' – another flick of inverted comma fingers – 'the weight.'

I don't believe it. *Welcome To The Day*. My favourite slob-out morning programme. I've always wanted to sit on the comfortable sofas beside Stephen and Suzy. To sip a glass of fresh orange juice companionably as they quiz me on my love life. To taste that day's offering from a celebrity chef. To clap along to the latest boy band. This isn't a wind-up. Nobody could be so cruel. I stare at Anthea, who smirks at me as she breaks a Ryvita in half and nibbles one corner. From now on, she'll do everything that I've ever wanted to do. She'll be my face. And I won't even get a clothing allowance. What is it they say? Always the bridesmaid?

SLIMMING TIP TWENTY-SEVEN

Lie about your weight

Two hours later and I'm back in the office. I don't care what Mike said about not mentioning the agreement, I have to tell Patti. The girl's booked me a personal shopping session at Harvey Nicks to sort out my on-screen wardrobe, for God's sake.

'But that's totally unbelievable,' she explodes when I tell her about Anthea. 'Does she even look like you?'

'Obviously not,' I point out. 'After all, she's slim. The perfect success story,' I add sarcastically.

'Well, what are you going to do about it? You mustn't stand for it.' She stamps her foot.

'What can I do?' I look at her in exasperation. 'They *are* giving me half a million pounds. I can hardly start making demands, can I? Anyway, they pointed out all these sub-clauses and legal paragraphs that mean that Abacus Ventures can do anything it wants in the interests of Light As A Feather.'

'But—' It's her turn to look exasperated.

'But nothing,' I interrupt. 'They're the experts. They're supposed to know what they're doing. And, besides, no matter what you think about Giles, he is meant to be the best in the business.' Patti snorts. 'Anyway, I haven't time to think about it now. It's almost time to sign on for today's session. By the way, haven't you got a lunch today? An urgent meeting with a journalist that can only take place in a wine bar? I mean, they are now open.'

Patti looks at her watch. 'Well, now you come to mention it, I'd better make tracks. Said I'd meet Tony Younger at quarter past in Jamie's wine bar on Gresham Street. He's having lunch with some journalists from the trade press, and wanted somebody to hold his hand. Make sure he doesn't say anything he shouldn't.' She winks. 'It's a dangerous job, but somebody has got to do it.'

'Oh.' A pang of jealousy hits me. Why didn't he ask me? I am, after all, senior to Patti, plus he knows now that I wasn't responsible for the City Hunk of the Week travesty.

'Actually,' she says as she re-applies her lipstick in a compact mirror, 'he was asking after you.'

'To accompany him?' I ask. ·

'No.' She replaces her lipstick in her bag. 'He was just wondering how you were. Said you'd had some sort of heart to heart a little while ago. I told him you were fine.' I blush when I think of how I opened up to Tony the day that Tabitha let 'slip' about Sebastian. I look sharply at Patti, wondering what he's told her about our chat, but she's busy packing notebooks and pens into her bag. She finishes her task and looks up. 'Anyway, as regards Light As A Feather, I don't think you should give up on this without a fight. I wouldn't. See you later. Don't wait up.' She swings her bag over her shoulder and walks off.

I log into the chat room. My mother and Lily are already in there, discussing a new, low fat Victoria sponge.

Mary >
It just doesn't seem to rise as well.

Lily >
Have you tried a dash of salt in it? I've found that helps.

Orla >
Hello.

Mary > Lily >
Hello there.

Tessa >
Hi. Have I missed anything?

Cecilia >
Sorry. Running late. Manicurist snapped one of my nails by mistake.

Orla >
So how did we all do this week?

Lily >
Stayed the same.

Cecilia >
Lost two pounds, but my husband never even noticed. He seems distracted this week. Rshole.

Bella >
I feel so much more energetic. I even went to the park at the weekend with my son. I've never done that.

Orla >
What did you do there?

Bella >
Had an ice cream.

Lily >
Was it one of my husband's vans? Larry's Luscious Licks?

Orla >
What about you, Mum?

Mary >
Lost five pounds.

Orla >
What? That's really brilliant. (@-@)

Mary >
Why are you stunned?

Orla >
How did you do it?

Mary >
I let your father make dinner on Saturday. He didn't realize he had to defrost the prawns before cooking them.

Tessa >
Can I have the recipe?

Orla >
What about you Tessa? How did you do?

Tessa >
Lost a pound, but I still feel unhappy. Are you sure we can't have a face-to-face session?

An idea comes to me and I type it before I think it through.

Orla >
No, but we could have a party. When everyone has lost a stone. The other clients can come too.

Realization suddenly dawns as the last letter leaves my finger. A party? That would mean that Anthea would have to be invited and pretend to be me. And I would be just another guest. I won't be Orla. How will that feel? Watching somebody else talking to my clients? I shudder at the image. Perhaps I can retract the party invite. Announce it is a silly idea. Maybe nobody will want to come. But I watch in horror as one by one the group respond favourably to the idea. Only Cecilia appears to have doubts. She wants to know if she can come without her husband. And then my mother . . . Oh my God. I forgot about her. She's just messaged saying that she'll look into flights. She can't come. I mean, even *my* mother would recognize that Anthea was not the child that she had borne. I'll have to talk to her separately. After the session. Explain the situation.

Orla >
I also have two bits of information for you. The first is that the knickers are in, and the second is that I'm going to be appearing on Welcome To The Day *with Stephen and Suzy this Wednesday.*

Lily >
That's my favourite. He's such a handsome man. Did anybody see the one where he demonstrated how to get the most from your lawnmower? Larry thought it was invaluable advice. Told all his friends.

Mary >
Will they want to interview me?

Orla >
Why?

Mary >
They often have the mothers on. Only last week there was a piece about three children, and they interviewed all their mothers.

Orla >
How old were the children?

Mary >
Just starting school, I think. Five?

It's times like this that Finn makes sense.

Within seconds of logging off, my mother's phone line is engaged. A little knot of dread ties itself in the pit of my stomach. If I know my mother, she will be on the phone to everybody she has ever met instructing them to video the show just so they can see her daughter talking to Stephen and Suzy. This is turning into a nightmare. Why couldn't I just have admitted to the Monday chat room session members that it won't be me? It will be a model posing as me. It would be so much easier. Only the Monday members, nobody else. But in my heart I know that I couldn't have because, as Benjamin Franklin once said, three may keep a secret – if two of them are dead.

Half an hour later and I finally get through.

'Mum,' I start, 'about the show.'

'Oh, Orla, I'm so pleased for you. It's absolutely amazing. Everybody over here is so excited, and listen . . . you'll be thrilled to know that I've picked up a few tips on public relations from you. The local paper is going to be doing a piece. Did you ever?'

'No.'

'Yes, aren't you proud of your old mum now. And you think I never listen.'

'Mum—'

'I always listen to everything you say. Now the paper wants a photograph of you, and I was thinking of your graduation photograph . . .'

'No. Mum—'

'Now why ever not? Sure you look lovely in it. And they told me that they have this hairbrush thing that can sort out pictures, because I mentioned that you'd had a perm at the time that I never really liked. I always preferred your hair when it was natural, as I constantly told you, but you children. Always know best. Never listen to your parents. Anyway, they said the hairbrush would fix it.'

'Mum, don't send any photographs.' My tone is firm.

'I never heard such rubbish. Of course I'm going to send photos. I was also wondering about that one of you in your First Communion dress. Might be the only time I ever see you in a white dress with a veil. It would be nice to see it in the papers.'

'Mum, I can't stress this strongly enough. Do not send photographs.' I adopt an even firmer tone.

'But why?' I can sense my mother's confusion. 'I can get them to hairbrush the spots away, although all teenagers get them. You shouldn't be embarrassed, and as for the braces, well, doesn't everybody have those nowadays? Heavens, even the bank manager had them when I went to see him yesterday. That reminds me, he'd like to see the show. I must call Brendan O'Reilly is his name. His baby sister was in your class.

192

Dervla. Do you remember her? Three children now, although he admitted to me that only two were after the wedding.'

'Mum,' I interrupt, 'it's not to do with the spots, or the perm, or the bloody braces. It just might . . .' I hesitate. I don't think I can tell her. In half an hour my mother has built up my appearance to such a monstrous degree that I suddenly feel I can't take it away from her. Right now. Can't I tell her tomorrow? Why can't I let her have today's excitement? To revel in the role of proud mother? Because, Orla, you eejit, tomorrow she'll have to call everybody and tell them that she made a mistake. Tell her. Before she embarrasses herself more. Tell her now. Now.

I ignore my conscience. 'It just might cause problems.'

I open my mouth again to explain further, but nothing comes out. I take a deep breath and start again. 'Mum,' I begin.

'Before you say anything, I just wanted you to know how proud I am of you,' she cuts in. 'You've made something of your life, and after all the heartache that Finn's caused me, it's great to know that one child will not disappoint. Who'll never let me down.'

Why did I ever think my life could change? It's the same old bundle of shit. On Wednesday morning, the person I care most about in the world will be desperately hurt and humiliated, and I'm too much of a coward to stop it. I'm not brave enough to save her today. I quietly replace the phone.

SLIMMING TIP TWENTY-EIGHT

Feel sick to your stomach

It's just before nine on Wednesday morning. I've rung in sick. Only it's not really a lie. I'm sick with nerves about Anthea's first appearance as Orla Kennedy. And sick with shame about my inability to warn my mother. Black rings circle my eyes. I've barely slept since our last conversation when she hung up so excited and thrilled that her only daughter was going to be on television. It was, she told Finn when he rang to tell her the truth, almost as good as being a grandmother. He didn't say anything. I was horrified when he told me of his failed mission. He's a bloody Buddhist for heaven's sake. They're not meant to lie. And he's spent the past months boring me about how any thoughts or speech that are rooted in delusion lead us away from Nirvana. They're bad. Finn's bad. He has deluded our mother. But he justified his actions, said that to tell her would harm her and would therefore push him away from Nirvana. He couldn't do it. I tried to force him, pointing out that by not telling her, his action was harming me and was therefore also bad, but he didn't waver. And then he turned practical. Pointed out that our parent's television was a small portable one, and maybe they wouldn't be able to make Anthea out properly on the screen.

'Of course, you could tell her,' he said, rationally.

'Of course, you could bloody pay rent,' I retorted, equally rationally.

Liz arrived about half an hour ago with Danish pastries and Styrofoam cups of rich, frothy coffee. She said we needed the sugar. Patti also offered to ring in sick and come round, but I told her that it wasn't necessary, even though I appreciated the offer. Imagine. That's how confused I am. Actually thanking the graduate trainee for thinking of bunking off.

The boxes of Undetectable Undergarments stand piled on top of each other in the corner of the room. On the floor in front of them, six piles of knickers are laid out in their sizes, ready for us to swiftly grab, pack into one of Mario's sandwich bags and send out to any viewers who order as a result of the show. An old-fashioned calculator lies beside them, a little roll of paper peeking out from its top, and a large handle on the side to pull down as the numbers are totted up. It looks like we mean business.

Finn is in my bedroom. He has laid out a green onyx Buddha on a linen cloth on one of my bookshelves and is venerating. The palms of both his hands placed together, raised high in front of his head. A string of worry beads is twisted through his fingers. I can imagine my mother, at this very moment, across the Irish Sea holding her rosary beads and praying that 'my' appearance will be a success.

'Orla, look. It's started.' Liz grabs one of my hands. Finn arrives, kneels by my chair, and grabs the other one. The opening credits roll across the screen. Stills of Stephen and Suzy in the garden. Smiling over coffee. Walking through a meadow. Laughing at a silly shaped parsnip. Chatting to Sir Elton John.

'I can see why people go out to work now,' mutters Liz. 'This looks boring.'

'Shh,' I hiss.

Suddenly the studio appears on the screen. Large vases of cerise pink gerberas and lemon roses sit, with a bowl of exotic fruit, on a sideboard at the back of the set. Through an oval-shaped window there are views of the London Eye, the Millennium Wheel, and the Houses of Parliament.

Stephen, sitting in a purple, wing-backed seat at the fore-front of the screen, is running through the order of the show. Along the side of the screen flashes a timetable.

'Next we'll be meeting a man who went for a walk and didn't come back for twenty years. Yes, we'll be talking to Frank Carter' – the camera pans to an elderly man on the comfortable sofa – 'who suffered such severe amnesia that he couldn't remember where he lived.' He smiles at Frank, who shrugs his shoulders as if he too can't quite believe it actually happened. 'Then in twenty minutes we'll be meeting Orla Kennedy.' The camera moves to Anthea, sitting beside Frank, carefully replacing a glass of fresh orange juice on the coffee table before them. 'A woman who was so determined to lose weight that she set up her own dieting chat room, Light As A Feather.' He leers at Anthea. 'Looking at her now, ladies and gentlemen, I'm sure you, like I am, are fascinated by how she achieved such a spectacular figure.' Anthea smiles coquettishly.

Bitch. But he's right. Anthea does look fantastic. Her hair hangs loose, sweeping over her shoulders. A perfect glossy mane. She's wearing a pillar-box red suit, with neat, pinched-in waist, which stands out dramatically against the yellow cushions behind her. Her legs, clad in sheer black stockings, are swept to one side at a perfect forty-five degree angle like a recent graduate of a wonderful finishing school.

'Bloody hell, Orla, you look fantastic,' mutters Liz. 'Your legs! How do you stand without snapping them?'

'Yes,' Suzy takes over the introductions. 'We learn that Orla was so determined not to be a fat bridesmaid for her best friend . . .'

'That's me,' cuts in Liz. She jumps up out of her chair in excitement, and starts clapping at the television. 'They're mentioning me.' She spins around to look at me. Her eyes are sparkling with pleasure.

'. . . that she shed three stone in weight. And she'll be answering calls in later. The numbers are on the screen now. That's in twenty minutes for this morning's phone-in.'

I turn the volume down with the remote control. A sense of doom in my heart.

'My wedding has been on television,' gushes Liz, still standing. 'Do you think *Hello* will be interested now?'

'I think I need a drink,' I finally utter.

'But it's not even nine thirty,' protests Liz.

'A large one. Sit down.'

I find a bottle of vodka in the fridge, grab two glasses and a carton of sterilized orange juice, and rush back to the lounge.

'Where's mine?' asks Finn.

'I thought you'd given it up,' I reply. Memories of Finn lecturing on how people don't drink for the taste, but merely to seek release from tension come flooding back. 'Isn't it one of your five precepts, or something?'

'This is an emergency,' he says, rushing into the kitchen to fetch a glass. 'I think Buddha will forgive me.'

Liz and Finn sip quietly. I take great big mouthfuls of drink in noisy glugs as I try to soften the inevitable pain that's about to hit me.

'She's back.' I pop up the volume and the three of us settle back to watch the first public performance of 'Orla Kennedy'.

'Welcome, Orla,' says Suzy. 'It's great to have you here.'

'It's great to be here, Suzy, and can I just say,' Anthea smiles. A small, trying-to-be-sincere smile. 'You look so much better in the flesh than you do on the small screen.'

Finn, Liz and I look at each other in horror. Then, simultaneously, we drain our glasses. Heads thrown back together. One big sip echoing around my small living room. Like a gasping Mexican wave.

'Er, thank you,' says Suzy, shifting uncomfortably in her high-backed chair.

'I mean,' Anthea continues. 'Whenever I've watched this show, obviously I'm a huge fan,' the camera pans to Suzy graciously nodding at the compliment, 'I'd always thought you were a size eighteen, but

197

now up close, I'd say that you were a size fourteen to sixteen. Am I right? And that purple trouser suit is simply divine. So well cut. It hides a multitude.'

'Well, Orla, that's very flattering, but we're here this morning to talk about you.' Suzy recovers some of her composure. A pinched smile fixed firmly on her face. 'So how did you do it? How did you manage an incredible three stones in weight loss?'

'It was nothing,' says Anthea, flapping her hand as if to indicate the insignificance of the task. 'Pure discipline. It's the only way.'

'Could you elaborate?' Stephen interrupts. 'Obviously you didn't have the discipline in the first place.'

Wow. Stephen, what big teeth you have.

He turns to Suzy and says, 'I think we should tell viewers that Orla declined to provide us with photos of her pre-weight loss.'

'Do you think he knows?' mutters Liz, glued to the screen.

'No,' I snap. 'He's being difficult because she's just embarrassed his wife before a live studio audience.' I grab the bottle and refill all three glasses.

'I threw them out in disgust at myself,' smiles Anthea, 'after using them as a little aide-mémoire to keep to the difficult job at hand. I set myself a calorie limit every day and a special task.'

'What sort of task?'

'A ten-mile walk. Jog around the park. An hour on the stepper.' She rubs her hand gently along her legs, emphasising her trim calves. Bitch.

'What?' I shriek at the screen. 'That's not proper advice. People should take it slowly at the beginning. Build up. A five-minute walk. Taking the stairs rather than an escalator.'

'I thought people should take it slowly at the beginning,' says Stephen. Good man. *'Set themselves small goals.'*

'Quite frankly, Stephen, I've never been one for small goals. Head

on, that's me. If people want to lose weight then they've got to get on with it. None of this poncing around saying "I just want to lose a pound a week". They need to act decisively and dramatically. Seize the moment.' Anthea grasps an imaginary rope in front of her.

'That's all the wrong sort of advice!' I scream. 'It's ridiculous.'

'We have our first caller,' says Suzy, smiling malevolently at Anthea. 'It's Marion from Isleworth in Middlesex. Hello, Marion.'

'Hello, Suzy. Hello, Stephen. Hi there, Orla.'

'Could you hurry up, please,' interrupts Anthea. 'We have other callers on the line.'

'Sorry.' Marion sounds shaken. 'I just wanted to say that it's not easy for people to lose weight when they're not paid well. All those diet foods cost so much money. How are we meant to afford them?'

'Good point, Marion.' Stephen smiles at the screen. 'What do you think, Orla?' He turns to Anthea. 'How can people diet on a budget?'

'Marion, what weight are you?' Anthea demands.

'Em, about sixteen stone, I think.'

'Goodness, you'd need to be ten foot tall for that to be your proper weight.' Anthea throws her head back laughing. Her hair flicks neatly out, and then lands back exactly where it started from. Stephen and Suzy look on in silence. 'Well, you didn't get to be that weight just eating cheap food. What do you usually have for breakfast?'

'Bowl of cereal, four slices of toast, tea and a muffin.'

'Mid morning?' She smiles at the screen.

'Couple of doughnuts . . .'

'Lunch?' She waves a finger, like a teacher reprimanding a recalcitrant child.

'Depends on the menu in the staff canteen. Yesterday it was lasagne and chips, and spotted dick for pudding.'

'Oh, Stephen.' Anthea throws her hand onto his knee, rubbing it softly. 'Can't we talk about you?'

'We're talking about Marion,' he snaps, carefully lifting her hand off and putting it back onto her knees. Suzy glares at Orla.

'Oh yes.' Anthea smiles at the camera, with an I'm-not-really-interested gesture. 'Sorry, got distracted.' She winks again at Stephen.

Suzy looks like she's getting ready to toss her glass of orange juice over her.

'Oh my God.' Liz and I hide our heads under our cushions as we cry out in unison. Finn looks on in horror.

'If you can honestly tell me that all that junk you shove down your throat is cheaper than fresh vegetables and fruit, or even meat and fish, then I'd be very surprised,' continues Anthea. 'It's probably cost thousands of pounds to get you to the size you are, and you're trying to tell me that diet food is expensive. Please. Next.' She throws her immaculately manicured hands into the air. The ten scarlet talons shimmer against the studio lights.

'I don't believe it.' I look at the screen in horror. 'She's offering the right advice, but she'd doing it all wrong. Marion is probably in tears by now. That woman is going to ruin Light As A Feather. What have I let Abacus Ventures do?'

'Our next caller is Michael from Wolverhampton,' Stephen continues, 'and I'm sure that Orla will have some more forthright advice for him. Hello there, Michael.'

'Hello, Stephen,' a voice wheezes down the line. 'I wonder, Orla, if you can help me.'

'I'll try.' She smiles graciously into the cameras.

'I need to get life insurance, but my doctor has refused to approve a medical. He says I'm obese' – a pause for a deep breath – 'and will die from a heart attack if I'm not careful' – second pause – 'and if that wasn't enough to worry me, he says I should think of the strain on my knees' – one giant pause – 'and the likelihood of arthritis.'

'Well, Michael, I'm surprised you even lasted the length of this phone call.'

'What?' He sounds shocked.

'What do you expect me to do? Tell you to find another doctor, get rid of that nasty man who dared to tell you what nobody else would?' Anthea adopts a sarcastic, child-like voice.

'Orla.' Stephen's irate voice cuts in, as Michael stammers with

indignation. 'I don't think it's necessary to be rude to the people ringing in. I must apologize to viewers who were offended by the comments of our guest this morning, Miss Orla Kennedy, the brains behind Light As A Feather. But you really didn't mean them, did you, Orla?' he snarls.

'No,' she sulks, 'but I am getting fed up with this culture of people who get fat and then turn round and blame it on their genes, their big bones or society. You only get fat by eating too much.' She emphasizes each word in the final sentence.

'But you were overweight,' interrupts Suzy. Emphasizing the final word with a sneer. 'You shed weight to become a bridesmaid. Surely you empathize with these people.'

'Oh, yeah, right. Sorry. Michael. I would recommend that you take more exercise and stop putting stuff in your mouth. I'm sure your wife already follows that last bit of advice.'

Stephen and Suzy look at each other in horror. I can read their minds. They are wondering how on earth 'Orla' promotes herself as caring about slimmers. The woman in front of them has about as much in common with dieters as Victoria Beckham has with singers. Suzy clutches her earpiece, listening to the commands from the floor manager. Suddenly she turns to Anthea and smiles.

'We have a surprise for you. On the line we have Mary from Dublin.' Anthea smiles. Oblivious to what is coming next. 'Your mother.'

Anthea visibly palls through her St Tropez fake suntan as Finn, Liz and I simultaneously scream at the screen, 'No!' I reach for the bottle, but it's almost empty. Enough for about two more drinks. I'll send out for reinforcements after the show.

'Hello, Mary,' says Suzy. 'Welcome to Welcome To the Day.*'*

'Thank you, Suzy, and I must say that I thought Frank was very inspirational. Wonderful piece. Imagine not knowing where you live. Admittedly it happens to my husband sometimes, but the landlord usually gives me a call.'

'Thank you, Mary. What have you got to say to your daughter?'

'Hello, Mother,' says Anthea awkwardly.

'Orla, what is going on?' demands my mother. 'You've changed so much. Marcella barely recognized you. Have you stopped eating?'

SLIMMING TIP TWENTY-NINE

Not everybody knows what they're doing

My mobile phone rings just as the commercial break cuts through Anthea's response to my mother's question. I grab it like an automaton, unable to tear my eyes away from the screen, which is now filled with happy, bonny babies bouncing around in nappies that prevent all sorts of leakages. Shortly there will probably be some woman climbing Mount Everest as she tells the camera that she never lets her monthly periods get in the way of a normal life.

'Orla.' Mike Littlechild's irate voice pierces through my handset. 'What is happening? What the hell was your mother ringing the show for? Are you trying to ruin everything?'

'Me trying to ruin everything?' I explode. '*Me*. I've just watched a blonde airhead act like a complete bitch on screen, and all in my name. And you have the audacity to say that I'm trying to ruin everything.' Finn and Liz look at me in dismay, then Finn slowly empties the rest of the vodka into my glass and hands it to me. He grabs his jacket and mouths at Liz that he's off to get another bottle. She hands him a ten-pound note.

'Giles thinks it went just fine,' Mike snaps, 'for a first appearance.'

'*Fine*? Were you watching the same bloody show? She was a nightmare. First she insulted the host, then she publicly upbraided callers and mocked their weight problems. You call that *fine*?' I take another gulp of vodka. Perhaps I should use it on my cornflakes in future. It really does give me spirit.

'I asked Giles about that.' Mike sounds defensive. 'He says

that Anthea's adopting an Anne Robinson image. She's strong and takes no nonsense. It's the new thing now. People like getting insulted. Fat people like getting told that it's their own fault. They are the Weakest Link. It's an image.'

'Did they sound as if they liked hearing it?' I scream at Mike. 'Because I didn't get that impression. I thought they sounded hurt and upset, but then maybe I'm just soft.'

Another phone rings in the distance and Mike excuses himself to answer it. 'That was Giles. Anthea's not being used in the next portion of the show. Apparently there's live coverage of the rescue of a prize-winning Persian tabby cat from a sixteenth-century oak in Kent coming in. They've decided to cut to that,' he says.

'Usurped by a Persian cat. Wow. Things are looking up for Light As A Feather,' I bark.

'I must say, Orla, your attitude is extremely disappointing. So negative. I thought a woman like you would understand about the need to raise the profile of a company. Anne Robinson is hot. Anthea will be hot.'

'I don't know if I can get this across to you, but she was not hot. She was not even lukewarm. She was nasty, grating, and hugely insulting. Anthea has adopted a public persona completely at odds with the style that I have in the chat room. Don't you remember telling me that your wife said I empathize with the slimmer? Anthea didn't. She showed enmity.'

'Well, anyway,' splutters Mike, trying to change the subject, 'you haven't answered my question. What the hell was your mother doing on the show?'

'She rang in to speak to her daughter.'

'But it wasn't her daughter.' He sounds confused.

'I know that.'

'But didn't she? Were you adopted?'

'No.' I sit back, exhausted by the tension of the previous hour. 'I didn't tell her that it wasn't going to be me. She obviously rang to find out what was going on.'

'Didn't tell her? Why?' Even more confused.

'You said to keep the arrangement secret,' I mumble.

'Not from your bloody mother,' he snaps back. 'There's client confidentiality, and then there's downright stupidity. Did you think she wouldn't notice?'

'No,' I reply, 'but I thought I'd tell her after the show. I never thought she'd ring in.'

'Well, she has. This could be a disaster.'

'A disaster? I think it was a disaster before my mother rang in.' I shake my head in despair. 'Is this how you make the numbers add up? By getting them down to zero?'

'There's no cause for that attitude,' retorts Mike.' The A-Team at Abacus Ventures is quite pleased with this morning's performance. All publicity is good publicity.'

'Is it?' I snarl. 'Well, let's just see what my clients think about it.' I break the connection. Liz is looking at me. Upset for me. Concerned that my chance to become a dotcom tycoon has been lost before it even was found. 'I'm just glad that I haven't handed in my resignation,' I say quietly. 'This could all go horribly wrong.'

My mobile rings again. It's Justin from Undetectable Undergarments.

'Orla, are you off set now?' he whispers.

'Er, yes.'

'I've just seen the show,' he declares. A short sentence that says it all.

'And?'

'You didn't mention the knickers. You promised you'd mention the knickers,' he shouts. 'How on earth are we going to increase our sales if we don't use every available avenue? *Welcome To The Day* was a perfect slot. Lots of women watching that will have bottoms sagging to their knees. They need our knickers.'

'I'm sorry,' I say weakly. 'It quite slipped my mind. Anything else?' Might as well get it all out of the way.

'Well, how can I put this without you taking it the wrong way?' He pauses to consider the matter. I can hear him tapping something with a pencil as he ponders the best way to tell me. 'You're not quite what I expected. I'd sort of imagined you as shorter, with perhaps a little more weight, if that's not being too rude.'

'No, you're fine,' I sigh.

'Also, well your voice seemed different. Had you had elocution lessons for it?'

'Yeah,' I lie. 'That's right.'

'Hmm, thought so.' He pauses. 'And, perhaps, you were a little bit rough on that last poor man.'

'I know,' I lie. What else can I say? 'I promise that I'll mention Undetectable Undergarments the next time. Scout's honour.'

'Well, you were a perfect advertisement for them,' he gushes. 'It hardly looked like you were wearing them. Your stomach was so flat; they really are miracle workers, aren't they?'

'Yeah, thanks, Justin. I'll call later this week, OK?' I hang up just as Finn returns with the new bottle. 'Give that here, Finn. What shall we say?' I lift the bottle up to the two of them. 'A third each?'

'Has Mum rung yet?' Finn asks as I pour the drinks. Liz stops me emptying the bottle, reminding me that we might just need it later.

'Not yet,' I admit, my stomach is turning at the thought of facing the phone call.

'I'll just check the chat room. In case anybody is in there,' he says, moving to the table set up with my computer. 'See what the reaction has been.'

I watch Finn log on and start checking out the site. Liz mumbles into her mobile phone, explaining to Jason about the events of the past hour. I hear her whisper the words 'unbelievably rude' and 'humiliating' into the phone, then suddenly a ferocious 'No' comes through the handset. She smiles at me, awkwardly.

Finn interrupts. 'Cecilia is in the chat room.'

'And?'

'Em, she doesn't seem happy. She thinks you've been stringing them along. That you've been thin all this time and have just been playing a role. She feels deceived.'

'What have you said?'

'What could I say?' shrugs Finn. 'I told her the truth. Told her that you used to be huge.'

Thanks.

'Did it help?'

'Not really. She says you now remind her of the women who work with her husband in the City.' He sees my distressed face. 'Don't worry, sis. I'll talk her round. You'll see.' He winks. 'When it comes for her regular chat room session, she'll barely remember all this.'

Hmm. I know Finn has discovered Buddhism and all that, but I don't believe he has discovered how to work miracles. I smile at him gratefully, although I fear he has an uphill struggle.

The phone rings. Liz, Finn and I all look at each other. One thought connecting us. It's my mother. She sounds subdued and upset.

'Orla,' she says quietly. 'What's going on?'

'Mum,' I start. 'I'm so sorry. I wanted to tell you.'

'I felt like a complete fool when that girl told me during the commercial break to get off the line. That she hadn't a clue who I was. She actually had the audacity to tell me, *me*, your *mother*, that I was a crank. Ringing up as some part of a sick joke.' Her voice is wavering and I can hear her catching her breath, trying to stop little sobs bursting out. 'Why couldn't you tell me you weren't going to be on the show? That it was some other girl called Orla Kennedy on today instead.'

'But that other girl was meant to be me,' I admit. 'They thought she looked better on television than me.'

'How could it be you? She spoke about sex on national television, for God's sake. You weren't brought up to behave like that. You weren't brought up to talk about sex in public. What will the nuns say?' She cries, humiliated at the memory. 'And the way she treated those people. I was ashamed. Ashamed to think she was my daughter.'

'Me too, Mum. Me too.'

'And your father . . .'

'I didn't mean to upset either of you.'

'He's down at The Yacht, and he's so embarrassed because everybody has been buying him drinks over the past few days to celebrate your appearance. What will he do now?' Do without free drinks, I'd say. I feel angry with my father. It's so typical of him to capitalize on my 'appearance'.

'When did they tell you that it would be somebody else instead of you?' Ah, the million dollar question. The chance to admit everything. To relieve my guilty conscience. But once again, I can't. With Liz and Finn watching me, I pick the coward's way out.

'Just minutes before we were due to go on,' I mutter. 'There wasn't time to call you.' Finn shakes his head and sighs. He doesn't approve.

'Well, at least that's something. I can tell Phyllis down the road that it wasn't your fault,' replies my mother. 'She's jealous, you see.'

'Oh?'

'Yes, her children have come to nothing. She hasn't even any grandchildren. She told Marcella that she was fed up with me boasting about my successful daughter in London. That she hadn't a clue what a public relations executive was, and when I told her about the chat room and the appearances on the television, well, God forgive me, but that woman's eyes were green. But I couldn't help myself. I was so very proud. I'm just sorry it didn't work out for you today. Anyway, I'd better go, I've got lots of calls to return to explain the situation. And I expect I'll take this video recorder back to the shop now. Your father and I won't be needing it after all. 'Bye darling.' She hangs up. I feel like a complete heel.

We sit there. The three of us sipping our vodkas. Liz and I staring into space, and Finn tapping away at the keyboard. Over an hour passes, as I contemplate what my mother said and Liz finally accepts that her wedding will probably not be appearing in *Hello!*

The phone rings once again. It's Patti. There's a lot of

background noise, and I can barely hear her. The mobile connection is shaky. 'Orla?'

'Yes.'

'What are you doing?'

'Drinking. Did you see the show?'

'Yes.' A simple word, but one that conveys so much.

'So you know why I'm drinking.'

'Don't be like that. It wasn't that bad.'

'Thanks. Is that what you rang to say?'

'No, I rang to say that you've got to come down here.'

'What? Where?'

'Jamie's wine bar in Gresham Street. I've sent a company cab to collect you, but you've got to get down here.'

'Why?'

'Just do what I ask. It'll be worth it. Oh,' she says as her battery starts to fade further, 'dress up a bit. See you in twenty or so.' The connection is lost. I press 1471, and try to recall her, but a disjointed female voice just announces that the phone is probably turned off.

'That was Patti,' I tell Liz. Finn looks up and smiles.

'She wants us to meet her in Jamie's.'

'Why?' asks Liz.

'She didn't say. Just said it would be worth it.'

'Well, I vote we go,' says Finn surprisingly. He stands up. 'What are we doing here? Mooning about? Worrying about what might or might not happen? You need to get out there, Orla. Face the world. It's not as if it was really you making a fool of yourself on television.'

Liz nods. I can't believe it. My brother occasionally makes sense.

'I agree,' she says. 'Get your make-up on. Shall I call a cab?'

'There's one apparently on its way,' I shrug.

The three of us rush around getting ready, which is difficult when we've drunk a bottle and a half of vodka between us. I find it hard to get my sandals on. My fingers lack the dexterity necessary to tie the buckles, so I throw them across the room and slip on a pair of orange mules. They look startlingly bright against the black of my trousers and jacket. Liz ruffles her fingers through her hair to give herself a wanton look, and declares herself ready just as the doorbell rings.

A quarter of an hour later we're walking into Jamie's wine bar. It's crowded with City bankers enjoying a lunchtime drink. Young waitresses in ultra short skirts zip in and out of the crowds, taking food and drink orders. We push through looking for Patti, who is sitting at a stool on one end of the bar, and she introduces us to two young male journalists. We order three large drinks. Patti looks strangely at Finn when he accepts his, but smiles when he mouths the word 'emergency'.

'Why are we here, Patti?' I finally ask.

'You'll soon find out,' she says mysteriously.

'It's not Tabitha and Sven again, is it?' The two male journalists look up in surprise. 'Off the record,' I mutter, waving a wobbly finger at them. They nod in agreement.

'It's better than that,' she smiles. 'In fact, I think you might be about to discover it.'

I turn as somebody taps me hard on my shoulder. It's Sebastian. And he's drunk. Very drunk. I look at Patti confused. Is this what she called me here to see? An abusive, incapacitated Sebastian.

'I shupposhe you thought that wash funny,' he splutters. I look at him in confusion. Liz and Finn watch quietly. Patti sips her drink. Carefully watching the two of us. Her companions look ready to break up our reunion if necessary.

'What was funny?' I reply.

'Thissh morning. *Welcome To the Morning* shhooow.'

'No, I didn't think that was funny,' I admit quietly. 'I thought it was a disaster.' I look across at Patti. Disgusted. This is some sick joke. As if the day hasn't been bad enough. But she shakes her head, muttering, 'Bear with me.'

'Caush I didn't find it amushing at all.' Sebastian loses his footing slightly, and staggers backwards before recovering. Don't tell me Marion from Isleworth is his mother? Or that he is related to Michael from Wolverhampton? 'In fact, I found it very coshhtly.'

'Costly? You've lost me,' I admit. 'And now, if you don't mind. I'd like to have a quiet drink with my friends.' I make to turn away, but Sebastian grabs my arm.

'My bosh ish off sick. In bed today.' He wobbles a bit more. 'And he shpent thish morning watching telly.'

I look at him wondering where this is going. What do I care about his disgusting boss who actually dared him to date me? I try to shake off his grip. 'So?'

'And he shaw Orla Kennedy. Now can't be too many women with the name Orla Kennedy. Can there?'

'No,' I admit, still a bit confused, although at the back of my mind, a small surge of realization is breaking through. Fighting through the vodka and the emotions.

'Sho he watched it. To shee the big fat bird his colleague Sebashtean had been dating. The big fat bird that had cosht him five grand. Only' – he waves his half empty beer glass in front of me – 'it washn't the big fat bird that Sebashtean had been dating. It was shomewon else. Sho he doeshn't believe Sebashtean. In fact' – his voice gets louder; Patti's companions rise to their feet, and move in closer – 'He now thinksh I wash lying. He wantsh his money back. *Tomorrow*. With interesht. What do you think of that?'

I look at him. Beautiful body. Lovely face, although reddened from today's excessive drinking. A dribble of beer slithers down his silk tie. How could I have been so blind to this man? He has a character straight out of a Grimm's fairy tale.

'I think' – I smile at him, removing his grip from my arm – 'it's the best thing I've heard all day.' Then I throw the remains of my drink over him. He tries to avoid it, but slips and ends up falling flat on the floor. Unable to raise himself up, he sinks back, alcohol slowly taking control of his body. 'Absolutely the best thing.'

SLIMMING TIP THIRTY

Grovel

Orla >
I don't know how many of you are out there today but I can only apologise for yesterday's appearance on Stephen and Suzy. I don't know what came over me.

Bella >
What came over you? You acted like a complete bitch. And you were slim! How do you explain that?

Orla >
They used a special camera, honestly. I am struggling with my weight as much as you all are.

Tessa > Lily >
Pah! And to think we gave up fat free desserts, because we thought we were all in it together. You've got a secret up your sleeve to accelerated weight loss, and you aren't even sharing it with us.

Orla >
Please believe me; I really haven't. There is no secret, and that's why we all need to continue supporting each other. It is a long and lonely process.

Tessa >
I don't know why we should carry on. You've cheated us. : (*) (I just said she makes me sick, Lily, in case you didn't understand.)

Lily >
I understood. :-o (no explanation necessary).

Cecilia >
I think Orla should carry on. We can't let her first appearance on television put us off. Think of all the TV presenters we'd never see now if they were judged by their debut.

Orla >
Thanks for your support, Cecilia.

Cecilia >
No problems. Finn explained the circumstances.

Orla >
He did?

Cecilia >
Of course, and I think going through the menopause at such a young age would be a terrible burden for anybody to cope with, particularly if they are going on television for the first time. Your hormones must have been all over the place.

Lily >
You poor darling. Shall I send over some Evening Primrose? It worked wonders for my hot flushes. Do you get those?

Orla >
Not exactly.

Mary >
Is this true, darling? Oh my God. Does this mean that I'll never be a grandmother?

Slimming tip thirty-one

Be strong and stick to your guns

Just over a week later and I'm sitting at the large boardroom table at Abacus Ventures. Felicity and Matthew are handing out folders to myself, Mike, Giles and Anthea. I almost tell them not to bother with her. I'd be surprised if she can read anything apart from shampoo bottles. Matthew is wearing a tie embroidered with little weighing scales. I'm sure he's trying to be witty, but if he comes any closer, the mood I'm in, I might just hang him with it.

Mike clears his throat, pushes his glasses back up his nose, and opens his folder. He takes out the first sheet, and glances down. 'Right, we're here in the' – he checks the paintings on the wall – 'Somme room, to discuss the publicity for Light As A Feather that the efforts of Giles and Anthea' – the two eejits clasp hands across the table and perform a little bow – 'have generated. He checks his notes again. 'There has been one television appearance . . .'

'Which was an utter catastrophe!' I interrupt.

'Only because your stupid mother rang,' replies Anthea. 'I was doing fine before that.'

'Fine?' I explode, but Mike cuts across me.

'Orla, there will be time for recriminations' – Giles glances sharply at Mike, who visibly palls – or not, later. Right, as I was saying, one live television appearance, three local radio interviews and two newspaper articles. Am I forgetting anything? Anthea?' She is leaning back in her chair, which is placed at right angles to the table, allowing her to lean an elbow and file

214

her French manicured nails, but looks up in an uninterested way and shakes her head. 'OK then, how does everybody here think they went?'

Giles rises slowly from his chair, leans both closed fists on the table in front of him, and begins. 'Personally, I am extremely pleased with what this young lady here has achieved.' He indicates Anthea. 'It is not easy stepping into somebody else's shoes.'

'Particularly hers,' mutters Anthea. 'They're hardly Jimmy Choo, are they? More like surgical shoe.' She extends one of her dainty legs in front of her, and examines her winkle-picker mules.

'The brand,' continues Giles, 'Light As A Feather is achieving recognition.'

'For the wrong reasons!' I shriek.

'Orla,' says Mike, in a warning voice, 'you will have your right of reply. Please carry on, Giles.'

'*Welcome To The Day*, with Stephen and Suzy, received six calls following Anthea's appearance.' I snort. 'There was also a review in one of the tabloids.' He lifts up a photocopy of the article.

'Did you read it?' I demand.

'Yes, of course I did,' replies Giles indignantly.

'Did you bloody understand it? Or, shall I read it to you?' I lift the copy, search down the page for the relevant paragraph and read it out. ' "*Welcome To The day* is traditionally a magazine style show, filled with trivia, innocuous news items and celebrities. Yesterday we were introduced to Orla Kennedy, a woman who, it was said, set up a dieting chat room because she wanted to lose weight before acting as bridesmaid for her best friend. The biggest surprise about that bit of information was that Orla Kennedy had any friends. She proved to be the worst kind of dieter. Like the reformed smoker who casually throws out sensationalist information about lung cancer and passive smoking to anybody careless enough to light up in their presence, Kennedy is a veritable mine of slimming tips. She also has a cruel, unforgiving attitude to people unfortunate enough to be in the position she was in just a year ago. I was appalled at her behaviour. Viewers ring *Welcome To The Day* for friendly advice, not a tongue-lashing. The show's producers should choose their guests more carefully in future. They have a moral duty to do so." So, Giles, I'll repeat the question: Did you understand it?'

Little beads of sweat are building up on his forehead. Giles pulls a silk handkerchief out of his top pocket and mops before replying, 'Light As A Feather achieved five column inches in that tabloid. Victoria Beckham achieved just four. I would say that we should be pleased. It is what we in the trade' – he smiles at Mike – 'call a *result.'*

'It is what we in the slimming trade call' – I start the sentence calmly, before taking a deep breath and letting rip – 'an unmitigated public relations disaster. And we haven't even analysed the radio appearances.'

'You can't blame us for those,' interrupts Anthea. 'We did offer you the chance to do the radio work. You refused.'

'Did it not strike you that any listeners who might have watched *Welcome To The Day* would wonder how my accent had changed so radically? Television, English accent. Radio, Irish accent.' I turn to Giles and add sarcastically, 'I can see why you get paid three hundred pounds an hour by Browns Black now.'

'Three hundred?' utters Mike in confusion. 'You told me it was four hundred pounds, Giles.' He gazes at me. 'How do you know his going rate, Orla?'

'Oh,' I fumble. Shit. Me and my big mouth. I can see Giles looking at me strangely. I can't admit now that I work there. He'll rush straight back to Tabitha, I'll get fired, and the way things are going with Light As A Feather at the moment, I'm not sure I have anything to go to. I have put on hold my plans to resign, just in case. 'I have a friend who's a journalist,' I stammer. 'She said it was the rumour.'

'How humiliating,' sniffles Giles, 'that people actually think I'd offer my services for three hundred pounds. An hour? My cleaner almost gets paid that.' He smiles at Mike. 'Journalists never bother to check their facts. Anyway, Orla, even you must admit that the radio interviews went well.'

'Oh yes. In one Anthea acted as a walking calorie counter, refused to take calls, but kept asking the presenter to test her. Very impressive. In another, where one of the listeners was practically crying that she couldn't find clothes big enough, Anthea offered her an old parachute that her dad had found during the Second World War. And even the presenter was floored in her third appearance when she advised one caller not to swim in the public baths in case it scared small children.' I smile at Giles. 'I suppose they went well because the producers didn't pull the plug early. As for the newspaper interviews, well, the less said about them the better.'

'I told you, Orla, after *Welcome To The Day*, that Giles is going for an Anne Robinson approach. Anthea is positioning herself as the dominatrix of the slimming world,' explains Mike.

'Fine, but the Anne Robinson approach is not going down well with my clients. The people we *are* trying to attract. I've had eighteen people close down their weighing scales and letting their feathers loose, and fourteen regulars have cancelled their food orders with Mario's. They think that I've been taking the piss out of them all this time. Your approach' – I point at Giles – 'is losing the site money. She' – I thumb at Anthea – 'is the Weakest Link.'

It was only Finn's efforts that prevented Cecilia from shutting her account. He told her that I was suffering terribly with first night nerves and 'my' television appearance had been very badly edited. Cecilia is a woman who has never before watched morning television, so she had no idea that the show was live. Anyway, Finn says she has other more important things on her mind, like whether her husband is having an affair. I haven't pried too much, but she seems to be confiding in him. Tessa was also pretty scathing about my public persona. I don't think she'll come to any party I might throw now. Anyway, the more I've thought about it, the sillier the idea seems. I can't imagine Anthea walking around a room filled with people trying to slim and actually being nice to them.

Amy also seemed outraged about my appearance. She told me in an e-mail that I displayed Jekyll and Hyde characteristics; that on the website I was attentive, caring and understanding, while on the television it seemed like I drank fresh blood for breakfast. It was hard not to admit all to her, but I have signed a confidentiality contract, and the bottom line is that if word gets out that Andrea is my doppelgänger then I can kiss good-bye to the half a million pounds investment.

But the worst reaction wasn't from one of my clients. Tabitha came bounding over to my desk the moment she saw the headlines in the tabloids, to thrust the paper in front of my face and laugh about the irony that two women with such different weights should share the same name. She has even cut out a photograph of Anthea and stuck it to her computer to taunt me every time I go into her office.

'Ah, well that's a worrying trend that I wasn't aware of,' says Mike, screwing up his face in concern. 'Are we still on target?'

'For what? Fifteen thousand clients or fifteen?'

'Stop being so sarcastic. Be serious.'

'I am.'

Mike looks across at Felicity and Matthew. 'What do you say, guys? What's happening to the traffic levels to the site?'

'Glad you asked that, Mike.' Matthew clears his throat. 'Felicity and I have taken the liberty of producing a selection of bar charts to answer this question.' He stands up and walks over to a large display easel in the corner of the room, and throws back the first page. A large graph stares back at us. It looks like one of those heart monitor displays in ER, where suddenly the zig zags end and the line goes flat. Only the dramatic sound is missing. And Dr Green shouting out 'time of death . . .' as bereaved relatives realize what has happened, and fall to the floor crying. 'We've taken the growth rate, pre-publicity' – he indicates a point on the graph – 'then extrapolated that growth rate across the time span.' He runs his finger up and down, tracing the zig zags, and moves along the bottom axis. 'Here' – he points to the horizontal part – 'follows the publicity.' Exactly. The part without a heartbeat.

I look around the table triumphantly, but Felicity takes over.

'Of course, while that base line might look disappointing, I've altered the differential coefficient to five in this chart.' She flips over a page. Eh? She's now talking gobbledegook. Gobbledegook that I invented. What is it with Abacus Ventures? Did they have to believe everything I originally said? And do they have to keep using it against me? 'And introduced a stochastic shock variable to take account the initial adverse reaction to Anthea's appearances.' She smiles nervously at her. The line suddenly shoots upwards to the top right hand corner of the page. 'We'll soon be back on track. So nothing to worry about, Mike, I'd say.'

Nothing to worry about? I look around the table at the others, who are all nodding sagely like they just understand what they've just been told. Talk about the Emperor's new clothes. I think of a question.

'And why have you altered the differential coefficient, Felicity?'

'Well,' she hesitates. 'It's all a bit complicated to explain.' Try me. Go on. Bluff a bluffer. 'But in essence it's to do with the knickers sales.'

'Eh?'

'Yes, there is probably more traffic now to the site for the extra items on offer, not just the chat room. I think knickers, bras, and pantyhose will push this site onto another level.'

'Well, if that's the case,' I snap, 'I have another point to make about Anthea's appearances. Those sales are being driven by word of mouth still, and Mario's sandwich bags. Anthea has never mentioned Undetectable Undergarments in any of her public appearances. The company is understandably irritated at that. I want to see her talking about the underwear.'

'Do you?' retorts Anthea, putting down her nail file and looking at me. 'And what item do you think I'm wearing now?'

'I don't know.' But I do. The matchstick woman in front of me doesn't need Undetectable Undergarments. She has probably never had a problem with a breast that won't stay within its cup. Or a belly that won't stay flat.

'Boys,' she simpers at Giles, Matthew and Mike. 'Would it surprise you to know that I'm not wearing any underwear at the moment.' A large bead of sweat drips down Giles' massive nose. 'Nothing,' she whispers, pausing between each word, 'at all.'

'Oh for God's sake, Anthea,' I bark, 'we all know you're beautiful. But if you're meant to be me you have to endorse these products.'

'You want me to lie? To your precious clients? To those poor little fat people out there?'

'I want you to endorse the products,' I repeat. 'As if you were me. That is your job, isn't it? To act as Orla Kennedy?'

Giles looks flustered. 'Well, now, I'm sure we can do something about that. Can't we, Anthea?' She shrugs. 'If it's important to Light As A Feather, then it's important to us. Isn't it, Anthea?' She shrugs for a second time before standing up.

'Giles, can I go? I've got lunch at San Lorenzo with Naomi at one. You know how I just lurve all this financial wizard stuff, but pretty please' – she pouts at him – 'let little Anthea leave. She'll put her thinking cap on about how to promote those *knickers*.' The final word is said with a sneer. Giles nods at Anthea, graciously allowing her to leave to eat four lettuce leaves and a bottle of designer water in Knightsbridge. Life in the fast track, huh? She puts both hands to her lips, and throws a kiss out to all the men in the room. 'Ciao, babies,' she says as she closes the door behind her.

SLIMMING TIP THIRTY-TWO

Always read the labels

Amazing. Two whole weeks and Anthea hasn't done anything to upset me. Her public appearances have been the very model of decorum and understatement. She has seemed genuinely understanding of the trials and tribulations of slimmers, and she is even managing to produce a small tear at the corner of one of her sapphire blue eyes when a caller to a Sunday morning programme tells of her great distress at her size. Watching it from the comfort of my lounge, curled up in my armchair, in pyjamas and towelling dressing gown, eating a bowl of Frosties and sipping a milky coffee, even I'm impressed by how great *I* look. And just thrilled that Anthea remembered to wear the waterproof mascara. One does have standards, after all. Especially if one is sobbing on national television.

'I must be the only person that actually loses weight on the small screen,' I say to Finn, who's busy checking the site. He smiles distractedly and returns to his task. 'Only wish that she'd mention the underwear more. It is the biggest money earner, after all.' Three errant Frosties slip off my spoon and land in a puddle of (skimmed) milk on my pyjama bottoms. I scoop them back up, then kill them with my bare teeth.

'Hmm,' says Finn.

'Wow,' I continue musing, as I watch my doppelgänger smiling and preening on air, 'I think Anthea is finally getting the hang of being me.'

'Poor cow,' mutters Finn.

'Sorry?'

'Nothing,' he continues on with his task. A little blush covers his face.

'Anyway, it looks like it's finishing now,' I say, putting the bowl on the floor. The presenter Alan lifts up a pile of newspapers from the glass-topped table in front of him. 'I can't believe it. Anthea has been on screen for almost twenty minutes and she hasn't offended anybody.' Alan selects a tabloid. 'Ooh, this is the juicy bit – the morning headlines. Wonder who's sleeping with who.'

I put my bowl on the floor, curl up into the chair, and switch the volume up.

'We at Good Morning Sunday *were rather surprised to open our* Sunday Exclusive *this morning and see page five, Orla,' Alan says. Anthea is looking flustered.*

'Page five,' I mutter, leaning over to flick through the unopened broadsheets on the floor by my seat. 'Did you get *Sunday Exclusive* this morning, Finn?'

'Of course not,' he snaps looking up at me. 'It is the most indecent paper out there. Full of salacious gossip and, quite frankly, articles that make me question what sort of a society we live in. Do people really want to know whom Patsy Kensit is dating? Or the secret of multiple orgasms?'

Yes. Yes. Oh God. Yes.

Yes. Yes. Oh God. Yes.

Yes. Yes. Oh God. Yes.

'Have you anything to say about this article, Orla?'

Anthea is shifting uneasily in her chair. A little bead of perspiration is daring to gather over her brow. She swipes at it, irritably. 'I felt it was my duty to tell the truth,' she says.

Truth?

I look at the screen in horror. Don't say that Anthea has revealed to a national newspaper that she is not really Orla Kennedy.

'Finn,' I call. 'Come over here. I think she's spilled the beans about her identity. Shit. What am I going to do?'

'Calm down, Orla,' says Finn, glancing at the screen as he walks towards me. 'If that was the case, then why is the presenter still calling her Orla?'

'Good point.' I look at him in surprise.

'But will your clients not be shocked by the truth?' the presenter asks her.

'Clients. So it does involve Light As A Feather. I knew this was too good to last. What the bloody hell has she done?' I grab Finn's hand for support.

'I think they have a right to know,' Anthea says defensively. A second bead of perspiration gathers on her forehead, and she starts to bite on her bottom lip. A little slither of scarlet lipstick stains the edge of one of her front teeth.

'To know what?' I scream at the screen.

'Will they not feel cheated?'
'I can't see why. There have been no complaints about them; instead there have been many letters of thanks.'
'But you're saying they're not for you,' prompts Alan.

'What aren't for you?' I scream again. 'Finn, run out *now* and get *Sunday Exclusive*. I can't take much more than this.' Obediently he gets up and leaves the room, before returning seconds later with his hand out for money.

'That's right.' Anthea wriggles a little more in her chair.
'In fact, this article says that you've never ever worn Undetectable Undergarments, that you've never needed to wear them, even though you regularly tell your clients in Light As A Feather's chat room that you find them indispensable.' Alan stabs a fat forefinger at Anthea.
'I tell people what they want to hear. If somebody's belly protrudes

beyond her knees, and she hasn't seen her trotters in months, then she really doesn't want me to tell her that mine is flat like a pancake – without Pull Your Tummy In Tightly Knickers. Does she?' Anthea snaps back.

My God. The absolute bitch. I asked her to boost the profile of Undetectable Undergarments, and this is how she goes about it. I look on in horror as Alan reprimands Anthea's sales techniques. What on earth is Justin going to say?

'Would you say that you're just as dishonest as one of those market traders who sell perfume in the proper bottles which just turns out to be coloured water?' Alan continues in a hostile tone.

'No, I would not. There is nothing wrong with the knickers. They work for fat people . . . but, as you can see, I am not fat.' Anthea stands up and thrusts her hands towards and then down her body. 'I'm slim.' She spells out the word dramatically for the two viewers who may find it hard to get her meaning. 'S. L. I. M.'

My mobile rings, and I reach out and grab it without taking my eyes off the screen. It's Justin.

'Orla?' he sounds angry.

'Yes.'

'What the hell is going on?' Very angry. Then he stops, and I hear the penny dropping despite the hundreds of miles that separate us, then one by one the cherries line up, and *bingo*. 'Peter,' he screams out, 'fetch me the brandy.'

'Calm down, Justin. Take a deep breath,' I instruct.

'But what is going on?' he shrieks. 'I don't understand this. You're sitting on live national television slagging off my products, and you're talking to me at the same time telling me to calm down. How can I calm down?' His voice continues to rise. 'I feel like I'm in an episode of the *X Files*.'

'That woman is not me,' I say quietly. Who cares about the legal agreement with Abacus Ventures now? This man will end up in an asylum unless I tell him the truth.

'But . . .' he falters, and I hear him taking a huge gulp of a drink, 'why is Alan calling her Orla Kennedy? Why is she talking about my knickers?'

'She's my double,' I say simply.

'What? Like a twin?'

'Not quite.' I take a deep breath. 'She's my body double.'

'Your what?'

'Body double. You know, somebody who pretends they're somebody else.'

'Schizophrenics?' Justin snaps. He's angry, but I can't say that I blame him. 'What on earth do you need a double for? Don't you like starring on national television?'

'Abacus Ventures, the company that lent me the money to buy your knickers and develop the site, decided that I wasn't suitable as a spokesman for Light As A Feather. They wanted somebody else because I'm not exactly skinny.'

A snort of derision comes down the phone.

The presenter is holding a pair of Hold Your Tummy in Tightly Knickers and has stretched them as far as they can go, quizzing Anthea on what is wrong with them. They're a gingham pink, with lace edging the waistband. I've always thought they were quite pretty – for big knickers. Asking her why she won't wear them. She slowly stands up and snatches the stretched pair from him, holding them up against her stomach. The knickers are at least eight inches wider than her waist. She begins to extol the virtues of g-strings.

It doesn't bear thinking about. With her bony little butt? It probably cuts through her walnut-sized buttocks like a cheese slicer.

'If you only knew how sick I feel at this moment,' I admit.

'How sick you feel? Those are my products she's slagging off. And anyway, I don't understand. It's a website for larger ladies. Why on earth can't a larger lady front it?'

Good point. But not one I cared to bring up when half a million pounds was at stake. I am such a doormat. I knew that Giles Heppelthwaite-Jones was giving the wrong advice, but once again I couldn't stand up to him. Obviously I tried at our last meeting, when I demanded that Anthea endorse the products, and act like me, but, by then, it was too late. She was already being associated with Light As A Feather. So now everything she cares to say or do damages my company.

I should have been firm with Giles and Mike Littlechild at the start. Insist that it was *my* company and that I promoted it. It's not as if I'm ugly or have an unusual feature on my face, like a massive mole with unsightly hairs, or a big protuberance that looks like another nose is trying to break through. I'm just fairly ordinary. Don't turn heads. Don't turn stomachs. So what if once I was three stone overweight? I'm not any more. My diet is succeeding. Obviously I haven't hit target yet, and I'm not Kate Moss, but I don't think I ever will be. And in truth I wouldn't want to be. Staying that slim requires such discipline; nights out would comprise crudités and fizzy water.

'Apparently people prefer to see images of slim women,' I admit. 'You never see an oversized lady parading down the catwalk, do you? And you don't promote Alcoholics Anonymous with a large bottle of gin.' I spout out Giles's winning line.

'No,' he snaps, 'and it's a crying shame. I am fed up dealing with the sizeist fascists that determine what is and what isn't attractive. Fed up. I deal in products for larger women. Real women. Who have mortgages. Broken marriages. Too little money. Bawling children. Varicose veins. Thrush. Why can't a real woman advertise for them? Not some walking, talking drinking straw.'

'I can't see what I can do,' I admit. Humiliated. 'She is meant to be me.' I pause, before adding firmly, 'I will have strong words with her.'

'Strong words?' snarls Justin. 'You'll have to have more than strong words or I'm going to cancel our agreement. I will not supply you with any more products. I'm giving you five days to sort out this mess. Five.' He slams down the phone.

I look over at the television screen. The credits are rolling up, superimposed on a shot of Anthea and Alan chuckling like old buddies over some article in one of the newspapers strewn across the coffee table in front of them. It's not fair. She's able to laugh. Free from any responsibility. To toss back her hair coquettishly while I'm close to pulling mine out. What stunt can I think of within three days to improve this mess?

My phone rings again. The number flashes up. Liz at home. I answer.

'I suppose you just saw the television programme,' I say, without stopping to greet her.

'I did.'

'What did you think?'

'It could be worse,' she says quietly.

'How? How could it be worse?'

'I take it you haven't seen the newspaper?'

'I sent Finn out to get it ages ago. Where can he be?'

'Hiding?'

'Eh?'

'I don't know how to tell you this, Orla.'

'What? You're really freaking me out.' My heart starts racing. 'Just say it. What?'

'Orla Kennedy who is not really Orla Kennedy, but who everybody out there thinks is Orla Kennedy.'

'*Yes.*'

'Orla Kennedy is topless.'

SLIMMING TIP THIRTY-THREE

Read a newspaper instead of eating Sunday lunch

Four copies of the *Sunday Exclusive* are spread out on my living room floor. Four of us are crouched down staring carefully at the article and wondering how in the hell we can sort out this catastrophe. I stare at my copy. Anthea looks stunning, pert bosoms with dark pink nipples sticking directly out rather than swinging from pendulous breasts, heading straight down to the floor. I settle myself on my haunches.

'I can't see a way out. There is no way that this situation can get any better,' I eventually say. 'What's Justin going to say when he sees the newspaper?' I shake my head in abject misery.

Patti looks over me, sensing my depression. She rushed over immediately after seeing Anthea and Alan, grabbing a large box of Belgian chocolates and a couple of bottles of champagne. Her idea of comfort food. The chocolates are placed in the middle of the floor, within arm's length. The first tier has disappeared, and there are big gaps in the second level. Little balls of silver foil are strewn across the floor. The champagne is cooling in the fridge, but I doubt that we'll open them. There is no cause for celebration. Liz's offering of vodka and cranberry juice is rather more appropriate.

'Have a chocolate,' Patti proffers, pushing the box even closer to my hand. 'And look on the bright side, Orla. Three million people think those belong to you.' She jerks her thumb at the picture before her.

'And they are magnificent,' mutters Finn dreamily.

'Aren't lustful thoughts against your religion?' Patti says, as she gathers her newspaper together and folds it up. Two little circles of red burn brightly on her cheeks.

'I wasn't being lustful,' insists Finn. 'I was being appreciative. There's a difference.'

'And so do all those men who go to lap-dancing clubs,' interrupts Liz. 'They're just being appreciative.'

'I don't know,' snaps Finn. 'I've never been to one. Look, I was just appreciating the human form.'

'Yeah, right.' I laugh. 'Men,' I say dramatically to the others. Liz raises her eyes to heaven, but Patti just keeps folding her newspaper. She seems a bit tense. I am just going to ask if she's all right when the phone rings. I grab it.

'What can I say, Orla?' Mike Littlechild sounds awkward and embarrassed. He has finally returned my eight phone calls.

'Sorry would be a good start,' I say.

'Sorry.' He says it quietly. I can sense his shame.

'And then, how about, "it seems you were right",' I persist. Sod his shame. Can he imagine my humiliation? Has he any idea? I don't think so. He's a man. To think when I first met him I actually thought he was cute. Married, but cute.

'But Giles said—' he protests.

'I don't care what bloody Giles said. Why did you ever listen to him?'

'He's a top public relations consultant. Someone told me he was the best.'

'Who? Who told you?'

There's a slight pause as Mike places his hand over the mouthpiece, and mutters something to somebody in the room with him. Bloody cheek. He's ruining my company and he doesn't even have the manners to give me his full attention.

'Mike,' I bark. 'Who told you that Giles was the best?'

'I can't remember,' he finally says. Sheepish.

'You can't remember? You took a recommendation and allowed somebody to come in and tell you how to run a company that you were investing in. Didn't Light As A Feather deserve a bit more attention than that?'

'I—'

'You bankers are all the same. You think you know it all,' I continue. 'Yet when it comes down to it, you take the recommendation of a person who, in turn, was recommended to you by someone you can't remember. Was it somebody you met in the pub? Did he try to sell you a car radio too? Or perhaps a Rolex watch?' Liz and Patti try to stifle giggles. Finn looks at me open-mouthed. I suppose that expressions of outrage are against his religion. Well, he can chant later to get rid of the bad karma. See if I care.

'Orla, please.'

'What do you mean "please"? All along I said I didn't like the idea that somebody as cold and unfeeling as Anthea was the mouthpiece of my company. And let's not even discuss how I felt knowing that I wasn't good enough to front the business I set up.'

'Nobody was trying to hurt your feelings,' protests Mike. 'This was a business deal. We were just trying to do what was best for Light As A Feather.'

'And so you have.' My tone is cold and determined. 'In five days, unless we can come up with some way to resolve this mess, Undetectable Undergarments are cancelling our order. Our biggest money-spinner with profit margins as wide as the knicker legs they supply will stop turning. And let's not even think of how many clients will cancel their subscriptions this week.'

'Maybe Giles—' he stutters.

'Don't even go there,' I snap. 'Did you not know that I was in public relations too?'

'You didn't say,' Mike says defensively.

'No, maybe I didn't,' I admit, trying to remember our earlier meetings when I'd been so desperate that nobody at Browns Black found out about my involvement with the site. It all seems so pathetic now. Would I really have cared if I'd lost my job? 'So perhaps this is ultimately my fault because I wasn't firm enough, but I'm damned if you're going to stop what I'm doing. I *have* helped people. Overweight people too ashamed at their size to leave their houses. People who worry that their husbands will leave them because they have put on weight. Who cry every night when he's late home from work. Did you know about any of that?'

'No,' acknowledges a penitent Mike.

'Did you know of the woman who lost two stone and found that she could walk up a flight of stairs for the first time in years?'

'No.'

'So what sort of research did you do into my site, Mike? Before you accepted all my blatantly inflated business projections and offered to lend Light As A Feather money?'

'I asked somebody I know about it,' Mike protests.

'Oh yes, your wife,' I snort. 'You said she thought I was very understanding to the views of fat people.'

'Not just my wife,' he adds. 'I asked my brother-in-law.'

'Great. The whole family. I'm glad you were so thorough,' I say incredulously. 'No wonder the dotcom miracle boomed with people like you throwing money at it. Well, let me tell you that Light As A Feather is a sound business proposition and I will save it. Me. Not you, and definitely not Giles.'

'Now hold on a minute, Orla. Abacus Ventures is poised to invest a lot of money in this. I must insist that you keep us informed about your intentions. Your half a million pounds in funding will be extended very shortly. If you check your contract, you will see that we have the right—'

'We've done the old contract line beforehand, haven't we? It worked then, but it won't work now. *I* will sort out this site, and now, if you will excuse me, I am about to have a discussion with my consultants about the best way forward. I will inform you when I have made a decision as to how. *I* will make your investment work because your advice has proved about as useful as a . . . as a hairdryer for a bald man.' I slam down the phone.

'Hairdryer for a bald man?' Patti snorts, almost choking on her chocolate. 'Is that the best you could do?'

'I was under pressure,' I say indignantly.' I was trying to be dramatic.'

'You were great, sis.' Finn looks at me proudly.

'Thanks.' I wink at him.

'Perhaps now we can open the champagne,' asks Patti hopefully.

'Go on then.' I concede defeat. 'And then when you've done that we all have to put our thinking caps on.' I turn to my brother. 'Finn, could you just check the reactions on the site, while I just throw this rubbish out.' I begin to gather the newspapers up. 'Unless of course you want to keep yours, Finn? Purely for appreciation purposes.'

'No, that's fine,' he mumbles.

One hour later and one bottle later, the four of us are still no closer to resolving the problem. My head is spinning. Mike Littlechild has rung back to say that he has dispensed with Giles Heppelthwaite-Jones's service. Anthea has not been seen since her television appearance this morning, and Giles is concerned. He has already received three phone calls from the tabloids requesting her. Mike has told him that if Anthea obliges then she will be sued for breach of contract. Abacus Ventures, he tells Giles, is also considering legal action over this morning's débâcle. Giles, Mike tells me, sounded worried. I hang up feeling pleased. And vindicated.

'I really don't like to admit this,' Liz finally says, 'but I can't see a way out. The damage has been done. Five days might as well be five hours. How many complaints did you say there were on the site, Finn?'

'Twenty-two,' he admits awkwardly. 'A few said they had forgiven you after your last television appearance, thinking it was nerves, but now they feel totally betrayed.'

'What can we do?' I say, rubbing my tired eyes.

'Open another bottle,' suggests Patti helpfully. 'I've just got to make a quick phone call.' She moves into the kitchen to fetch the champagne and I can hear her muttering into her mobile. Lucky her. She's probably organizing a date with a dashing journalist for later on this evening, working out an excuse to get out of my flat and make a dash to freedom. A few minutes later Finn, who is obviously getting rather thirsty, walks into the kitchen to hurry her along. They reappear with four glasses and the much needed champagne, minutes before the phone rings again. I answer it anxiously. My number is in the phone book and an irrational fear has just gripped me. I could get stalkers. Men who think that body in the paper is mine.

'Orla?' It's my mother. My heart sinks. I think I'd prefer the stalkers.

'Mum—' I prepare to make my excuses.

'Now, before you say anything, I'm just telling you that Father Andrew is putting a little message into the parish newsletter next week, explaining to everybody that my daughter did not flaunt her breasts in a national newspaper. As if a Kennedy would ever do such a thing. The very idea.'

'But what about the confidentiality clause?' I protest, but it's no good. I can tell that she is firm about this.

'Darling, I had to do something. Your father was looking at the paper in a state of shock. The poor man couldn't work out which side of the family that strumpet got them from. Anyway Marcella soon put him straight. She got them from Harley Street, that's what Marcella said. Her friend Oonagh, you remember her, nice woman, always wore the little hats, I think she had a bad perm one time, anyway she had hers' – my mother drops her voice – 'done. Apparently the Good Lord gave her a set that were different sizes, and it was costing her a fortune in cotton wool. She went to a little man in Harley Street. Nice chap. Jewish. Think she said his name was Finkelstein. Or was it Cohen? No, it was Smith. That's right, isn't it, Marcella? Anyway he did Oonagh's, and she told Marcella that she'd recognize his handiwork anywhere. And when we got out a magnifying glass – no dear, we did send your father down to The Yacht first – we could see tiny little scars.'

'Really?' I think I'm keeping up. But I'm getting a headache.

'Father Anthony is also going to make an announcement at the end of evening mass today. Just to let people know that my

233

daughter hasn't gone off the rails. 'Tis a terrible burden, you know, having two children who live in London. You hear such things about the place,' she sighs, but then quickly pulls herself together. 'The nuns were so upset. They couldn't believe anybody could complain about the Pull Your Tummies In Tightly Knickers. They've revolutionized the convent. They can fit another two nuns down each side of their dinner table now. Sister Agnes is delighted. She used to have to eat in the kitchen. Actually I think they're about to put in a large order for the Bounce Free Booby Bras after I told them that they hold the breasts back. They're looking to get another few pews into the convent chapel, you see.'

'But Mum, I think Anthea—'

'Who?'

'The strumpet. I think she's ruined everything. Undetectable Undergarments are threatening to cut off supplies.' I tell her about my earlier phone call with Justin. 'He's given me five days to sort out everything. To make amends.'

'Plenty of time. Imagine. It took the Good Lord six days to create the universe. Think what you could do in almost the same stretch. Now I better go, dear. Marcella and I have to be somewhere at four. Is Finn OK?'

'He's fine.'

'Is he eating?'

I look across at my brother stuffing a chocolate into his mouth. 'Yes.'

'And you're making sure that he brushes his teeth every night? After he says his prayers.'

'Mum, he's a grown up boy,' I interrupt, 'and I'm his sister, not his keeper.'

'You women these days. So liberated. When I was a young woman, we loved looking after our menfolk. We saw it as our duty.' She lets out another big sigh. 'Society today. I blame the telly. Never see any of the girls in soap operas putting a meal on the table for their husbands, do you? They're always eating in cafés or the pub. How can they afford it? That's what I want to know. They never seem to have any money.'

'Mum,' I prompt gently, 'it's half-past three. You've got to be somewhere at four, you said.'

'Oh yes.' She gathers herself together. 'Speak to you soon, and don't worry. I'm sure things will turn out fine.'

SLIMMING TIP THIRTY-FOUR

*Sometimes you just need to resign yourself
to the situation*

I *hate* Monday morning. Every Monday I wake up feeling
lethargic and unrested. My eyelids always somehow feel heavier, as if I'm just about to come down with a heavy head cold.
And it doesn't matter how early I go to bed on the Sunday, it's
just *never* early enough. I'm no lover of the European Union,
but if it wanted to win me around then I would suggest stop
meddling in the curvature of cucumbers and instead introduce
Monday Morning Blues legislation. So when I wake up on a
Monday morning and need an extra hour or two in bed, then it
would be fine. All I would need to do is to ring up the
personnel department and claim an EU lie-in.

But this morning it feels different. I leap out of bed the
moment the alarm clock rings out and dash around getting
ready. I'm filled with energy and enthusiasm for life because
last night I made a momentous decision. Today I, Orla
Kennedy, spinster of Goswell Road, am going to resign. I am
going to leave Browns Black and never return.

It came to me last night when I was lying in bed, listening to
the sound of Finn's gentle snores from the living room. My
mind was turning over the events of the previous week,
analysing them, debating them, and suddenly I realized that
the only way forward was for me to resign. It was pointless
waiting until the company was fully up and running because,
the way things were going, it might never be. If I delayed any
more Light As A Feather might actually fold. I'll draw a salary
from the funding provided by Abacus Ventures, and spearhead

the website's recovery. The only trouble is that I'm just not quite sure how I can pull it off. Anthea's fired, no question about that, but how do I suddenly announce that somebody with exactly the same name is replacing her? The excuse that we wanted to save on business cards seems rather fatuous.

We failed to come up with any solutions yesterday. Liz finally went around six, hugging me fiercely as she left and muttering that, like Mum, she was sure it would all work out fine. These things were sent to try us and all that. Patti left about twenty minutes later. Finn walked out with her on his way to fetch some items from the local Open All Hours supermarket, which really opens at seven and closes twelve hours later. Our supply of Mario meals has run out, and the fridge is well and truly empty. Apart from a bottle of vodka, my mascara, and three pots of bio-yoghurt, with a sell-by date that I can't even find on this year's calendar. I leave them there now just in case I ever want to lose weight really fast. For a date or some other such unlikely event.

Patti isn't at her desk when I arrive, although her jacket is hung over the back of her chair. I vaguely remember her saying yesterday that she had to host some journalist breakfast morning. A pile of articles about Browns Black in the weekend press are stacked on her desk. She must have been in really early this morning, I think, feeling rather proud of her. But I know she's disillusioned with Tabitha's ineptitude and, although she wouldn't say anything to me, I expect she's already having job interviews. It's a pity really, because she'd be a great replacement for Tabitha if the witch ever resigned.

I can see through the glass walls of her office that Tabitha is on the phone, so I flick through the press cuttings while waiting for her to hang up so that I can hand over my resignation letter. There is one mention of Sven. A property deal in Slovakia. Funny. I thought that was completed months ago. I remember him nagging me to get coverage about it ages ago. In fact, if my memory is working correctly – and I couldn't be at all sure that it is because I am rather nervous at this precise moment – I think that's the deal that he expected great coverage for. When he went out and bought loads of new ties just in case a photograph was required. I read the article carefully, in case there's something new in it. Ah. That'll be it. The deal is now one hundred million dollars. Wow. It was only ten million to start with. Sven must be doing something right. For once. I read the details of the financing, but haven't got a clue what it all means. Patti must have handled this one. It looks really good.

Shit. I pick up three articles in quick succession, which all relate to the long standing rumours that Browns Black has a black hole somewhere. A black hole that is sucking away the bank's money. What on earth has prompted these rumours to start again? Tabitha is quoted in each article, refusing to comment on the allegations. Challenging the journalists to put up or shut up. I sigh. Her combative tone will just set them all off trying to prove the rumours. I read the articles again. How can this bank run a serious press office when two of the three members don't even know what the rumours are? Patti would have said something to me if Tabitha had told her about these stories, and the witch definitely didn't say anything to me. I seethe with indignation about being kept out of the loop before remembering that it doesn't matter any more. In less than an hour I will be free.

I glance across at Tabitha. She is no longer on the phone, but is sitting back in her ergonomic chair, tapping a pencil on her teeth as if deep in thought. I take a deep breath. Time to give her something to think about.

I knock on the door.

'What?' she demands, pen in mid-flight. 'Can't you see I'm busy?' She points at a pile of papers on her desk, which give the illusion of a hectic office but which I know are props. Arranged every Friday lunchtime before she leaves for the weekend.

'I wanted to have a private word,' I say firmly.

She looks at me in horror. Her scarlet red lips in a moue.

'You're not going to try any of that female bonding rubbish, are you? I know there was a memo that came around last week discussing mentoring for junior staff, but I really am not interested.' She waves her hand at me to indicate I should leave the office. 'Not interested.' She turns her attention to a small document on her desk, leaving me facing the top of her immaculately coiffured head, adding, 'And it is way too soon to try asking about this year's bonus or assessment. Way too soon.'

Ah, what the hell. I'm resigning.

'Tabitha, if I was looking for a mentor then I can assure you – without a shadow of a doubt – that I would not even have you in my top hundred potential candidates.'

'Well, really' – she looks up at me indignantly – 'there's no reason to be offensive.'

'No, Tabitha,' I say slowly, 'there is no reason to be offensive, and yet that has never prevented you. I am tired of your snide comments. Your bitchiness. The way you constantly assess my clothes with a sneer on your face. Tired of your laziness, and your complete willingness to claim responsibility for all the work that Patti and I produce. And finally I'm tired of you.'

Way to go, Orla.

I take a deep breath, my heart racing with the adrenalin rush from finally breaking free. The object of my detestations is going red. From my standing position six foot from her desk, I can almost feel the heat gently rising within her. Like a pressure cooker coming to the boil. A wave of panic passes quickly over me, then I suddenly feel calm and serene. Nothing she says matters any more.

'How dare you?' she finally explodes as she scrambles to her feet, then she clenches her fists, bangs them face down onto her desk, and leans on them as she confronts me. 'How dare you march into my office and say such dreadful things? Who the hell do you think you are?'

'I'm the employee that is resigning,' I say quietly.

'You can't resign,' she replies sharply, shaking a scarlet talon at me.

'I just did.'

'Well, you can't because I'm going to fire you.'

'On what grounds?' I look at her, bemused.

She hesitates for one fleeting second then suddenly shouts, 'Insubordination.'

'I think you'll find, Tabitha, that to do so without any official warnings would contravene employment laws.'

'Don't give me employment laws,' she screams, as a bead of perspiration gathers on her forehead. 'I can't believe your ingratitude. I have taught you everything you know. How *dare* you treat me like this! I am going to call security and get you escorted off the premises.'

'That is your prerogative,' I say calmly. 'The work is all up to date. Patti has sorted through all the weekend cuttings and written a report on the press coverage. It is on her desk. I should mention that several papers have written about black holes . . .'

Tabitha shrieks, 'Why the hell can't they let that story drop?' I might be mistaken but, for a moment, I swear that a look of panic brushes over her face. Then, as quickly as it arrived, it disappears. She turns back to her phone and starts to dial. 'I want you out of this building within ten minutes. Please leave your security cards, company credit card, mobile telephone, pager.' Tabitha points at her desk. 'Now get out of my office, you ungrateful cow. Go and sign on, because nobody else would employ you.'

'Actually I am going to be self-employed.' I advance towards her desk. She looks uneasy. 'I am actually going to take control of my very own company. You may have heard of it – Light As A Feather.' I rip the newspaper cut-out of Anthea from her screen. 'She was *just* my stand in, but I'm the one who is going to earn millions.'

'I knew it,' she sneers triumphantly. 'I knew anybody called Orla Kennedy had to be fat. It's in their genes; I guessed she was an impostor.'

'Do you know, Tabitha, a couple of months ago those comments would have upset me, but today I'm almost down

240

to size twelve for the first time in ten years, and I feel bloody marvellous. Nothing you can say can wound me.'

'Get out!' she shrieks.

'I'm going,' I shrug. 'Say goodbye to your lover boy Sven for me.' Tabitha looks at me in horror. 'I gave his wife your number. Ciao.'

Ten minutes later I'm walking through reception with Bert, the security guard, who has one wooden leg and a pet tarantula that he keeps in a cage in his kitchen. Not that I've ever visited his house or his kitchen, but he told me one time when we were both doing fire drill duty. He is carrying a black bin liner, into which we unceremoniously dumped the contents of my desk drawers. I rediscovered one pair of shoes and two pairs of sunglasses that I thought I'd lost, plus eight toothbrushes that I bought in panic before different evening events when I was sure that the garlic that I'd eaten at lunch would overpower the other guests.

'I'm really sorry, Orla,' he says, as we walk out through the security turnstiles and I suffer the ignominy of colleagues avoiding eye contact as I walk past with my escort, 'but you know when that witch orders you to do something, then you do it.'

'Hey, Bert, no sweat,' I reply. 'Actually it's quite fun really. I always wondered what it was like to be "escorted off the premises".'

'Normally, I'd make them carry their own bags,' he grins, 'but you're special.'

We get to the main glass entrance just as Patti runs up the steps into the bank. She's holding a tabloid newspaper in her hands and is out of breath. Two steps behind her, Tony Younger is walking into the building.

'Orla,' she says as she reaches me.

Bert hands over my bag, gives my arm a little squeeze and my cheek a quick peck. 'Good luck, God bless,' he whispers before walking back inside.

'Orla, what's happened?' says Patti. Tony nods as he walks past, a look of confusion on his face at the black bag by my feet.

For one fleeting moment, I think he's about to stop and say something, but he doesn't. I feel a strange mix of disappointment and relief.

'I've resigned. I'm off to run Light As A Feather full-time, try to salvage some of the wreckage. Finn rang this morning. We've had eight calls asking about our returns policy.'

'What did Finn say?' she asks.

'That all items returned must be thoroughly washed and perfumed with a fabric conditioner.'

'Not about the returns policy,' Patti says sharply. 'Did he say anything else?'

'No.' I start in surprise at her tone.

'And did you have any more ideas after I'd left last night?' asks Patti, 'apart from resigning?'

'Nothing,' I admit.

'Well, it's just as well that somebody has,' she suddenly beams, thrusting the tabloid newspaper into my hands. 'Page nineteen. I think you should take a look.' I look at her in horror, my heart sinking at the thought of another bout of Anthea exposure, but she just waves me on.

I flick through the pages, my fingers unable to move quickly enough, until I reach page nineteen. I look down at the photograph in disbelief. Hot tears sting my eyes. A large one plops onto the newspaper and drips down the page.

'Orla.' Patti's voice is concerned. 'What do you think?' She looks at me carefully, trying to judge my reaction. 'It was an idea that came to me yesterday morning when Finn rang me from a phone box asking had I seen the papers. He was so worried about what your reaction would be. We spent ages trying to think of something to do and then I thought of this. That call I made from your kitchen yesterday was to check it was all going according to plan. She organized it all. She was desperate to help. Say something please. What do you think?' Patti covers her hands over mine, which are still glued to the newspaper, and squeezes.

'I think she's amazing,' I finally say, as I stare down at a large black and white photograph of my mother and Marcella

in their bras and knickers, under a two-inch thick headline declaring WHY UNDETECTABLE UNDERGARMENTS WORK FOR
US.

Listen to mother – just once

There are three empty boxes lying by my desk when I return home. Finn has marked them up in black marker pen. Returns: Clean. Returns: Unworn. Returns: They're having a laugh. He is nowhere to be seen. I rack my brains, but I can't remember him telling me that he was going out this morning. Then again, I'm only his sister. Not his mother. I fall into one of my armchairs and, for the fifth time since Patti shoved it into my hands, re-examine the newspaper article about my mother and Marcella. It reads like poetry, the two of them singing the praises of Pull Your Tummy In Tightly Knickers. Patti explained how she had rung my mother and asked her if she was willing to show her support for her only daughter, had even used emotional black-mail about how I would never settle down and have children if I wasn't happy with my life, and how I definitely *wasn't* happy after Anthea's latest appearance. Apparently it only took one quick phone call to the Dublin office of an English tabloid, desperate for stories to fill their pages, a second call to Father Andrew to check they weren't breaching any religious rulings on showing sixty-year-old thighs, and at four o'clock yesterday afternoon they were sitting in the studios getting made up in preparation for their pictures. The only stipulation was that they didn't pose topless. The tabloid insisted.

I don't think I'll ever be able to thank my mother for this. All the times that I've hurt her over the years with harsh com-ments or by rebelling against her interference in my life, but as soon as I'm in trouble she's there for me. Without hesitation. I suppose that's what they mean by unconditional love. I just hope that one day I'll experience it, and reward my mother for her unstinting love with a grandchild.

Anyway I can't spend time analysing my relationship with my mother; I've got to save my knickers order. Five days to sort out the mess that Anthea and Giles have created. My mother's efforts will help, but I need something really dramatic to save the day. My heart sinks as I realize that I still don't know what.

It doesn't hurt, I think, to do a little housekeeping on the website. I must have many very angry clients who don't know whether to trust me or despise me, so I log on and write a message.

Dear All

You may have seen some of the recent press coverage regarding Light As A Feather. I want to apologize for the comments attributed to myself, for any hurt or distress they may have caused. I am afraid that, on the advice of my public relations executive, I allowed my place in all advertising to be taken by a model. Her behaviour has been contemptible.

I want to assure you all that I empathize at every step along the way to losing weight. I am struggling on the journey too, but the support that I have enjoyed from the chat room discussions and individual e-mail relationships have helped me pass through many milestones. I have now lost almost eighteen pounds and I'm thrilled. I am starting to walk like a slim person now, at speed and with ease.

I know that many of you have enjoyed similar success and I urge you not to give up now. Not to allow the catty comments of an out-of-work model to put you off because then she will have won.

I think that our mutual success deserves some reward, and that is why I am holding a celebratory party for all clients who can make it. It will take place in Corney & Barrow in Moorgate on Friday week. Starting at seven. I would be delighted to see you all taking a night off from the diet.

Keep the faith

Orla

PS I do wear Undetectable Undergarments and I think they're wonderful.

PPS I am afraid that I won't be able to monitor the chat room sessions this week; the pressures of building this business are too great. Apologies and good luck.

I am just about to log off when a little envelope pops up in the corner of my screen. It's an e-mail from Amy.

To   Orla@Lightasafeather.co.uk
From Amy@Hotmail.com
I was touched by your honesty. Perhaps such a story deserves a larger audience?
I'm keeping the faith and will see you at the party.
A x

I read the e-mail carefully a few times, an idea starting to form at the back of my mind. A larger audience? Perhaps Amy has got something there . . .

Three days later and I'm sitting on a comfortable sofa in the middle of a television set. It is nine in the morning, and I've been here three hours. Explaining my story. Rehearsing my answers. Having breakfast of fresh fruit and yoghurt; I would have gone for a fry-up (purely for the energy), but my stomach is so filled with butterflies that I worried that I'd throw it up mid-sentence.

A make-up artist is applying last-minute powder to my nose in an effort to eradicate a resistant sheen of perspiration that settled there the moment that I took my seat under the bright studio lights. Suzy and Stephen are standing to the left of the studio, going over their lines and checking on the order of the show.

Three dabs of cover stick have hidden the persistent spot on my chin, and my eyes have been brought to life with a palette of lilac and purple eye shadows. When the artist shows me her work, I can't help feeling a dash of pride. I might not be as thin as Anthea, but the way that she's applied the make-up gives me at least the chance of matching her on the looks front. And anyway, when I ran around Oxford Street yesterday in a mad dash to buy a new outfit, I found that I didn't need a size sixteen any more. The black (because after all, it is still slimming) trouser suit that I'm wearing is a fourteen jacket, and a twelve trousers. Okay, so I might not be able to *quite* do up the top button, but with the jacket closed over them I don't think anybody has noticed.

'OK people,' shouts the producer, 'places please.' Suzy and Stephen run to their purple seats and I flick a hair off my trousers as he counts down, 'Six, five, four, three, two one' then 'action.'

Suzy begins. 'Good morning, and welcome to today's show. Coming up in twenty minutes we have Oswald in the kitchen, who is today being taught by guest chef Mario, who runs his own London delicatessen, how to make fresh ravioli and not ruin his diet.'

'And it's a diet show today,' Stephen continues. 'We have the tale of a woman who was told she was too fat to publicize her own dieting chat room.' I can feel the camera pan over to me, and I force a smile and suck in my belly as it moves up and down my body, praying that in these metric times the camera has stopped adding a stone to people. Stephen turns to me. His face one of concern as he drops his voice a level and says in a solicitous tone, 'Orla Kennedy, would you like to tell us what happened?'

'Yes, that's right, viewers,' pipes up Suzy, before I can reply, 'Orla Kennedy. Is that name familiar to you? Rings a bell? Let me refresh you with a clip of a programme we showed just over three weeks ago.'

In the distant monitor I watch a repeat showing of Anthea abusing callers. Even now I can feel Suzy bristle once again in indignation. She and Stephen turn to me when the clip ends and ask in unison. 'Is that not Orla Kennedy?'

Cue me. I explain that it isn't, how I came up with the idea of a dieting chat room to lose weight before my friend's wedding next year. I feel a twinge of concern. Liz would love to be here today, watching from the wings, but she hasn't returned any of the messages that I left to tell her of my appearance. Jason was rather vague, claiming that she was busy with wedding stuff, but I wasn't convinced. I'm worried. I really do think she may be having an affair with one of the contenders for City Hunk of the Week. It's just an uneasy feeling I've had, actually since that night we went out with those three candidates. She's been evasive and distant. I suspect she knows that I'll challenge her, demand to know if she fully understands just what she is putting in jeopardy. She knows that I'll lecture her on how lucky she is to have found a partner like Jason. Somebody who'll do anything to make her happy, even, as he told me last night, selling his Arsenal season ticket and prized football shirt signed by the team so that she can have a string quartet during her champagne reception and a honeymoon in the Maldives. And he's done it all behind her back, in secret, to make her dreams come true. Imagine that. Having somebody who cares enough to work behind the scenes to help her out. She doesn't know how lucky she is.

'And so I was persuaded by a public relations executive that fat people don't sell goods,' I continue.

'That would be Giles Heppelthwaite-Jones,' interrupts Stephen. I nod. He turns directly to the camera. 'We invited Giles Heppelthwaite-Jones to participate in this show, but he declined, citing work pressures. His company, Smiths, is involved today in a major City scandal, which those of you who have read this morning's financial press will undoubtedly have heard about.'

Oh? I look at Stephen in confusion, but before I can fully consider what he has just announced, he turns back to me.

'We also invited Anthea Heppelthwaite-Jones.' What! She's a bloody relative. I've going to make him pay. Big time. 'But she did, however, issue this statement.' He lifts a piece of paper and reads, ' "Fat people should not be on television. End of story." So Orla, how did you feel about your stand in?'

'Awful,' I admit, bringing a small tear to my eye, a trick I've practised over the past two days, 'and ashamed. Ashamed that I wasn't good enough. Ashamed that I was letting down my clients, who believed I was trying to lose weight with them, but then saw a thin woman on television acting as spokesman. They felt betrayed, and I felt terrible because the site was working for me. I have lost eighteen pounds since launch,' I say proudly.

'Congratulations.' Suzy does a mock round of applause. 'But you couldn't tell your clients, could you?'

'No. She couldn't even tell her own mother,' interrupts the woman sitting on my right hand side: my mum, who booked a flight from Dublin yesterday evening just as soon as she heard that this television appearance had been scheduled. Wouldn't hear of letting me go through the ordeal on my own. What are mothers for? she demanded. And what could I say? Only yes. Come on over. I'll even pay. And Marcella too. I mean, what do you say to two women the wrong side of sixty who have just posed in their underwear for a national tabloid to help you out? Apart from please don't do it again. 'She had signed a confidentiality agreement and my daughter was brought up to abide by the letter of the law,' she snaps indignantly.

'I'm sure she was,' soothes Suzy. 'Which rather explains your confused telephone call to the show. But tell me, you led the battle to save your daughter's company.' She holds up the tabloid photograph of my mother and Marcella posing.

My mother looks delighted. Her face glows with pleasure. 'Undetectable Underwear is, quite frankly, a miracle worker. Honestly, dear, I couldn't believe it when that thin one knocked it in print. It's amazing stuff. I can almost fit back into my wedding dress when I wear those knickers. The only trouble is that it was a short dress, and I have trouble with,' – she drops her voice into an elaborate whisper – 'the old varicose veins.'

'Was the newspaper reluctant to print the pictures?'

'Well, seeing as Marcella and I have enough up top to fill four page threes, I don't think so, my dear. And sure aren't they used to putting in pictures of old dears in their underwear? I mean, that Joan Collins, she's older than me, you know. And she's always in the papers.'

'I think,' says Stephen, adopting a serious I'm-going-to-make-a-worthy-point tone, 'that your acceptance as an older role model just emphasizes how badly Orla Kennedy was treated. We complain about the size of our models, moan that eating disorders are the disease of our teenagers and then, when an attractive,' he smiles at me, 'larger lady is available to promote her own company, she is rejected by those supposed experts who claim to know better in favour of a thin woman with absolutely no sympathy or understanding for overweight people.' He shakes his head slowly as if he's just said something deep and profound, then smiles brightly and announces that it's time for the commercials. 'But join us again after the break when we'll be talking some more to this lovely young lady' – he pats my knee – 'meeting five models showing how to wear Undetectable Undergarments, and' – he adopts a serious face – 'a Peter Wilson from Leeds, a man for whom haemorrhoids were not just a pain in the backside. Back after the break.'

Twenty minutes later and Justin joins us on the bright yellow sofa to discuss the outfits that the models are wearing. I rang him two days ago with my idea and he dashed down on the train to make his debut appearance on *Welcome To The Day*. It was, he told me on the phone, his lifetime ambition. Along with meeting Dale Winton.

Justin was not what I expected. He's whippet thin, dressed in tight leather trousers, a shiny mesh T-shirt, which clings to every muscle in his chest, and pointed lizard skin cowboy boots. His black hair is gelled back into a quiff and kohl lines the bottom lids of his startling green eyes. His companion, Peter, is the exact opposite, dressed in lumberjack shirt that hangs loosely over his sagging jeans and protruding belly. He is standing in the wings watching. I suspect that he was forty-inch waist, thirty-two inch inside leg who tested out an earlier version of Pull Your Tummy In Tightly Knickers.

'First along the catwalk, we have Marcella,' Justin announces. My mother bursts into applause, causing Marcella to wave. 'Marcella, who is, I must point out, not a trained model, is wearing a summer tea dress in a delicate pink rose design. As Marcella gives us a twirl, you can see the way the bias cut skirt swings around her hips, emphasizing the looseness of the dress. Now, I think it's just coming on your screens at home, there is a photograph of Marcella in the same dress, but without those knickers. See how the skirt clings to the extended contours of her hips?'

He looks at Suzy and Stephen who nod in agreement, a sombre expression on their faces. Suzy walks over to Marcella and pulls the skirt out, illustrating the inches that have disappeared from her hip and thighs.

'Next we have Sister Mary Claude, who is on her first trip to London, in a Bounce Free Booby Bra. See the way it emphasizes the contours of her body under her black habit.' I watch in horror as my old headmistress marches down the catwalk.

'We thought this would be a nice surprise,' hisses my mother. 'She wanted to go to the Oxfam summer sale, so this kills two birds with one stone. I told you she was a great fan.'

'And these bras have saved Sister Mary Claude hundreds of pounds, haven't they?' asks Justin. She nods. 'Because she was going to have to buy two new habits, as they were getting tight across the bust.' Another nod.' And now she can fit them quite comfortably. Would you like to pull on the garment again, Suzy?' She shakes her head in embarrassment. Suzy may be quite willing to discuss another man's haemorrhoids at length and in detail, but when it comes to tugging on a female of the cloth, even she has principles. I can see Stephen twitch, though. This might just be a fantasy of his.

Two hours later and the show – dedicated to losing weight sensibly and salvaging my reputation – is over. Stephen and Suzy are shaking my hand and congratulating me on how things have worked out. Marcella, Sister Mary Claude, and my mother are having a pot of tea made for them by Mario. Justin and Peter are getting tips from the studio's make-up artist.

I'm on a high. The show's researcher has passed on messages

from dozens of viewers, offering support for my plight and asking for details of Light As A Feather. There's a congratulatory one from Mike Littlechild at Abacus Ventures, saying the half a million pounds will be in the company's bank account tomorrow morning, and that he'll see me at the party. Tessa also rang, apologizing for having doubted me, promising to come to the party even though she has only lost ten pounds, but it has made a dramatic difference to her life. Her son is no longer getting bullied. And then there's one from Liz, asking if I have seen the newspapers.

SLIMMING TIP THIRTY-SIX

Panic

And then I recall what Stephen said earlier, about Giles Hep-pelthwaite-Jones and a financial scandal involving one of his clients. Browns Black is the only financial client he has. It couldn't involve the bank, could it? I feel a sense of dread as I rush over to Stephen, who is now accepting congratulations for 'once again a wonderful and informative show' from the producers. He flicks back his hair nonchalantly, winking at the admiring studio guests from Bournemouth's Derby & Joan clubs, and calls over to his assistant for a glass of chilled champagne.

'Stephen,' I say nervously, 'what financial scandal were you talking about? The one involving Giles. Do you know any more details?'

'Oh that,' he answers in a bored tone. 'Something about a black hole. Does that make sense?'

I nod. Slowly.

'At Browns Black.'

'Browns Black.'

'Yep, I remember now because I thought it was funny that there was a black hole at a bank called Black. Coincidence and all that.'

Funny? A black hole? It's about as funny as root canal work. What happens if it is too large and the bank's balance sheet can't take it? Oh my God. Is Patti's job safe? What about Tony Younger? He's only just joined. He's too nice a person to be caught up in a mess like this. And Patti's only really starting out.

'Have you got the newspaper?' I ask.

'Yeah, it's somewhere behind there.' Stephen gestures towards a director's chair and I rummage through a pile of crumpled newspapers. It's the front-page story on the third one down, under the headline PR AND EASTERN EUROPEAN BANKER UNDER INVESTIGATION AS BROWNS BLACK UNCOVERS MASSIVE TRADING HOLE.

I read the story. A property deal in Slovakia has turned out to be fraudulent. The deal Sven constantly hassled me about. The one that I realized last week had increased dramatically in size. It turns out the money invested in the property deal was being siphoned off by the contracting companies appointed by Browns Black and put into an offshore account in the Cayman Islands. The deal was merely a front for making money.

Sven is named in the story as the banker behind the transaction. It cites a series of convictions for fraud that he incurred in Slovakia and hints that his brother was involved with the contracting company. Tabitha is mentioned. Her affair with Sven is noted. Although she is not accused of wrongdoing, the article implies that she was aware about rumours of trading losses for some time, but had failed to mention them to her bosses. In fact, she had not even bothered to check out the truth, but instead, along with her £300-an-hour public relations adviser, Giles Heppelthwaite-Jones, had issued a firm denial. The article implies that the losses had been accelerating in recent weeks as her affair with Sven hotted up and that he had offered assurances he did not know anything about financial difficulties of any deals. The bank's new spokeswoman, Patti de Jager . . . eh? Rewind. New spokeswoman. Wow. No wonder Patti has been so elusive recently. She's been getting promoted. Patti tells the newspaper that Tabitha is accused of nothing more than naïvety, but that her inactivity may have unnecessarily cost the bank hundreds of thousands of pounds. Nonetheless, her contract has been terminated while Sven has been arrested.

I read on. Sven is quoted as describing his body as a gift from God, who most admires the qualities of honesty, integrity and humility. Haven't I read that before? I cast my mind back. Yeah. Patti and I read it in Sven's submission to City Hunk of the Week, when Liz told us she was working on a longer investigative piece. Is this it? Has it been syndicated by the magazine to a national newspaper? I check the by-line. It reads Liz Jackson and . . . Finn Kennedy?

My mobile rings as I'm dashing over to my mother to show her the article. Justin and Peter are just making their excuses; they want to take in some West End sights and hope she doesn't mind them leaving early. Sister Mary Claude and Marcella are leaving to visit the sales. They are still high from the experience of marching down a catwalk. As Sister Mary Claude says, when you become a bride of Christ, you don't really expect to have a flourishing fashion career. 'There's not too many supermodels that can do both now, is there, dear?' she asks Justin.

I answer the phone. It's Liz.

'I wondered where you'd got to,' she says, in an excited voice. 'Have you seen it? Our masterpiece that has taken several weeks of intensive investigation and collaboration?'

'I've seen it,' I admit, still in shock. 'I'm just trying to take it all in.'

'Come to Starbucks,' she instructs, 'on Moorgate in half an hour. We'll fill you in. Oh, and Orla.' She moves the handset closer to her mouth and whispers, 'I think Finn has given up on the Buddhist idea. He's been enjoying the good life of the City too much, along with the rather attractive attentions of the new press officer at Browns Black.'

My mother and I walk into Starbucks fifteen minutes later. She's recognized by our black cab driver, and I watch five pounds tick onto the clock as we sit in the cab outside our destination while she explains about how wonderful her new knickers are. Unfortunately, she tells the disappointed driver, she's not really planning to do any more glamour modelling. If truth be told, she and Marcella had found it all rather boring and a bit chilly.

Finn and Liz are drinking cappuccinos, notebooks spread out

in front of them as they try to compile a follow-up story. Finn is wearing his navy blue, one hundred per cent wool suit. His date suit. I watch my mother hug her long-lost son and wait until her tears dry up.

'Now,' I say, as Liz places two more cappuccinos on the table, 'does somebody mind telling me what is going on?'

'It's all down to Finn, actually,' starts Liz. My brother has the grace to look embarrassed. 'He's got to know many of the Light As A Feather clients while he's been monitoring the system, and in particular Cecilia.'

'Not like that,' Finn says hastily, as he sees our mother's eyes lighting up with the hope of future grandchildren. 'She's married.'

'Precisely,' continues Liz. 'To an Eastern European banker, who was cheating on her with another woman, but who had been silly enough to let slip a few secrets about his business.'

'Sven!' I cry.

'The one and only, and Cecilia was a woman scorned and all that,' smiles Liz. 'Anyway Finn contacted me, and the rest, as they say, is history. We've spent so many evenings wining and dining people that we thought might be able to help us.'

'But,' I stammer, 'I thought you were having an affair.'

Liz snorts in surprise. 'Actually Jason was concerned you might be wondering that. He says that you've sounded incredibly consoling whenever he tells you I'm out.' I blush. 'But we couldn't tell you. Don't forget that until Monday you were the person really running Browns Black's press office. It would have been too much of a conflict of interest. You'd have felt obliged to tell the senior management, there'd have been a cover-up and we'd have lost our scoop.'

'But what about the engagement ring?' I say indignantly. 'You took it off.'

'Ah yes. I was having a bit of a laugh with you, sorry. Jason cocked up on the sizing and it's a bit too small. It was just about cutting off my circulation. I was having it enlarged. I felt too silly to admit it. After he went to all the trouble of burying it in a box of popcorn.'

'So, what is happening to Tabitha?'

'Out without compensation,' spits Finn, 'and quite right too. Patti was telling me about the work she has done which that witch has taken credit for. Did you know Patti even wrote the advertising slogan?'

'I'm having a little trouble following all this, dears,' my mother suddenly pipes up. 'Are you eating, Finn? How are you doing for money?' She moves to take her purse out of her handbag. 'Would a few pounds help? Buy yourself a haircut?'

'Actually, Mum . . .' Finn puts his hand over hers, indicating that he doesn't need her money. 'I'm fine. I've even got a job.' He smiles at us both. 'I'm joining Liz's magazine as a junior reporter.'

Throw a party

I'm perched by the chrome bar in Corney & Barrow in London's Moorgate, sipping a glass of water in an attempt to calm the butterflies swarming around my stomach. Lines of glasses stand ready on the bar, filled with wine, set out in little blocks like an army of soldiers about to go into battle. I check my watch. In ten minutes people should start arriving. I drain my glass.

'Another water?' asks the attentive waiter, who is shining glasses with a dish cloth and placing them on shelves under the bar. 'Or do you fancy going on to the hard stuff? Calm your nerves.'

'Do I look nervous?' I suddenly panic.

'No more than anybody else I've known who is hosting a large party. How many are you expecting?'

'Don't know,' I admit. 'Could be a couple of hundred. Could be a handful.'

'I'll keep my fingers crossed for the former answer; we're on commission,' he smiles as he hands me a glass of champagne and mutters, 'On the house.'

'Ooh, we're not too late, are we?' I turn to see my mother and Marcella coming in. 'It's not all over, is it?' She looks around the empty room. 'You did say seven, didn't you?' A look of confusion flicks across her face.

'Don't worry,' I smile, 'you're the first to arrive. Welcome to Light As A Feather's inaugural party.'

'Listen to you,' smiles my mother, 'the grown up business

woman. I remember the time when I had to open all the windows while I changed your nappy. She was on iron,' she whispers to Mary before turning back to me. 'And don't you look lovely today. I like that suit. It's you.'

I'm wearing the same trouser suit that I wore on television, but today, what with all the running around over the last few days, the button on my trousers does up. What's more, the waistband is slightly loose. Not too much, just comfortable enough that I can have a big pig out and not have to sit in agony for the rest of the day. I've got a silver lycra scoop-necked top on underneath and sparkling strappy sandals on my pedicured feet. Even Tabitha, I tell myself, would be envious. Of course, I'm not yet her size and I'm not sure that I ever want to be, but I definitely feel more confident. More alive.

'Well, I do like that banner.' My mother points to a large sign that I had made up earlier in the week, with a large feather swirling through all the words. 'Oh Marcella, look there's Mario. Let's go and try out his nibbles again. And he said he'd give me his mother's recipe for minestrone soup. Come on.'

They wander off, and I stand there feeling awkward and alone until the door opens and three people walk in. I recognize two women from that night outside the slimming club.

'Lily?' I approach the short, but not so dumpy, woman. She looks at me puzzled, before recognition dawns.

'Oh, my dear. You look lovely. Doesn't she, Trixie?' She turns to the tall, slim woman at her side who gives me a quick up and down look, shrugging her shoulders. 'This is my daughter, Orla. She works in the City and said she'd join me for a quick drink before she goes off to meet her boyfriend Ciaran. He's from Ireland too. You probably know him.' I shake my head. 'Well, Tessa and I wouldn't have found this bar without her help. Very confusing place, the City.'

'Tessa.'

I look at the smiling woman in front of me. The ten pounds have made all the difference. The jowls that I vaguely remember have gone, replaced by a smiling face. Her eyes are twinkling. Is this the same Tessa who moaned each time about her loneliness? She's throwing her head back and laughing at some of the waiters in the corner, who are busy trying to blow up some balloons.

'Tessa, you look sensational,' I say. 'So vivacious.'

'Isn't it amazing what love can do for you?' She smirks.

'Love?'

'Yes, love,' she squeals in delight and does a little clap. 'Would you believe it? It was right there under my own eyes and I never saw it. Lily's husband Larry has a colleague, Jimmy, and, well we'd talked, but nothing ever happened. I always thought he was nice, a bit big—'

'He's massive,' interrupts Trixie.

'We don't use that word in this party,' I say firmly, waving a finger; in truth, to catch another glance of my manicured nails.

'Anyway, one day I was round Lily's moaning about how life sucked and then it happened. Cupid's arrow. Bull's eye in my heart.' She shivers with the memory of it all.

'And three bottles of champagne,' mutters Trixie quietly.

'Well, you all look brilliant,' I enthuse. 'Is Bella coming?'

'She couldn't get a babysitter. Cecilia said she'd be along later after she's had a meeting with her divorce lawyer,' explains Lily. 'She's going for the juggler.'

'Jugular?' I suggest. 'Mary and Marcella are over there. Why don't you join them?'

I'm left to greet all the guests. Some have not lost much, others have stayed the same, but many have shed life-changing amounts of weight. They giggle at the life-sized cut out of Anthea, which I've had laminated as a darts board and go off to try their luck. The place is buzzing, with people swapping recipes and meeting their chat room colleagues for the very first time. The party is going well.

Liz and Jason arrive, and he goes off to demonstrate to new clients all the functions of the website, some of which I don't even know. Liz stands nearby, watching him, admiring him, playing with the newly fitted engagement ring on her finger.

Patti calls to say that she'll be running late; some journalist needs the answer to a complicated question within the hour and she's got to talk to the chairman to get the information. Finn rings to say that he's running late; he's just posed a complicated question to the press officer at one bank, and she's got to talk to the chairman to get the information. It'll take at least an hour. I smile. I think I get the picture.

I'm wandering through the crowds, smiling and chatting to Light As A Feather clients, introducing myself, when I notice that Mike Littlechild has quietly arrived, and is sitting at one of the high circular tables chatting to a woman. I start to move over as she turns and I'm stopped in my tracks. It's Emmie. The woman who arrived for Tony Younger, the first time Patti and I met him. I'm confused. What is she doing here?

'Mike,' I say uncertainly. 'What do you think of the party?'

'It's buzzing,' he smiles. 'And I see that Justin is doing great business on his underwear stall.' I nod, willing him to introduce me. He doesn't. I take a deep breath.

'Hi there.' I extend my hand. 'You're Emmie, aren't you? We met before? Several months ago. With your boyfriend, Tony Younger?'

Emmie and Mike burst into laughter.

'My boyfriend?' Emmie asks. 'Whatever gave you that idea?'

'I . . .' I can't say a word.

'I'm sorry, we shouldn't laugh,' she smiles. 'It's only that it would be incest. Tony is my brother.' I look at her in confusion. 'Ah, here he is.' She waves to somebody. I turn. Tony Younger is approaching. Dressed in a charcoal grey suit, with pale blue shirt, he looks stunning. Stunning, but out of place. What the hell is he doing here?

'Orla.' He kisses both my cheeks. 'You look great. Absolutely fantastic. I thought your television performance last week was amazing. The tabloids just lapped it all up, didn't they?'

'Yeah,' I say hesitantly.

'And I see you've met my sister again?' He greets Emmie.

'Yeah.'

'And her husband?'

'Eh? Mike is your brother-in-law?' What a small world.

'I think that's how it works,' he smiles.

'And that's why you're here? He invited you?'

'No, you did,' Tony grins.

'No, I didn't,' I say in confusion. 'I haven't seen you to invite you.'

'I didn't say you'd seen me,' he adds, mysteriously. Tony delves into his inside breast pocket and pulls out a business card. 'There you go,' he says, presenting it to me with a flourish.

'I don't need your business card,' I add. How much have I drunk? This conversation is totally losing me.

'It might help,' he says enigmatically.

I look at the card. Anthony Michael Younger. Analyst. Browns Black.

Yeah? So?

I read it again.

Anthony Michael Younger.

Realization starts to dawn.

Anthony. A.

Michael. M.

Younger. Y.

'You're Amy?' I shriek in horror.

'Yep,' he nods.'

'But you don't need to lose weight. You never did. What was it? A joke? Did you think it was funny to befriend me, to make me feel that I had an ally in dieting?'

'You did have an ally,' he says quietly.

'How? What did you do for me apart from laugh when I confided my feelings about my weight?'

'I never laughed.'

'How do I know that? So what was it? A bet?' I snarl. 'Don't tell me, you're also related to my old boyfriend. The one who took money to date me?' Mike and Emmie look at me, startled. 'Is that all round the trading floor now? Everybody laughing about me?'

'I never told a soul,' Tony says. 'I promised that I wouldn't.'

262

'So what did you get out of it?'

'I got the satisfaction of thinking that I was helping, in some small way, a beautiful young lady, who lacked the confidence in herself and in her ability, who perceived herself as too fat and unworthy to make her way in this world. To build a business. I fed a few ideas, and watched her seize them and make them work. Heard how she stood up to my brother-in-law, and I laughed and felt good about her. I didn't like what happened with Anthea, but Mike was adamant that he had the top public relations guy advising him. I told him all along he should be listening to you.'

'So who are you then,' I snap, 'Mother Bloody Teresa?'

'No,' he shrugs. 'Just somebody who felt very guilty about the way he once treated her. The way he scorned her in front of two of life's most disgusting people. And how humiliated he felt when he learned that she had just been covering up for her colleague.'

'But how did you learn about the site?' I said, a sheen of blush covering my face.

'You mentioned it the first time we met. Said a friend was starting one up. I had a feeling it was you, so I just surfed until I found it.' He shrugs. 'But I didn't really have to be Inspector Morse; there were lots of flyers all round the place. The staff noticeboards were packed with them.'

'So you became Amy to make amends for my humiliation?'

'In the beginning,' he concedes. From the corner of my eye, I can see Mike and Emmie moving away. 'I thought you needed some help and made a few suggestions. I had told Mike all about the site, and Emmie was a fan, so it was just a question of putting you in touch with him. But then I began to get to know you. To listen to your worries, hear about your troubles, and I began to want to help you more. Not because of what had happened, but because of you.'

'Oh.'

'And besides, every time I spotted you in Browns Black, you'd run a mile.'

'I thought you hated me.'

He throws his head back and laughs. 'Even after the flowers? How many clues can a man give? Orla, I thought you were great the first time we met, when you interviewed me and were fretting about your size, but then our relationship went awry.'

'We don't have a relationship.'

'Yes, we do. We have an internet relationship. What we have to do now is to turn it into a real one. If you'd like.'

'How do we do that?' I ask.

'Well, we start like this.'

And then he kisses me.